A Breed Apart

'There was five of us in the gall'ry, all huddled against a wall,
In the terrible silence that followed the rush and the roar and
the fall.
Not a muscle moved amongst us - not a sound, not a sigh, not a
breath,
For we knew that there in the darkness we were face to face
with death!'

March 29th 1890, Morfa Pit, Glamorganshire. (unknown)

Mike Bowden

A Breed Apart

This book is dedicated to the miners

and their families,

of Great Britain.

Who were indeed;

<u>A Breed Apart</u>

A Breed Apart

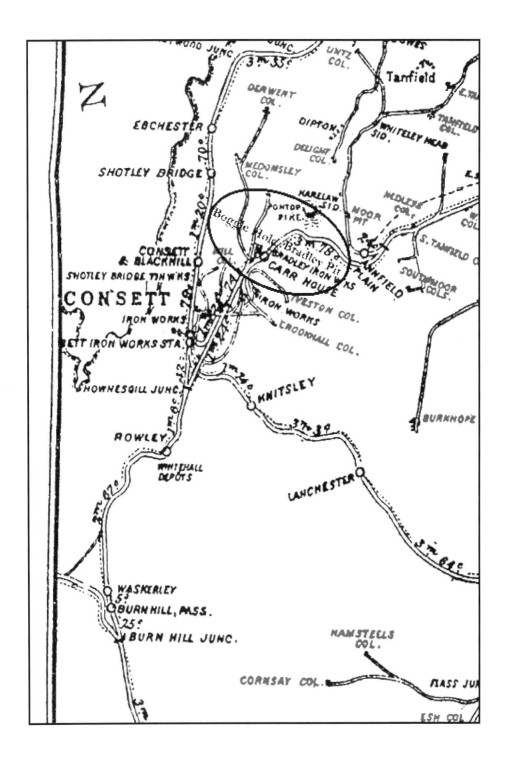

CHAPTER ONE

Monday 24th June 1906

Jack was getting ready for his shift. He glanced at the bedroom door as another cry of pain interrupted his preparations. He knew something was wrong in there and he was worried about Ada. On his way home from work the day before, he had seen a magpie at the top of a tree. He had scoured the area to find another, but in vain. It was a terrible omen of sorrow to come and it had unsettled him. Long ago he had decided not to listen to such nonsense, but what if he was wrong? Why couldn't God just let her have her baby? Life was tough enough as it was.

The brutal struggle between miners and coal left many victims, husbands and sons crushed to death or blasted apart, hundreds of feet below the earth. Three generations of a family could be wiped out in one disaster underground, son, father and grandfather, gone in an instant of fear and agonizing pain. Afterwards it was the lingering grief that had to be endured, the families who had no one left to work at the pit faced eviction and the workhouse along with their loss. But the people accepted the dangers as all part of the job, for in return they were given a home with free fuel, a garden to grow fruit and vegetables, perhaps even a chicken run where a few Rhode Island Reds provided the luxury of fresh eggs. The chicken's diet consisting of boiled potato peelings, and maybe corn scrounged from the stable lads for a few pennies. Churches and reading rooms were constructed for the welfare of the mining communities, but not out of generosity. The landowners provided these amenities based on the theory that if the miner was happy, then they would get more out of him and it was true, the pitman and his family were generally happy with their lot. Working in seams as low as fourteen inches, they hacked the black gold from the bowels of the earth. This was Jack Walker's world, as it had been his father's, and his grandfather's.

Jack had first met Ada at the harvest festival held in the tiny village chapel. Her sultry hazelnut eyes and slight figure had bowled him over. He smiled at the memory. That was three years ago and now she was due to give birth to their first child. Why she had never fallen pregnant sooner only God knew, because their passion burned like a whinny bush fire on a pit heap. His love was matched only by his physical desire, which was readily returned by his willing wife. But when the cramps started and pain filled her eyes, he felt helpless and it hurt him because he couldn't help, and more so because he didn't know what to do. In his clumsy way he would cuddle her in his muscular arms, his hard hands smoothing her hair and his mind willing the pain to ease. But she was in good hands, there wasn't much that Madge didn't know about birthing and she had hardly lost a child yet. She was famous for her skills but had told Jack that his wife's hips were too slender and she expected a difficult time ahead. Anyway, it was women's things and a man had best keep out of the way at those times.

He kissed his wife and then automatically ran his hands around his thick leather pit belt, his mind subconsciously identifying the equipment as his fingers touched the items, water bottle, bait box and sheath knife.

She did her best to smile.

'It'll soon be over now Jack, I think he's on his way.'

He didn't argue this time about whether it was a boy or a girl, they had had many a laugh over the child's sex, but he could see she wouldn't appreciate it this time.

'There'll be a bonny bairn waiting pet, when your shifts over,' she said.

He hesitated.

'Go on, get, Madge will look after me.'

He nodded and left.

Ada sighed with relief at not having to pretend in front of her husband, she grimaced as another spasm grabbed her abdomen. She could tell that something was wrong because of the way Madge was looking at her. It should have been a time of joy, but a deep frown of worry was creasing the woman's brow. Ada began thinking about her husband when the pain eased a little. He was a good man she thought, strong and hard, but gentle as well. She smiled inwardly when she thought of his hugs, and her protests that he was breaking her ribs, but that was part of being a miner's wife, pitmen were hard they had to be, in a dangerous and unforgiving world.

Jack left the bungalow and entered a bleak wet world, the rain was pelting down. He looked up at the sky wondering if it was ever going to stop, it was the wettest year anybody could remember.

The summer of 1905 had been glorious, but that was last year, and the relentless grey swept above him, heavy rolling clouds shoving each other out of the way to get their chance to rain on him, no one else, just him. Flaming June? Not bloody likely, he hadn't seen the sun all month. He grimaced at the thought, hunched his shoulders and ducked his head as though it would offer protection from the rain.

He peered through the gloom as he headed down Pit Bank towards the Annie pit, named after the owner's wife, but his thoughts were on his own wife, not some well to do posh woman, who had probably never had to lift a kettle without a servant there to do the job for her. A nagging knot of worry gnawed at his guts, because something didn't seem right, but he thought it was probably just him, he always worried needlessly, or so his parents had told him after a beating. His father would stand over him with his belt in his hands, swaying unsteadily with a drunken leer on his face, bawling at him. He remembered the words like yesterday.

'That'll teach you a lesson boy, It's over now, just forget it, it's pointless worrying about it, its history,' his words slurred, but Jack never knew what he had supposed to have done wrong.

He shook his head to clear away the memory, to go down that road brought only feelings of hate and sadness, and no, enough, he thought, as the memory of his revenge against his father demanded to be recognised in his head. He blocked it out, as he had done so many times before, pulled his cap hard down on his head and leaned into the driving rain and on to the pit.

The drift mine was finished now, worked out, the miners

were working on the new pit nearby. This one was different though, it was a deep mine almost three quarters of a mile to the bottom. Jack had never worked that far below the earth, and if he was honest with himself, he was nervous about it, not that he would show it in front of anybody, a man just didn't do that.

He was working on the Heapstead, the building at the top of the shaft, but only as a labourer under the direction of the mining engineers until the shaft was sunk. He would worry about being nervous later, not that it would make any difference, he would still have to go down the shaft. The rain became heavier, stotting off the ground. In his thirty four years he had never seen the like, even the streets and rooftops of the pit bungalows had been washed clean of the ever present coal dust. At first it had been a refreshing sight, but now it was just a bloody nuisance, he was permanently damp, his chestnut wavy hair slicked down on his head, his cap soaked. His clothes were always hanging over the fire at home, but never completely drying out in time for his next shift, always stinking of wet, foisty it was called, but like everything else, you just got used to it, because there was no choice.

A movement caught his eye, he looked up at the top of the coal heap. A cloud was closing in, lower and denser than the rest. He stopped, frowning as he tried to penetrate the gloom and figure it out, it didn't look right somehow, he took off his cap to try and see better.

The other miners were crossing the stone bridge by now and one turned back.

'C'mon Jack, you're ganna be late man,' he said, in the unmistakeable accent of a Gateshead man.

'Aye Tom, I'm on my way, don't worry,' Jack's accent was softer and more rounded, typical of North West Durham.

He turned to look at the cloud again, but it had gone, in fact it had never been there. What he was staring at was every mining community's nightmare, it wasn't a cloud at all. Due to the persistent rain the pitheap had become waterlogged and the peak had broken free and was sliding down towards the pit pond.

He spotted a group of school kids crossing the rope bridge, always a good short cut. He had helped with the construction a few years ago, but they shouldn't be crossing in this weather, they should be using the old stone bridge, it took a bit longer but it was a lot safer. They must be late, he thought, then the alarm bells started ringing and the penny dropped.

The trickle of water from the pit pond overflow had created a stream, but over the last month it had become a fast and dangerous river, the pond was at bursting point and higher than the surrounding land.

When the heap slide hit the pond the water had to go

somewhere, and the children were now in a hell of a lot of trouble. He started to run, waving his hands frantically. The boy at the front was walking along the heap path, they had crossed the bridge and he turned to see Jack waving and waved back, pleased that a respected face worker would recognise him, he was due to start at the pit on Monday. He was thirteen and ready to follow his father underground, but wait a minute, why was he still waving and why was he shouting? Jack was pointing back to the rope bridge that the children had crossed only moments before. The boy turned in time to see a wall of water bursting over the top of the pond as the slag slid gracefully into the water. The river had turned into a flash flood and was sweeping towards them, at an alarming rate.

'Bobby,' screamed Jack, 'into the old drift entrance, run like hell boy, go.'

The boy felt a surge of pride because Jack knew his name and that pride changed into courage. He turned to the children, all younger than him, their faces turned up to him in the rain, their eyes bright and trusting, water dripping from their homemade canvas hats onto their noses. Jack could only stand and watch helplessly as the boy took control.

'Into the pit all of you, run like you've never run before,' shouted Bobby grimly.

He tried to stay calm, he was thirteen, and couldn't

show fear. The children ran down the narrow incline, the brick walls funnelling them towards the drift entrance as the water raged behind them. Jack watched them disappear down the slope, the torrent close on their heels, but it looked as though they had made it.

Jack started running, he would get into the drift through the main entrance and make sure they were safe. It had been a narrow escape for the bairns, but the lad had taken control and acted fast, he'd tell his dad what had happened, Bobby looked like a good'un.

The boy was last down the incline, but something was wrong, why were the little'ns still there, fear grabbed his guts as his brain registered what was wrong. His heart began to race, the panic rising, his bowels churning as he saw that the big square door was closed, blocking the way into the drift. He started beating on it as the water surged around them, the children were crying out now as the water began to rise over their heads, the youngest shrieking in fright and bewilderment. He beat savagely at the door as the other children screamed in terror.

It was only moments before the flood water filled the incline. Bobby held his breath as long as he could, but finally he exhaled, and the life began to seep away, all concern for those around him gone as he fought desperately for life, but he was lost. He tried to breathe in but all his aching lungs received was water, and death. Slowly he sank down on top of the little bodies below him, the cries had stopped and he gazed unseeingly on the children he had led to their deaths. A final gob of air burst from his lungs as he rolled over in the water, his arms wrapping around a girl of ten as though he was comforting her, their wide staring eyes met. But in death there was no recognition.

CHAPTER TWO

Seth Ridley was generally considered to be a bit of a bastard. He was, not that anybody would consider telling him that to his face. He wasn't bothered about what others thought of him, at least he forced himself to think that. After the disaster he had changed, in fact many said that he had a screw loose but his reputation for breaking men was second to none. He didn't do it out of spite, he just generally hated humanity. No bugger cared a shit for him, so why bother about them? He looked up at the sky and scowled at the rain, it annoyed him and when he was annoyed he became angry and when he became angry he took it out on the miners. A group of men were struggling to get a derailed coal tub back onto the tracks.

'Get your fingers out you useless arseholes,' he shouted at them.

As he got closer he swept his yardstick, a three foot

length of ash with a brass ferrule, from under his arm.

'I said get your fingers out you useless bunch of shites,' and began to swing the yardstick at the men, who seemed to gain extraordinary strength and heaved the tub back onto the rails.

'Better, much better,' he growled and stormed off.

As he approached the old drift mine he looked up again.

'Good God,' he said to no-one in particular, 'It's friggin pissing down.'

A boy was bending over struggling to pick up the end of a heavy chain.

'Get out of the piggin way arsehole, its bloody raining stair rods and I'm getting wet.'

The boy didn't hear so Seth kicked him up the backside sending him sprawling in the clarts.

'What the hell are you playing at?' said the boy, but lowered his eyes when he saw who it was.

A long incline ran down to the drift entrance, bricks from the local works lining the sides as the incline became steeper. At only twelve feet wide and five feet high at the entrance, the tunnel bored its way down to thirty feet under the earth and then a honeycomb of galleries spread out in all directions from the motherway as the tunnel was known. It wasn't a haphazard operation, as the coal was mined, pillars were left in place to support the roof. When all the coal was gone the pillars were also taken as the miners retreated. It was known as the bord and pillar method of mining. Seth entered the drift, instinctively bowing his legs to compensate for the height of the tunnel. His back was straight and he rolled along with the distinctive walk of a veteran miner. For the last twenty years he had been overman of the pit, only the assistant manager was his boss and that was debatable. Anything that happened underground was his responsibility and he made sure that everyone knew that.

Seth preferred not to remember the disaster, but it was insinuating itself into his mind as he walked along the deserted tunnel in the pitch black darkness. No matter how hard he tried he would always relive the events of that terrible day.

It was a miracle that he was alive today. He remembered the explosion and the tub cartwheeling towards him, bouncing all over the roadway and that was when the friggin thing hit him. He could remember the appalling heat that began to roast his flesh under the upturned tub that covered him, but then the water had come, oh God the water. He had struggled free as the water began to get deeper. He stood up as it got higher and higher, the roof of the roadway getting closer and closer, his face touching the roof of the tunnel as he filled his lungs with precious air. He could hear the shrieks of the survivors as they panicked, and then the sounds faded away. His last memory was the searing agony in his face. He wanted to scream and shriek in agony but there was no air left to breathe, just the water, the hated water washing around his mouth as he struggled for breath. Then darkness, then silence.

The water disappeared down the main shaft and into the sump at the bottom. Only one man survived, barely alive and babbling incoherently. When he had regained consciousness in the hospital he knew that he had been left to roast alive, abandoned and left to die by the miners trying to save their own miserable lives. When he was told he was the only survivor he had reasoned that they had been punished by God for abandoning him, but God had saved him he had decided. He had chosen him to bring the black gold out of the earth, to supply the machinery of empire that allowed Britain to reach the far flung outposts of her possessions, so that the savages could be taught the way of true salvation.

Perhaps it was just as well that God loved him, because no-one else did.

A new shaft was on its way down into the earth, searching for the seams of coal that lay deep underground and the miners were employed by the engineers as labourers, setting the headgear with its huge wheels towering into the sky that would drop them into the bowels of the earth where the huge reserves of coal lay waiting for them.

He turned a corner, to his right, a short tunnel led to the old shaft that was still open, a three hundred foot drop for the careless, or for those who didn't fit. Miners had their own justice, and an experienced collier could fall over the edge, recorded only as a shaft accident. He walked on, unwittingly bending his back. He suddenly straightened up again, a bent back meant a bad back, and as far as Seth was concerned a bad back was no bloody good in the pit. Some of the kids coming down the mines these days had started washing their backs after a shift, the stupid buggers, any decent pitman could tell you that if you washed your back you would weaken it which was no bloody good at the coalface.

He soon covered the two miles which was in total darkness, stopping to light his carbide lamp when he neared the last curve in the roadway. He released the thumbscrew at the side of the lamp to let the water drip into the lower chamber, it only took a few seconds for the carbide lumps to react, he shook the lamp gently and put his finger close to the gas outlet. He always cleaned the lamp before he started work and had already used his pricker to make sure the vent was clear. The stink of rotten eggs showed him that the gas was escaping. He reached into his pocket for a box of matches, he smiled when he thought of the old ones he used to use, Swan white pine vestas, they were called, made from wooden splints soaked in wax, the bloody things would have your fingers singed if you weren't quick enough.

The new Swans were made from pine, unsoaked with a sulphur head and were shorter but burned more slowly. He struck the match on the wall of rock and cupped it in his hand until it got a hold then carefully presented it to the gas vent on the lamp. Whoosh, the gas ignited and the dark tunnel took on a ghostly light, shadows flickering along the walls as he started moving again. There were many who said they had seen Auld Nick underground but Seth reckoned it was purely a trick of the light. Anyway, the good Lord was on his side and the devil wouldn't dare interfere with his work.

The drift had always been considered as a safe mine and there was little chance of firedamp and open lamps had always been used, they gave a better and brighter light, and apart from that, a miner with a bit of nowse in his noggin could heat up his cold tea if he knew how to do it. His last job on that day was to seal the drift. The rain over the last few weeks had caused a problem, the air vent opening out near the stream would have to be closed. If the river flooded then the workings could end up flooded before all the equipment could be removed, and Seth didn't like water, in fact he was scared of it, no, more than that, he was absolutely bloody terrified of it and those buggers had better have done what he told them to do, or by God there would be hell to pay, begging your pardon lord as he realised what he had thought. He could see a light in the distance that shouldn't be there, he glowered at it. What the hell were they playing at, the entrance should have been closed off by now, right, you useless bugger's, he thought.

Bob Curly, a veteran of many years was relaxing, his back against the wall, happily puffing away on his clay pipe. Pipes weren't allowed underground but he knew that the drift was safe, there had never been an explosion in all the time he had worked there and that was when the place first opened.

Anyway, it was easy to sneak his baccy and pipe underground, he simply clenched the pipe between the cheeks of his arse when he came on shift. The baccy was for chewing only, but if you shaved it thinly enough, then it gave a man a decent smoke underground. He noticed a faint glow down the roadway and recognised it as the light of a carbide lamp approaching. He struggled to his feet, the others startled by his sudden movement.

'Watch it lads, shitface is coming,' he pointed his finger at Bill Brophy, a new man, built like an ox.

'Say nowt son, I've worked with this bugger for years and he's an evil sod, so watch your mouth, right?' he snapped.

Bill shrugged his shoulders in a so what attitude. Bob

shook his head sadly, the stupid bugger, he thought, he's going to try it on, well, his loss eh.

'What the hell do you lot think you're doing,' growled Seth as he entered the gallery.

'We were just showing the new lad what was what, while we had some light,' said Jim, an older man on light duties, his voice friendly.

Seth soon put paid to that. He swung his head from side to side looking at each man in turn. Then suddenly he drew his yardstick from under his arm, and jabbed Jim in the chest.

'You,' he drew the word out, 'you of all people should know, that when I tells you to do something, you piggin well do it.'

'Sorry Seth,' replied Jim, he knew when to shut up and he wasn't going to risk his cushy number by shouting his mouth off, leave that for the young'uns, he thought.

'Now get that bloody opening closed afore I lose my temper. What's that?' he almost shrieked as he jumped backwards. The men followed the direction of his pointing yardstick, a steady stream of water was running down the incline into the pit. The new man spoke up.

'It's only water.'

'Water, only water? You stupid bugger, get it shut, now,' his voice had an edge of panic in it.

Bill was about to retaliate but Bob Curly elbowed him in the ribs so hard that it took all of his time to get his breath back.

'C'mon,' said Bob,' his voice resigned, 'get it shut afore he blows his top.'

The three men forced the door closed. Odd that, thought Bob, he'd never seen Seth frightened like that before. The flow of water was getting heavier making it difficult to get the heavy wooden door closed but they finally heard the reassuring click of the sneck dropping into place. They lugged the heavy railway sleeper into the iron brackets, then Seth, his hands shaking hooked the padlock through the hasp and staple and snapped it shut. He looked down at his feet the water almost covering his boots. What the hell was going on, he thought. It's time to get out of here. He was certain that he had managed to cover the panic in his voice, but he must write down the number of times he had blasphemed. As long as he got the number right then he knew that God would forgive him, and not that arse of a priest that took his confession, what would he know, God spoke to him, Seth Ridley directly.

'What?' he snapped.

'I said, I can hear voices on the other side,' said Bill.

Now what's he on about, thought Seth angrily.

'What are you talking about?' he responded.

'I can hear cries, like children yelling.'

He suddenly grabbed the crossbar and started to heave, 'Give me a hand,' he shouted.

'Stay where you are you two or you'll have me to answer to, come away from the door son there's nothing there,' he said in the kindest voice he could summon up. The water was pouring through the gaps now and no way would he allow that door to be opened, not likely, if there was somebody on the other side then it was tough luck on them.

What the hell was that racket going on up the line now? He thought. He turned to stare into the gloom when suddenly, Jack burst into the gallery.

CHAPTER THREE

Jack ran down the cinder track and onto the old humpbacked bridge, his heavy pit boots clattering over the old stone. Then on and upwards to the pit entrance passing between the two gateposts, the gates long gone. He was breathing heavily now as he ran down the incline and into the drift's main entrance, ducking instinctively through years of habit. Suddenly he was surrounded by darkness, only a rectangle of light behind him that grew smaller as he ran further down the tunnel. But he knew the pit like the back of his hand, and didn't slow down. Bugger he thought, its two miles inbye to where the children had disappeared, too far on foot. He hauled on an empty coal tub in a siding and heaved until he had pulled it out and onto the track. He began to push, gradually the tub picked up speed and Jack jumped over the side and crouched down inside. The speed increased until the tub was rattling down the slight incline, weighing four hundredweight anyone in the way wouldn't stand a chance and he prayed there was no-one on their way outbye. Jack tried to judge the speed but by the screeching of the wheels the coal tub was going faster than it was ever meant to. Too fast by any means he reckoned and he was wondering how he was going to get out of the damned thing. The faint light of a carbide lamp hanging on the wall warned Jack of a bend up ahead.

He hurtled towards the bend knowing that the tub wouldn't sit on the rails, he prepared to jump. Remembering the headroom, he would have to make the leap in a crouched position, but he'd done it many a time as a boy. The wheels began to protest and squeal loudly as they took the bend, and the tub began to buck like an awkward pit pony and finally reared up as Jack leaped over the side. He hit the ground rolling fast, his water bottle digging in to his side winding him and making him gasp in pain.

Struggling to his knees Jack just had time to pull himself into a passing place when the tub came bouncing along the wall back towards him. Unseen and lethal in the darkness, a splinter a foot long whipped passed his face and clattered to the ground. The iron chassis had separated itself and was bouncing uncontrollably around the tunnel. It rolled up the wall and part of the way across the roof.

Jack tried to make himself as small as possible as the chassis dropped, but most of the inertia had gone and the wheels rolled slowly to a stop in front of him. The coal tub slowly keeled over on its side with a groan. The roadway was filled with dust and Jack was coughing loudly. He looked into the distance and frowned.

Something was wrong, it was too dark surely, there should be light up where the old entrance was. A sickening feeling welled up, no, surely not. He saw a faint light from a carbide lamp, so there must be someone there, thank God, he thought. He started to run again, frustrated at the cramped conditions that forced him to stoop, but the light was getting closer, but why was it still so dark, of course it's the rain he convinced himself, but he knew there was something wrong, sometimes a man had a feeling that things weren't as they should be.

He burst into the gallery and took in the scene about him, his eyes frantically searching for the Children. Then he saw the barrier across the entrance, a railway sleeper sat in two heavy steel brackets and a huge padlock hung from a big hasp and staple. He turned in dismay as his eyes scrutinizing the four men.

'Christ almighty, what have you done? He hissed.

'Blasphemy,' shouted Seth, 'you'll rot in hell Jack

Walker.'

Jack rested his hands on his knees as he bent over to get his breath back, coughing the coal dust out of his throat.

'Get that bloody door open,' there was no answer. 'Now,' he roared.

Seth slowly turned his attention to Ned, his eye glinting in the dark, his head angled slightly to see better.

'You'll give no orders down here Walker, this is my pit and you'll hold your bloody tongue or lose your job my lad.'

Jack turned to Seth, his finger stabbing at the door. 'The river burst its banks and there's kids on the other side,' he hissed.

'I told you I heard voices,' said a man who looked in his thirties, Jack didn't recognise him.

'What?' roared Jack. He grabbed the railway sleeper that held the door shut and started to heave. 'Give me a hand you lot, now!'

'Hold hard,' shouted Ridley, 'you'll do no such thing.' But by now they were forcing the sleeper out of its iron brackets.

Jack spotted the huge padlock, a Squire, four levers and built like a brick shithouse.

'The key,' it was a command not a request.

'You won't get the key Walker, I've got my job to do and

the door stays shut.'

Jack grabbed the mashy hammer used to bash the hasp onto the staple and swung violently at the padlock. The heavy club of steel crashing down on the lock, but it was designed to stop just that. He threw the hammer down in disgust and hung his head in defeat. Then he lost his temper.

Seth didn't see it coming, neither did he expect it, Jack's fist crashed against the side of the overman's head bouncing it off the stone wall, instantly stunned, he slid to the floor. Ned had the keys off him in a crack and had opened the lock before Ridley could gather his wits. He used the hammer again to the hasp and staple apart and the door burst open letting in the grey light from outside. The water, lower now, rushed past in a torrent and down into the old workings.

The miners stared at the pitiful heap of bodies. Bobby was on top, he would never achieve his ambition. Jim Wilson and Bob Curly turned away, they knew what they had done and they also knew that no matter what they said they would be outcasts forever if they stayed in the village. Their lives were forfeit now, and miner's justice would be carried out if they didn't get out of the area fast. They looked at each other, and as if on cue bolted for the surface.

The new man and Jack stood speechless. The man looked at Jack, but he shook his head slowly.

'Why?' he whispered, 'why didn't you do something?' said Jack, his voice trembling with anger and sadness.

'I tried.'

Jack shouted at the man, his anger rising again. 'Well you didn't bloody well try hard enough, did you,' his face showed the disgust he felt for the man.

Behind them Seth was struggling to his feet, he was overman, and he didn't have the job by being soft, and he wasn't soft, anything but, it was time to sort these useless shites out, God was on his side and he knew he was right.

'Good God, what have we done?' said the new man, his eyes turned to Jack's as though asking for forgiveness. 'I tried, honestly, I tried.'

Jack ignored him, he didn't even deserve consideration.

'What's done is done,' said Ridley, on his feet now, 'You two,' get outbye now, It's going to be a pleasure sorting you two troublemakers out.

Jack stared at him in disbelief.

'Is that all you're bothered about? Can you not see what's in front of you on the floor?'

'What's done is done.'

'You murdering bastard.'

Seth sneered.

'Who the hell do you think you're talking to, you lot

breed like rabbits, there'll be plenty more of that lot to take their place,' he said, pointing at the bodies.

Seth was standing in front of Jack, they were face to face.

'You're going to lose your job Walker,' a sneer on his lips, 'you're a pile of shite and I'm going to get rid of you, and him,' he added as an afterthought, pointing at the new man.

Jack wiped away the tobacco laden spittle off his face.

'Well then you bastard, I've got nothing to lose then have I?'

He swung his fist again but Seth was ready for him, and blocked the blow with his arm, bringing his yardstick up ready to whack Jack across the head, but for some reason he hesitated and then a hand grabbed the stick

'Get back boy, this is man's work,' but the man tore the stick from Seth's hand. The distraction was all that Jack needed, he brought his knee up into Seth's crotch and as the man doubled over gasping in agony, Jack clenched his fists and brought them up under his jaw snapping the man's head back. Seth went down, the fight was over. Jack looked at the other man, nodded his head and walked off towards the surface, looking back only once to capture the image of the bodies in the entrance. Why? He would never know the answer to that, but he would always ask the question.

A woman was waiting at the surface, he couldn't see her

eyes for the headscarf she was wearing. He brushed past wondering why she was there, then something made him stop and he turned to face her. She nodded.

CHAPTER FOUR

'Jack, you're needed back home.'

He looked into her face, a crease furrowing his forehead trying to see inside her, there was something wrong, he could see it in her eyes, her bearing, her voice. He knew it must be the baby but he refused to accept it.

'What's up?' he said, hoping that she was an apparition and would just bugger off and disappear.

He squinted through the drizzle, his face close to hers now. He recognized her, one of Madge's helpers.

'Ethel, I said what's up, is there something wrong?'

His voice trembled as he tried to keep control.

She simply stared at him.

He ran.

It had to be the bairn, he thought, oh please no, he had to get back to Ada, she needed him. He raced back over the stone bridge, running with all his strength up the slope to his home. What's all that? He asked himself. There were people standing outside his gate.

He stopped and saw the faces of his neighbours, why were they looking like that?

'What's going on? Is she all right?'

But the faces showed only pity and slowly turned away.

Then something else struck him, what was it that Madge had said about Ada's small hips? He looked around at the people again, no, please no, not Ada.

He threw the gate open and jumped down the three steps into his backyard and then into the scullery. The door to the living room was closed, he grabbed the knob but someone else was quicker and the door flew open and a woman rushed past with an enamel bowl filled with bloody rags. She stared at him for an instant, then recognition crossed her face, she lowered her eyes and brushed past him intent on her errand.

He was about to enter the bedroom when Madge appeared, closing the door gently behind her. She ran her hand through her damp hair.

'Madge? ' He whispered.

She looked up, dismay filled her eyes.

Jack shook his head slowly.

'Madge?' he said again, this time his voice sounded

pleading.

'I'm sorry bonny lad, the poor bairn never had a chance.

Guiltily Jack felt sudden relief, at least Ada was all right, that was the main thing, but why was Madge staring at him like that?

Then a terrible thought insinuated itself into his brain.

'Madge, Ada's alright isn't she?

She put her arms around him, her silence giving him his answer.

'No,' he roared, 'no,' and struggled free of the woman's arms. It was a mistake that was it, simply waiting for him to sort things out as usual. He burst into the bedroom and stopped, it was quiet, too quiet, apart from the tick tock of the old mantle clock. The fire was still glowing in the grate. The scent of her body lingered in the air, but there was something else, it was something he readily recognised, he'd smelt it often when a man or boy was crushed under a rockfall or smashed by a loose tub. The acrid smell of sweat, urine, faeces and blood, the undeniable stench of agonising death.

His clothes were giving off a wet rain smell as they warmed in the cosy bedroom, the little fire crackling and spitting as the coals began to turn from red to orange as the flames died down.

The bedroom they had shared so joyously and guiltily in

their innocence.

He moved to the side of the bed and looked down at Ada. He gently removed the penny from each of her eyes so that he could look at the face of his dead wife. He leaned over and kissed her, suddenly her eyes fluttered open. They had made a mistake, he cried with joy only to be replaced by a terrible wail when he realised it was only a reaction after removing the coins, he sank to his knees by the bed.

He would climb into bed with her he thought, that might do the trick, he got up and moved the blankets aside but a hand clutched his shoulder.

'Jack,' whispered Madge gently, he turned to her and she shook her head, 'come on lad, there's plenty who would want to look after you and I need to tend to your wife, we'll talk later pet, much later when you're feeling a bit better.

'No, I, I can't leave her like this, she's my missus and she needs me.'

'She's in a better place than this now Jack, believe me.'

He reluctantly stood up, he noticed the sheet over the dressing table mirror. At least her spirit would not be trapped for all eternity in the glass.

'Madge,' he whispered, 'has she really gone?' his eyes pleading that she would say no but knowing what the answer would be.

Madge nodded her head gently.

'C'mon pet, she whispered gently, 'it's time to go.'

CHAPTER FIVE

It was raining. The sky was overcast, a shadow hanging over the small community. The hearses dripping with water and the horses shaking their heads to clear away the rain as they slowly made their way to the church. The trees bowed downwards as though out of respect, the branches unable to contain the weight of water were sagging over the ancient tombstones lining the avenue, a damp smell hung in the air. The pathway, usually hard packed earth was claggy with mud.

The owners had spent money extending the graveyard. They knew that the extra space would be needed. A miner's life could be short and brutal, but to forget that nature could also be cruel was folly. She could lash out at any moment, taking what a man thought as permanent and suddenly leaving him naked, his emotions exposed to everyone else, but a man had to hide those feelings. It wasn't good enough to just try, he had to do it, to cry in public wasn't acceptable. But he wanted to cry. But he didn't.

It was dry inside the church. He stared at the roof as the coffins were brought in, he drifted away to better times when he was courting Ada. The look in her eye when no one was watching had told him all he wanted to know, but the warm feeling in his guts whenever he saw her was like nothing he had ever experienced, all he wanted was to care for her.

He became aware of singing around him, The Lord is my Shepherd. Well, he certainly wasn't his shepherd, all the shite that had been doled out to him. He swallowed as a great wave of grief surged through his mind and body, using all his control to stop the tears rolling down his face. Before he realised it, the funeral was over. The mourners leaving the churchyard, the children more important than his Ada. He was standing by her grave, only vague faces slipping past him as they offered their condolences, the vicar offered him a cursory smile of sympathy. Jack wondered if the man really did feel sorry for the victims, or was he just happy for the business.

He lived well enough by the look of him, baldy and tubby, a well fed vulture feeding on the miseries of the miners.

The fresh earth was piled on top of the grave. A breeze had picked up and soon after it started to drizzle but Jack didn't really notice, the rain fell through his hair and down his cheeks, the tears flowing with it, no one could see now and if they did they would think it was the rain. His body heaved as the sobs wracked his muscular frame. Neither of them had any family that they knew of, they had only each other and now she was gone. The baby was by her side in death, at least he would have a hand to hold on their way to God. He felt dead inside, or was it disbelief, or was it grief, or was it, what? He didn't have an answer, he just wanted her back, oh God how he wanted her back, why did it have to happen like this.

The children were lying in a mass grave nearby, he heard the wailing of the mothers', the angry threats from the men. His own loss a minor affair as far as the villagers were concerned, but they had shown respect, he couldn't hope for anything more, but what difference did it make anyway.

There was to be a gathering in the welfare hall, where the women had put together pickles, cheese and sandwiches and jugs of beer for the men, no doubt they would tell stories of the good times with their children but he would not be there, he wanted to be by himself.

He finally tore himself away from her grave. He looked up at the cross carved out of the stone above the church door and suddenly a surge of anger coursed through him.

'You didn't have to take her,' he shouted, 'why didn't you take me instead?' His fist thrust out, threatening the cross.

Then the anger left him as quickly as it came and was replaced by a deep and desperate longing.

He had stayed away from the pit for a week. The first night he had glugged himself to sleep on Ada's gin. She had hidden it under the bed, it had helped her when the pain had been too much, he had always known it was there but had never said anything. But the next morning the impact of total loss had hit him again. He was ashamed at first but the tears refused to stop so he had let them come, then the crying turned into great heaving sobs. He didn't leave the house and nobody troubled him, they had enough problems on their plates.

He ate cheese and stale bread. Maybe he would starve to death, that would sort out a lot of problems he thought. But slowly he began to realise that she was gone and was not coming back and he would have to get on with life whether he liked it or not. Then there were the children, maybe if he had left them alone they might have survived, was it his fault they had died? Maybe if he had minded his own damn business, but how would the parents react when he saw them again. He grabbed the bottle of gin and drained what was left and fell into a fitful sleep tormented by the faces that drifted past him.

In the distance he heard a banging that was getting louder and louder, his father was standing over him with a pint glass of beer in one hand and his pit belt in the other. Jack was trembling with fear his father's laugh mocking him, his face a grotesque caricature of what he had really looked like.

'It's pointless worrying about it,' the face snarled. The banging was much closer now, his father's face faded away and Jack floated slowly to the surface, reality taking over from the fantasy of his nightmares, was that a voice? There was someone shouting outside and banging on his door.

CHAPTER SIX

The knocking was steady and persistent.

Who the hell is that thought Jack, why can't they leave me alone?

'Go away,' he shouted.

The knocking stopped for a moment then started again.

'Bugger off and leave me be.'

Silence, then knock, knock, knock. Right, he thought, I'll sort this lot out, and stood up angrily. He swayed, the room turning the wrong way for some reason, he grabbed the mantelpiece to steady himself and then made his way to the back door.

'What you knocking for, it's never locked, what do you want?' he shouted through the door.

'Jack, it's me, Madge.'

Hurriedly Jack tucked his shirt into his pants, buttoned

up his fly and straightened his braces. He took a deep breath in and opened the door.

'Yes, Madge, what can I do for you?' his manner was angry and impatient.

She looked up at him.

'By God Jack Walker, you've made a right mess of yourself, haven't you? You should be ashamed of yourself,' her voice was now rising in anger.

'What d'you think your Ada would say if she could see you now? Look at the state of you.' Her words were clipped and harsh, she pushed past Jack and strode into the living room.

'Look at the state of this place, it's disgraceful, you should be bloody well shot.' She turned to face him, he simply stared at her as if she was a stranger. She had seen it plenty times before, it always amazed her how a strapping miner could be humbled by the loss of his woman. What if men had to stay at home and women did the work instead, the soft buggers. No she thought, that's unfair, and anyway the poor man was standing looking down at the floor as though he was ashamed, which he probably was.

'Sit down Jack and let's get you sorted out.'

'There's nowt to sort,' he mumbled.

'That's as maybe and that's how you're feeling for now, but the first thing you're going to do is have a bath because you stink to high heaven.' At this she started to clean out the grate ready to light a fire.

'You'll not stand in here while I take my clothes off woman.'

'Aye well, it's nowt I haven't seen afore, but if that's how you feel I'll leave you to it,' she stood up and turned to leave.

'Madge, no, please I'm sorry pet, I didn't mean to sound, well like, truculent, please, you're here now you might as well stay, all right?'

His voice had become gentle, or was it finally acceptance, she thought.

She stopped and turned.

'Get some coal pet and let's get this fire going. When did you last eat?'

He shrugged his shoulders and smiled sheepishly. Good enough she thought, it means he's on his way back from wherever he's been. She knelt down again and began to clear out the cinders in the grate.

An hour later Jack was sitting with a cup of tea in his hand while Madge lifted the black kettle off the range and poured the steaming water into the tin bath that was in front of the fire. She then poured the two buckets of cold water that were standing on the hearth into the bath. She stuck her finger in the water.

'Aye that's fine.'

Jack looked at her and wondered why she was doing this, it had been a while since he'd had a bath and he was actually looking forward to it. He stood up and waited. Now what? She was about to ask, then realised that this was indeed a very private man. She smiled gently.

'Give me a shout when you're in and I'll fetch some more water,' and left the room.

He stripped off his clothes, it was evening now, the flame from the gas lights on the wall at either side of the range sputtered as the pressure fluctuated, but the fire was glowing now. The red coals radiating warmth and comfort, while orange and blue flames licked at the new coals that were beginning to heat up and catch fire. The shadows fluttered around his naked body, his muscles hard and lean, his flesh glowing in the flickering light. As he stepped into the tin bath the warmth of the water spread through him, he eased himself down into a sitting position, the belt weal's on his backside still livid after all those years, but he wasn't thinking of the beatings now, the nightmares had gone for a while. He luxuriated in the warmth almost enjoying himself, but suddenly the pain hit him, the memories, the loss, he felt guilty somehow, but he was beginning to accept the truth now, she was gone, never to come back. The living room door opened and he hastily shoved the flannel over his manhood.

'Is that nice Jack?'

'Yeah but you shouldn't see me with nowt on, it's not right.'

'Don't be daft lad, one day I'll probably lay you out for your funeral, it's nowt I haven't seen before, and anyway, that flannel isn't big enough to cover what you've got,' she raised her eyebrows and thought, I wouldn't chuck him out of my bed. Seeing her expression, Jack tried to sink into the bath, but a burly man doesn't fit easily into a tin container measuring four feet long by two feet deep and two feet wide.

'Madge! You shouldn't be saying things like that.'

'Oh shut up and enjoy your bath, here give me the flannel and I'll do your back.'

He began to protest but handed her the wet rag and hastily covered himself with his hands.

'There,' she said, as she rinsed the lifebuoy soap suds off his back, 'I'll get you a towel.' She pulled the towel off the airer that hung from the ceiling in front of the range, it was warm and dry.

'There you go,' she said.

'You can go now, I can manage that myself.'

'I'm going nowhere lad until you're sorted out, now stop being soft and stand up. I'll shut my eyes right?'

'You promise?'

'What? Oh alright, I promise.'

Jack stood up gingerly, one hand covering himself. Madge had her eyes screwed shut, well that's what it looked like anyway, at least to Jack.

By Madge, she thought to herself, he's a fine figure of a man and he's packing as fine a set of tackle as I've ever seen, it's been a long time. She sighed out loud.

Jack heard the sigh and grabbed the towel wrapping it around himself.

'You were squinting weren't you?'

'Are you telling me I can open my eyes now?' She answered coyly.

'You never had them shut.'

'I don't know what you're talking about,' Madge swung her hips and swirled around in the way only a woman can. She opened the door to the kitchen, looked over her shoulder and gave Jack an exaggerated wink before she finally left the room.

Jack was astonished that such a woman would do something like that, although she was still a handsome piece, he thought. He smiled, then suddenly wiped it off his face, apologising to Ada for having thoughts like that and dried himself vigorously. He was sitting by the fire when she returned.

'I see you're dressed now, well you can take them off

again, I've ironed some clean clothes for you, it'll tidy you up a bit, you're looking better already.'

'I suppose you're going to shut your eyes again.'

'How dare you,' she said in mock anger, and left the room again.

Jack shook his head in confusion, how can a man work out what goes on in a woman's head, after some deliberation he decided it was impossible. Imagine if they got the vote, what the hell would happen to the country. Anyway, it wouldn't happen, would it? What was that smell? A waft of pork frying in dripping assailed his nostrils, he'd forgotten about food, the smell was making him hungry, how long was it since he had eaten, he couldn't remember. It must be for him, hurry up Madge, he thought.

'Right lad,' Madge popped her head around the kitchen door, 'do you want to eat in here, or where you're sitting?'

'What? I mean, at the table, sorry Madge, I'm just a bit mixed up lass.'

'That's all right lad, you'll be in a canny fettle when I've finished with you.'

Jack wondered what finished with you meant, he'd just lost his wife dammit. She came back carrying two plates of pork chops, fried onions and sliced potatoes, the aroma was wonderful. Madge smiled when she saw the look in his eyes.

Aye, the way to a man's heart is through his belly, always had been and always will, and this was one man that wasn't going to escape until she had had him between the sheets. Nobody would know, except themselves of course, and Jack wouldn't say anything so soon after his loss. It amazed her how a man would seek comfort in a woman's arms after losing someone, then apologise later as if he were guilty of something. Life goes on and if they wanted to make excuses for what they did, that was their problem, she ran her tongue over her lips, but it wasn't at the prospect of her pork chops, she was thinking of something much more meatier. Jack tucked into his dinner. Madge placed a black bottle and glass in front of him.

'Have a drink,' she said, 'it'll do you good, and don't gollop your food, take your time, I'm not going anywhere.'

Jack poured the thick black stout into the glass, the creamy head threatened to spill over but settled back at just the right moment, it took skill to do it like that, to let it go wrong would attract disapproving glances from others in the bar, not that he was in a bar but the rule still applied. A warm glow spread through his body, the house was warm and cosy, his stomach rumbled with satisfaction. The heavy stout went straight to his head, never a heavy drinker but like most pitmen he still enjoyed a robust drink and the combination of good food, a good drink, and a good woman gave him a feeling of –

Wait a minute! What was that? A good woman? Now just a minute Walker, steady yourself.

Madge was sitting by the fire watching him, was she wrong to take advantage like this? But why not, life had dealt her a rough deal anyway, surely she was entitled to some pleasure. Anyway she couldn't help it, just like his bloody lordship when he cast appraising glances all those years ago. She knew what it meant and before anyone knew she was pregnant. It was all hush, hush of course, none of your tarring and feathering, it was astonishing what money and power could do. She was still a good looking woman at thirty four years and knew that men still looked at her, the dirty bastards, they were all the same, rutting for their own pleasure without consideration for anyone else. It was only the ones who suffered that momentarily showed compassion and that was just the way she liked it. For a moment she wondered what her son was doing now, wherever he was, but then blocked it out of her mind. Jack was staring into the orange embers of the fire, his hazel brown eyes sparkling with the reflection giving him a mischievous look.

'You alright pet?'

'I'm fine Madge, I'm just tired now.'

'C'mon I'll take you into the bedroom.'

He laughed out loud, not drunk yet but comfortable

enough to make him careless.

'And what are you going to do then?' he asked, a smile on his face.

Got him, she thought and a shiver of anticipation ran through her body. He held out his hand and let her lead him into the spare bedroom. He stood for a moment collecting his thoughts, I shouldn't be feeling like this, but hell, I need someone to wrap my arms around, just to feel the warmth of a woman and anyway, he didn't want to be alone tonight, just this once he would let himself go. He began to unbutton his shirt letting it slip to the floor, his hard muscles gleaming in the faint glow of the gas lamp on the wall. He turned to pull the blankets back, Madge had slipped out of her simple cotton dress and stood naked before him. She was more than just handsome, he thought as his loins began to stir, which was not unnoticed by Madge when she lowered her eyes.

'You don't look as though you want to go to sleep yet,' her voice husky now.

He lay down on the bed and held out his hand.

CHAPTER SEVEN

George Bassett stood looking out of his office window, everything he could see was in his power, his control. A sad smile crossed his face at the thought. He knew the men called him Fat Geordie, but he didn't mind, the term was affectionate rather than derogatory, and anyway I'm not fat, he thought, as he glanced in the full length mirror across the room. The reflection showed a heavier man than he once was, but what did he expect with a job like he had now. A fine figure of maturity he thought. His side whiskers were turning grey but he wasn't concerned, at forty nine it was to be expected. His thick moustache was still black and was his pride and joy, it gave him an upper class look, he thought, especially when he wore his hat. He turned sideways, the mirror showed that his belly stuck out at just the right distance, not too much to look as though he wasn't bothered about himself, but enough to look prosperous.

He poured himself a scotch from the decanter on the sideboard, a fine single malt from the isle of Jura in Scotland, he loved the flavour, the sharp burn then the gentle warmth that coursed through his body.

He remembered when his belly was hard and flat, he had been a strapping lad and turned the heads of many a bonny lass, aye, and bedded them as well, he thought. He had married one of them, she was a real beauty and still was, but she wasn't interested in him now and sometimes he wondered why. He also remembered the hard slog of working underground and the constant fear of death, and he was thankful. His life was relatively comfortable compared to the men he controlled and through hard work and determination his days of hard brutal grind at the coalface were long gone. There were men that George used to know who still worked underground, men who had started their working life when he did, and they were buggered, neither use nor ornament. If they survived they would end their days with bandy legs and bad backs, earning a pittance in the screening sheds picking out the stones and bad coal on the belts before the coal was dropped into the hoppers and then into the coal waggons. They would work twelve hours a day in the noisy dusty room until some disease or infection carried them away to their maker, a hell of a way to end, he thought, but not me.

Now there's a word, he thought, derogatory, imagine talking like that underground, the men would have sneered at him in their ignorance telling him it was a useless word, mainly because they wouldn't know what it meant, it wasn't pitmatic, the strange language of the mines. An outsider wouldn't be able to understand the conversation between two men down there, but it was different now, he moved in circles he had never even dreamed of, whether he liked it or not was another matter, but needs must. But his middle class bosses never let him forget that he was working class, but so what, they could look down their snooty noses at him, but he reckoned if he went boo! to them they would run like stampeding ponies, or kicking cuddy's as they were known locally. What would they know about the life his men had to live, he would like to see one of those soft bellied bastards spend a shift underground. He smiled at the thought and let himself drift back to his past.

He was ten years old, was it really thirty nine years ago? Didn't time fly? He was a trapper then, a lad who opened and shut the canvas doors crossing the roadways, which regulated the ventilation of the workings. Many a time he had sat wide eyed and terrified in total darkness waiting for the clatter of the tubs on the line as a putter would push them through the opening, hoping for a friendly word but much of the time the putter was too preoccupied with his own survival. He had cried a lot then, in the darkness, twelve hours a day, but always when he was alone. He eventually moved on, his boyhood and the tragedies he witnessed underground turned him into a kind and compassionate man, tinged with a hint of sadness at the plight of the collier. Many would joke at the death of a comrade to cover their own fear, but Geordie could see past the immediate horror and see the terrible effect it would have on the victim's family, most probably eviction, the workhouse, or even whoring to survive. Tragic, tragic, he thought as he shook his head slowly which brought him back to the present and the bloody persistent rain that ran down the sash window, when was it ever going to stop? It was bound to affect the sinking of the new shaft. But thinking back he had come on a canny way, ending up as deputy, then overman, assistant manager and finally pit manager, Fat Geordie, the man in charge, but what had he lost in getting there. Shut up he thought, you're talking shite, just get on with the job in hand. But for a moment he couldn't shut up. Aye, he thought, it's been a long time since I was down there amongst the lads, but he could never be there again, he knew. He had crossed the barrier, he was one of them now as the miners would call him, just the same as he had done when he was at the coalface.

But never mind, what about those poor kids, drowned by accident or intent, he didn't suppose he would ever know, he was a queer bugger Ridley, you never knew what was going on inside his head, Geordie doubted whether even Ridley knew, but he was a bloody good overman. He wondered for a moment if he would be blamed for the poor mite's deaths but shoved it aside, the owners wouldn't let anything like that happen, it would affect production, the cold hearted bastards, it would be interesting to see what they came up with.

He had been at the funeral but the people seemed unfriendly towards him, it was probably just the sadness he thought, and could you blame them? No dammit.

But still, they seemed, what was the word he was looking for? Disrespectful, that was it, and then it dawned on him, they were blaming him for the deaths, but he wasn't even there, why should they be like that to him?

But George wasn't stupid and he began to put two and two together. Something was wrong and he began to wonder what really happened, was he too ready to accept Ridley's story?

The investigation had kept everything neat and tidy and the verdict of accidental death had been met with nods of approval, it just so happened that the magistrate was one of the owners of the pit, how very convenient thought George, but he had a feeling that the matter wasn't going to be dropped so readily by the pitmen and their families, he knew what they were like and they had their own ways of meting out justice. He decided to watch his back for the time being.

Never mind though, that was a week ago, now he had things to do and the sight of Seth Ridley striding purposefully across the pit yard towards his office brought him instantly back to the present, and the matter of Jack Walker and Bill Brophy to sort out.

CHAPTER EIGHT

Jack turned over and spread his hand across the bed, he was climbing out of a deep sleep, deeper than he had experienced for a while now. Something wasn't right, he felt as though he shouldn't feel this good, then suddenly everything flew back into his head. But last night? Where was she, he realised that she was gone, then it dawned on him that it was best that she had left, her reputation would have been destroyed forever, she wasn't daft. He felt guilty and yes, sad and ashamed and unfaithful, as though he had gone behind Ada's back, but she was gone now and he would have to get on with his life and he owed Madge, or Margaret as she had insisted he call her last night. He smiled at the memory, what a night, but it's over now, rightly or wrongly, the deed was done and he couldn't change things. Not that he would ever want to forget. He finally gave up trying to analyse his feelings.

He jumped out of bed and headed to the back door and across the yard to the netty where he opened his fly and pittled luxuriously through the hole in the wooden boards. After a satisfied grunt, he ran back across the yard and into the scullery. He filled the kettle and took it into the living room. The coals were still showing signs of life so he grabbed the poker and gently moved the black bits into the embers. The flames burst around the unburnt coal. Champion he thought, I won't have to lay a new fire. He went back into the scullery and cut himself two thick slices of Madge's homemade bread, famous in the village. He stuck his toasting fork into the first slice and sat in front of the fire waiting for the bread to turn brown. He had just finished the first delicious slice, when he was startled by an urgent banging on his door. Why the hell can't everybody just leave me be, he thought, but nevertheless he stood up and went to the back door.

'Who is it?'

'It's me mister Walker,' announced a voice.

'Aye I know you're me, but who the hell is me, you daft bugger.'

'I'm not you mister Walker I'm Bobby Samms.'

Jack opened the door and looked down to see a coal smeared face staring up at him, the boy's eyes bright and white in contrast.

'Well?' said Jack staring sternly at the boy who quailed under the glare. Jack's face softened, the lad wasn't a full shilling, bless him, it was Jim Samms's lad, people said his mother had dropped him on his head when he was a baby and he'd never been the same since. The lad had the job of running messages for the manager. Fat Geordie was a soft bugger underneath, but nobody would take advantage of that fact, thought Jack.

'Err, av got a message mister,' Bobby's face broke into a wide grin cracking the dried coal dust on his face giving him the look of an older man.

'Well, spit it out son, what's this message that's so important?'

The bright eyes stared at him as though waiting for something. Then Jack twigged on to why, the message still remained in the boy's scrambled head.

'Come in lad, here you go,' as he handed the boy a threepenny bit, 'I suppose you'll want a slice of toast as well.'

Bobby's grin became impossibly wider threatening to split his cheeks.

'Sit down lad and hold the fork.'

Bobby sat as ordered and held the toasting fork in front of the fire, too close and the bread would burn, too far away and it would end up merely warm. Bobby concentrated to get it right. Mr Walker must be important so he would have to be careful.

'Well?' said Jack

'Well what?' said Bobby.

'The message?'

Bobby stared vacantly for a moment, Jack saw the penny beginning to drop as the lad lowered the fork to pass the information on.

'Hold on son, sort your toast out first, here, there's a bit of pork fat and jelly left, you spread that on and I'll get you a drink of Oxo and you can give me the message when we're sorted, all right?'

'Thanks mister,' he studied for a moment then said, 'Walker.'

Jack smiled and wondered if the lad's face ached on a morning with all the smiling he did, perhaps they should all take a lesson from him.

The sun was shining through the window, at last the rain had stopped. Ada would have loved it, she enjoyed the sun so much. There was nothing she liked better than to stroll through meadows on warm summer days and then lie in the grass staring up into the sky, the smell of hay and wild flowers, the buzzing of insects as they searched for nectar. Stop right there he thought, there will be time in the future to remember the past, at the moment he needed to get over it.

'Right son.'

'Eh?'

'The message?'

'Oh right, yes,' mumbled Bobby through a mouthful of toast and pork fat. He thought for a moment, the word was very important, but what was it? He formed the word on his lips but somewhere between his brain and his vocal chords it had become lost, until his eyes lit up with pride as he remembered the word. Jack tried to hide his impatience and said nothing.

'Straightaway.'

'Straightaway?' asked Jack.

'Fat Geordie, sorry, I mean mister Bassett said he wants to see you now.'

'Now?'

'Yes mister Walker.'

'Why didn't you tell me before, you daft sod?'

'I just did,' said Bobby, his face showing alarm at Jack's voice.

'Forget it son, wipe your mouth, it's up to the eyes in fat.

Jack rinsed his face in the zinc plated sink in the scullery, he poured the remains of a kettle of warm water into a tin bowl and quickly lathered his shaving brush with the bar of lifebuoy soap at the side, then spread the foam over his stubble. He rinsed his safety razor in the water and scraped the bristle off his face, enjoying the luxury of a clean shave. He quickly donned his jacket, an old Harris Tweed favourite of his and stepped into the yard, he stopped and turned back inside.

'How old are you son?'

'I think I'm thirteen,' said Bobby, his grin spreading because he was proud that he could remember that number.

'Aye, you're probably right, bonny lad, thanks for bringing the message, have yourself another slice of toast, but don't burn the house down or you'll get a knuckle sandwich,' he waved his clenched fist at Bobby and left.

Outside, he crossed the little yard and climbed the three steps to the gate, lifted the sneck and stepped into the back street. He lived in number forty five with the romantic name of First Street. On the other side the dwellings were logically named Second Street, fifty bungalows each side of the hill leading to the bottom where the pit stables were. At the top of the hill a quarter of a mile away, the winding wheels of the new deep pit stood starkly against the sky.

The sun was out now and steam was lifting from the outhouse walls and pavements. The air had a fresh clean smell without the taste of tar and coal, the unmistakeable smell of a pit village. Miner's wives already had lines strung across the narrow back lane and were hanging out damp clothes in the hope that they would get the chance to air and dry them properly.

The street looked clean which was unusual in itself. Jack was used to seeing coal dust everywhere, not the romantic version that the upper classes liked to think, he had seen their paintings in the library, the solid and forthright miner of the empire staring towards the pit wheels with a look of determination in his eyes. His comrades behind him ready for the toil, some with picks on their shoulders and miners lamps in their hands, what a load of shite, he thought. The silly buggers knew nowt, had they never heard of a lamp cabin where you collected your pit lamp and your tally was hung on a tag. The tallyman would soon see if anyone was missing or so badly crushed or blown apart that he was unrecognisable by the tag left hanging on the wall of the lamp cabin, its owner gasping for air or screaming in agony hundreds of feet below ground. The owners didn't give a damn about the men and boys who worked for them, production was the be all and end all of pit life. If someone was killed a replacement would be found immediately and the bereaved evicted to make way for the next family. The fact that those left behind could starve to death or end up in the workhouse didn't concern the owners at all. It was wrong and Jack wished he could do something about it, maybe he would one day if he was given the chance, but he couldn't see it, he was trapped in the cycle of a miner's life. The owners owned him, he wasn't naive enough not to realise that, however they waffled on about good conditions and good housing. It was there purely to enslave them until they were worn out, blasted apart, gassed, drowned, you name it the miner had it all. He smiled at his cynical thoughts and realised that he was already striding up pit bank and nearing the grand entrance to the pit.

CHAPTER NINE

Bill Brophy stirred under the blankets, he knew he had to go to the manager's office, perhaps he was going to be promoted, he smiled at the thought, chance would be a fine thing, but he reckoned it was something to do with those poor drowned kids. That bastard Seth was the culprit and he was sure the manager only wanted his version of what had happened so that the bugger would be punished, and deservedly so, what was it Ridley had said? They breed like rabbits, that's when that man hit him, hell of a roundhouse punch. Even Brophy, who had been in more brawls than he cared to remember, was surprised at the power of the man, anger could do that, but it was the way he controlled himself. His face had shown no trace of the anger he must have felt, he just clobbered the man, should have broken his neck the bastard, poor kids. What a hell of a thing to say at a time like that, breed like rabbits, the overman deserved everything he got and if he could help, then he would do his damnest to make sure he was punished, even though he'd only been at the pit for two weeks.

Brophy had gone over the incident time and time again, he should have done more, but what, he asked himself. He had tried to force the heavy door and when Seth bawled at him he knew there was nothing more he could do. But there was a funny atmosphere around the village, whenever he went into the corner shop or the Co-op, people stopped talking. He knew it took time for a stranger to be accepted, but this was different and he had realised that they were blaming him for the deaths as well. The older couple who he rented a room from had become subdued in his presence and there wasn't the friendliness that he had experienced at first. He was beginning to think that the whole idea of moving here wasn't such a good idea after all, but then again he didn't have much choice did he. How was he to know the girl was younger than she said, she certainly didn't look it and it didn't take much to get him going, a flash of eyes, a knowing smile was all he needed, but he didn't expect the whole damned family to come after him. The crafty little bitch must have gone running to Daddy straight away. Anyway, he thought, it had been time to move on and with the increase of shaft sinkings in North West Durham he had found the perfect place to disappear.

There was a sharp knock on the bedroom door.

'Breakfast,' said the woman, her voice toneless.

'Right,' said Bill thinking that her manner was a bit curt, he was obviously right about what he had thought earlier, he might have to move on again, anyway the pretty brunette he was seeing was starting to get careless. She knew the system, a piece of coal on the wall in the same place when her husband was out, but the daft bugger had done it the other way round and when he walked into the bungalow, there he was sitting by the fire as large as life, with a look of surprise on his face. The surprised expression soon turned into a look of suspicion when he had babbled out some cockeyed story about why he was there, and then to one of anger. Bill had left quickly and had decided to let the dust settle if it ever did, before he would go back.

He dressed and went into the kitchen, it was the same old stuff, porridge made with water and sprinkled with salt, the woman ladled it into an enamel dish and pushed it towards him as he sat at the table. He picked up the spoon and dipped it into the porridge noticing the black smuts of coal from the roaring fire that had floated down into the goo in front of him. Her husband, now in his 70s was getting ready for work and hadn't spoken. It was even worse this morning, he thought, you could cut the air with a carving knife.

The husband came across to the table, a big craggy man, still strong and well-muscled, he could still fill his share of tubs at the face and was respected by the miners. Bill looked up at him ready to smile, but the look on the man's face changed his mind.

'We want you out lad.'

'But.'

'Hold on son, and let me say my piece. There's many who are taking you to task for what happened lad, and me and Polly's getting a bit of grief over it, now I'm not saying I agree or disagree but we're too long in the tooth to have to put up with any trouble and that's why we want you out. You're a canny lad from what I can see but you're ganna have to gan, so if you've got owt to say, best say it now lad.'

Brophy didn't realise he was nodding his head as though emphasising what the man said, but ganna have to gan? He mulled it over for a moment then realised what he meant.

'If that's your decision then I'll have to abide by it. It's your house and you make the rules so when do you want me out,' he said.

'Soon as you can,' it was said matter of factly as the man turned away and continued his preparations for work.

He was annoyed that such good people would think such bad things about him. He hadn't done anything wrong, why blame me? He asked himself. Where was he going to live now? If this was the village attitude towards him then he would be sleeping under the stars. But wait a minute, the man who hit Ridley, he would get the sack and there would be a house free and he would be next in line. He worked at the pit and would probably get the place, so there was nothing to worry about.

* * *

At the same time another man was contemplating what he had done. Why had he run away from the scene? Bob Curly had worked many years as a miner but had never seen the likes of what had happened to those kids. He admitted he was frightened of Seth, he was an evil and bitter man. But had decided long ago just to do what he was told in the hope he would be left alone. But it was all over now for Bob Curly. He noticed a group of men coming towards him talking amongst themselves, he knew most of them and carried on whitewashing the wall where the shaft dropped another four hundred and fifty feet down into the earth. It was disused and there were many who didn't know that it was there, so the walls were whitewashed as a warning to the unwary, but accidents still happened.

The men were beside him now.

'Hello Bob,' said Geoff Hayes.

'Hello Geoff.'

Geoff stared at him, there was an odd look in his eyes. Well, he had lost his daughter in the drowning, thought Bob. He was still pondering on the matter when Geoff elbowed him sharply in the ribs.

'Steady on man, you nearly shoved me over the edge.'

The other men became quiet.

Bob's voice took on an edge of panic, there was something wrong here, no, it couldn't be, they wouldn't.

'What are you playing at?' he said trying to force a smile.

But they were the last coherent words he ever spoke. His terrible shrieks of fear echoed around the drift as he was shoved over the edge of the shaft and fell the four hundred and fifty feet down to the stinking twenty feet of stagnant water filled with pit pony shit, human shit and the stinking carcasses of anyone else who had 'fell' over the edge. If he heard the words of Geoff they didn't register in his brain, he was too busy frantically waving his arms in a desperate attempt to slow the fall. Four hundred and fifty feet gave a man just long enough to know what is going to happen when the bottom is reached and he began to scream for God, his Mother, anybody. Then he hit the bottom.

'That's for my daughter you bastard,' Geoff had shouted

as the man fell to his death.

The deputy took out his notebook, licked the end of his pencil stub and wrote. Shaft accident 9.30a.m. on Tuesday 15th July 1906.

* * *

That same morning another man was getting ready for work. His wife was moaning and groaning about why she should have to do this and that, he hardly listened to her now, how long was it? Good God, sorry Lord, he must remember to say sorry at church on Sunday. Anyway it was almost forty years since he had met her, but she was different now, wizened and bent. Hell, if he had known how she would turn out he would never have married her. He spent most of his time in the club now just to get out of her way, nag, nag bloody nag that's all she did. One of these days he would jarp her lug, he'd hit her before and he would do it again if she didn't shut her mouth.

Arthur Hardman had been down the drift with Bob Curly when that business with the kids had happened, he had wanted nowt to do with it and had cleared off as soon as Walker had turned up. Best out the way he had thought, and it had worked, nobody had said anything to him since.

What was the skinny cow going on about now?

'What man?' he shouted at her.

'I said don't forget your bait.'

'I wish I could forget you,' he snarled at her.

'You bloody sod,' she hissed, 'if it wasn't for the fact that you bring money in I would have left you years ago.'

'Aye, right, whatever you say, what's in my bait?'

'Rhubarb leaves.'

He stared at her in astonishment.

'You really would try to poison me, wouldn't you, you bitch.'

She turned around, for an instant he caught a glimpse of the pretty girl he had chased after but it was gone almost as fast, years of looking after the house had worn her out.

'If I thought I could get away with it, yes. I hate you Arthur Hardman, you're a horrible man and I hope you drop dead.'

He slapped her across the face.

'That's the only way you can handle it isn't it, you're clever at thumping women, but a coward amongst men,' she cried, the tears trickling down her ragged face.

'Shut your face you stupid cow,' and he stormed out of the house.

His wife stared at the door, a look of pure hatred on her face, a moment later she heard his voice raised outside. Now what was he up to, she thought, and quietly opened the back door, crossed the yard and peered over the low wall down into the back lane. She liked living in Second Street, it was on the high side of the hill and gave her the opportunity to watch what everyone was up to. Heavens above she had little else to do, but what she saw made her clamp her hand over her mouth as though preventing herself from shouting out loud.

Three men had a hold of her struggling husband, he was shouting and threatening them but they held on grimly. One of them punched him in the gut and he doubled over, another brought his fist down on the back of Arthur's neck and he fell to the ground where the men quickly bound his wrists together. A crowd had formed, a woman dragged an old tin bath across the street and was helped to lift it onto a set of pram wheels held together by a wooden framework. They lifted Arthur into the bath and stripped his clothes off using pocket knives to cut the garments apart.

'What the hell are you doing?' roared Arthur, 'I know who you are and I'll get you for this you bastards.'

One man slapped him across the mouth.

'Shut up Hardman, you know what this is for, and don't swear in front of the women, you should know better.'

A barrel was being wheeled up the backstreet in an old handcart, it stopped next to him and the lid was prised off, the smell was familiar thought Hardman and the acrid taste in his mouth made him cough. Then he suddenly realised what it was and began to wriggle frantically in the bath, but he was held down by the men.

His eyes widened in fear, flickering backwards and forwards, looking for a way out.

'No, please, why are you doing this?' but he did know why and he also knew he wasn't going to get out of this. He twisted his head round to see if he could escape into the safety of his home, a desperate idea for a desperate man. He saw his wife and his eyes pleaded for help from her, she felt the urge to help him and then rubbed her cheek which still stung from the belt he had given her and shook her head slightly, a smile of vengeance creasing the worn skin on her face. Let the bugger pay, she thought and settled down to watch the fun, while her husband began squealing like a stuck pig.

The barrel had been lifted above Arthur's head and the tar was slowly rolling out in waves over him. He had the sense to shut his mouth as he was finally covered completely in the sticky stinking clag. He hung his head to clear his mouth and breathe again.

Three women approached carrying old pillows.

'You know what these are Arthur?' said a voice close to his ear.

He shook his head.

'Pillows Arthur, pillows of the bairns you left to die. You ran away you pile of shite,' hissed the voice,' and now you're going to pay.'

The mothers of three of the dead children held up the pillows and the crowd began to chant.

'Murderer, murderer,' over and over again.

The pillows were slashed open and goose feathers surrounded Arthur and clung to his tar covered body, the greatest humiliation anyone could suffer. The families of all the children who had died carried saplings, gorse branches and reed whips. They approached and began to beat the helpless man while the chanting went on.

'Murderer, murderer.'

Someone pushed the pram wheels and the contraption began to roll down the hill gathering speed, the crowd running with it, the relentless beating making Arthur scream in agony. Finally he hit the bottom of the hill and crashed into the midden across the road. He was flung violently into the pile of rotten vegetables and chicken manure, and lay there broken, stinking and beaten.

He lay for a long time, now and again children would come to gawp at the funny man dressed up like a bird, but decided he wasn't much fun and threw stones at him instead.

He crawled further into the midden covering himself with household rubbish and lay still for what seemed a very long time. He understood that he had only just escaped being beaten to death by the villagers and had to get out somehow, but how? Then the dawning of an idea penetrated his muddled and frightened brain.

It was dark now and Arthur's wife heard a quiet tapping on the door.

'Elsie, it's me,'

'Aye I know who it is, what do you want?' She was sitting by the range, the fire crackling and sputtering, her rocking chair creaking backwards and forwards in the gloom. In all honesty, she thought, she had been worrying about him, why? She would never know but there it was, she supposed after forty years you got used to someone, it was comfortable in a funny sort of way.

'Howay in,' she whispered. He stepped through the door, a black goose feathered apparition, bits of rotten vegetables and who knew what stuck to him from the midden.

'Phew, what a pong, look at the bloody state of you, stay where you are till I get an old blanket.'

Elsie went off muttering to herself and wondering why she felt a little happier now the sod was back. She returned with an old woollen blanket and spread it on the floor.

'Right Arthur sit on that.'

He obeyed meekly. She raised her eyebrows in surprise.

'The first thing we've got to do is get that stuff off you,' she produced a wooden skillet out of her apron,

'Here, start scraping.'

He rolled his eyes up to her and nodded, he began to scrape.

'I didn't think you would let me in,' he said quietly.

'And why wouldn't I, you're my husband aren't you?'

He nodded silently.

'I'm sorry pet.'

'Shut up and get on with it, you've never said sorry to me for years, you daft bat.'

'Well it's been a long time coming and I mean it.'

'Oh Arthur, if only that was true.'

'It is lass, I know I'm a funny bugger but this has put things right for me and I hope it's not too late for you. I never wanted those kids to die and I would have helped, it's just that, well,' he hesitated for a moment. 'It's just that, I'm not the strongest type in front of others.'

'Do you think I don't know that after all these years Arthur?' It's time you realised I know more about you than you do yourself, now get on scraping that stuff off ,I'll be back in a jiffy.'

Elsie went into the scullery and picked up a long bladed knife, it was blunt but it would do the job. She came back quietly, her mind trying to sort out what he had said. She sat in front of him and raised the knife, he flinched and closed his eyes, beaten and defeated, he had nowhere else to go and didn't care anymore. He felt the blade on his chest and opened his eyes for the last time. Well, he thought it was the last time, Elsie started scraping the tar off his chest.

'Come on,' she said, 'start scraping with that skillet.'

'But.'

Suddenly she realised what was going on in his head and stopped.

'You stupid arse, you really thought I was going to polish you off didn't you.'

'Well what did you expect me to think you silly cow,' he said his voice raised.

She pointed the knife at him and said. 'Watch it son or you'll get this,'

Hours later he lay in bed, his skin red raw and sore, Elsie had covered him with calamine lotion to cool and sooth his skin and he had eventually drifted off into a troubled but deep sleep. His snoring loud and erratic as his nightmares tormented him .

Elsie stayed with him until the sky began to lighten and then went to put the kettle on. When she came back he was sitting up in bed.

'Here you go pet, I've laced it with a drop of that navy rum you like.'

He took the cup of tea and gratefully swallowed a mouthful almost gagging on the stuff.

'Good god woman, there's enough rum in this to supply the bloody navy,' he gasped.

'Shut up and drink it, we've got some things we need to sort out.

Two days later in the early hours of the morning, Elsie and Arthur slipped quietly out of the village, walked to the railway station half a mile away, and boarded a train. They were never seen again in the village

CHAPTER TEN

Jack glanced up at the great wheels turning, the cages constantly riding up and down the shaft below, he couldn't remember how many times had he been dropped into the earth. At first it was a terrifying experience when he was a boy, the veterans pulling his leg about the cable breaking, his face determined yet not able to hide the fear of being dropped eight hundred and fifty feet into the earth, and then the sudden stop and the good natured banter of the men as they laughed and joked about it.

'You'll get used to it son, you've got no choice,' his own trembling voice telling them that he wasn't afraid and the condescending, 'yes we noticed,' followed by more chuckling.

He had reached the top of Pit Bank and was turning into the entrance of the pit yard where a scene of organised chaos confronted him.

There were men everywhere, the miners were working as labourers now under the direction of the pit engineers. Railway lines were being laid, two huge hoppers were being erected, giant square funnels where the coal was tipped and then emptied into the big coal waggons, up to thirty at a time hauled by the powerful steam engines that would take them to the mainline and then onto Newcastle or Sunderland to be loaded into coal barges and carried to all parts of the country.

The shaft was now two hundred feet deep, the sinkers working round the clock, a dangerous job but paid accordingly, which was little consolation if the shaft wall collapsed while they were working, and it did, often with tragic results but there hadn't been any deaths, but there was a long way to go.

The hawthorn hedges on the surface were trying to produce new leaves and the scrubby blackberry bushes were throwing out suckers. The rain had washed them clean and they had burst forth with a new lease of life, but it would be temporary, soon the coal dust would reduce them to the scraggy excuses of what was once a farmers hedge, luxuriant foliage and juicy blackberries every late August, but alas the pit put paid to that, what was once open farmland was now a vast site of mans industrial might.

Jack wondered for a moment if the land would ever return to its original state, not that he could do anything about it or wanted to, it paid his wages, but he couldn't help think that they were doing something wrong, the earth shouldn't be like this, he had heard that experts had said that the coal would run out in a hundred and fifty years, which wouldn't affect him, but what would happen then, he thought, maybe things would be better, who knows, but anyway he would be with Ada by then.

He was crossing the yard now, wooden scaffolding was everywhere. The lamp cabin was going up fast, two dozen bricklayers' working day and night. The cabin was one of an important series of buildings that would allow the smooth running of a deep mine, the pit pony surface stables were almost finished. The pit ponies were sturdy little animals and worked hard underground only coming to the surface for an occasional holiday in the summer.

George Bassett watched the powerful form walking across the pit yard, and smiled to himself. He's a tough bugger that one, he thought, the man made it look as though he was out for an afternoon stroll. But he also knew that he was a tough bugger as well and that matters had to be sorted, and he was the man paid to do it. He wasn't happy about it but the word happy was an elusive emotion, was anyone happy, really. He doubted it, but like the men and boys who worked for him happiness didn't win coal and didn't feed their families so most simply got on with their jobs. An example had to be made, but we'll see, he thought, hoping that an agreement could be sorted, but when he saw the look of pleasure on Ridley's face he thought it wasn't likely.

He had never liked Ridley, but he was good at his job, and at the end of the day that was what he was paid for and he intended to do what was necessary even if it meant people's lives would be changed forever. Production at the old drift had been excellent and he intended that the same would apply when the shaft of the new deep mine was completed. He also knew from old that if you were soft then the miners would take advantage. The overman was in charge of all underground operations and had to be one hell of a tough character and that's why Ridley was the man in charge down there. Right thought Bassett, I know what needs to be done, then satisfied with his decision he turned and sat at his mahogany, leather topped desk. He had bought it himself from Farnons of Newcastle and cherished it like the wool carpet from Hugh Mackays of Durham that adorned the office floor. No-one was allowed to walk on it unless they removed their boots or shoes and pulled on a pair of slippers, which sat in a row outside his office door.

He noticed Ridley fidgeting, his one eye twitching, the disfigured skin on the left side of his face red with excitement, it looked like melted candle wax, he thought, and why had he dressed like that, a gaudily coloured paisley waistcoat and a faded single breasted serge suit that was obviously past its best, even his tie was knotted badly, never mind, thought George, he probably thinks he's dressed to the nines.

Brophy was sitting three feet away in front of the leather topped desk, he was uncomfortable, he wasn't used to being in posh surroundings like this. He took in the wallpaper, dainty little pale roses and not a thorn in sight, the smell of polished leather gave the room an air of authority and the thick woollen carpet felt soft and luxurious through the old slippers he had been made to wear before he entered the room. He was in no doubt that this was where decisions were made, decisions without any thought of the miner, a man could be broken on a whim by the all powerful pit manager sitting behind his desk. The man was portly with a round kind face, but there was still a power in his body that came from working underground, his eyes were hard and bright and very alert, this was a dangerous man, thought Brophy.

The manager lifted his pocket watch out of his waistcoat and then looked at the big wall clock as though checking the correctness of his watch, which was an unnecessary act as it was always accurate.

Jack knocked on the outer office door.

'Come,' said a reedy voice.

Jack opened the door and entered the room.

'Take your boots off and put those slippers on,' commanded the clerk, a slight man with thinning wispy hair.

'Hello Cyril,' said Jack cheerfully, although he didn't feel it, 'still got your head up the boss's arse you slaverry bugger, still scraping and bowing eh?'

'How dare you Walker, you'll be laughing on the other side of your face when you come out of there,' he poked his thumb over his shoulder to the door behind him.

'Name,' he said holding his quill poised over a big ledger.

'You know my name, weasel.'

Cyril looked over the top of his round spectacles in what he thought was an angry glare, but only made him look like a petulant child and wrote Jack's name down.

'Stay there,' he said and stood up, walked across the floor of his little empire and tapped on the door.

'Come in,' called a strong voice.

'Mister Bassett sir, it's Walker sir,' Cyril was bobbing and bowing all the time, Jack half expected him to curtsy.

George simply nodded, one day he would get a proper clerk, he thought, not the snivelling wretch he had now.

Cyril held the door open for Jack who purposely squeezed the man against the door frame making him whimper, an action noticed by fat Geordie. The door closed behind Jack and he saw Brophy for the first time.

The surprised look was not lost on Bassett, he motioned Jack to sit down.

'I'd prefer to stand mister Bassett, if you don't mind.'

'I do mind, and I'll ask you to sit with the rest of us,' whereupon he sat down followed by Ridley who hadn't picked up on the managers hint at first.

'Right, that's better.'

Jack knew he had lost the initiative now, not that he had any chance of getting the upper hand, he was amongst the men who controlled every action in his life, they decided where and how he would work, where he would live. They could even decide to fine him out of pure malice for short weights on the tubs he sent to the surface, he could even end up in debt to them by having to use the Tommy shops, the despised system where a miner when fined would only be able to use grocery stores owned by the management because he didn't have any money. Rather than let his family starve he would tick on at these stores paying double the normal price for goods and end up owing the owners more than his next fortnightly wage, the tally being deducted before he received anything, sometimes it increased the man's debt so that he had nothing to take home. I would rather starve to death, he thought. Anyway he was out of his depth, the posh surroundings were from another world, a world alien to him, pictures on the wall, proper cloth curtains and the desk, well that was something else, a bit different from the rough wooden table he was used to. This was polished and shiny and smelt of, what was it? Well off was the best he could come up with. He was annoyed with himself because he shouldn't feel inferior but generations of working class people ran through his veins and it was just something that made you feel as though you were different from these, these, he struggled for the word and ended up with simply posh buggers.

Someone was talking, his voice edged with annoyance.

'What?' said Jack impatiently, until he realised that he was being spoken to directly.

'I said what you have got to say for yourself?' said Bassett, a touch of annoyance in his voice at the thought that anyone could possibly ignore him when he spoke.

'What about?' said Jack.

Bassett became more than annoyed now, how dare anyone ignore him.

'He wants to know what happened when you thumped Ridley,' said Brophy, trying to diffuse the situation.

Jack turned and looked at the man next to him.

'I'm neither deaf nor stupid, I heard what he said and I'll answer him in my own good time, so I'll ask you to shut your trap.'

'I'm sorry,' he said looking across the room at the manager.

'That's all right Jack,' said Bassett gently, 'let's get things sorted out.' Mister Ridley has accused both of you of assaulting him whilst he was carrying out his duties, I have no reason to doubt the man and I'm more concerned as to why you did it. '

Bill's face showed indignation and disbelief at the same time.

'He's a damned liar.'

'That's enough,' said Bassett. His voice rising, 'I'll have no insults and no arguments about this, so watch your mouth.'

Ridley had stood up and was bobbing up and down, his excitement was becoming obvious.

'Mister Ridley, please sit down,' said Bassett.

'Yes your honour, I mean sir,' said the excited man and sat down abruptly.

Jack wondered what he would have done if there wasn't a chair behind him and secretly smiled to himself at the vision of the man sitting on the floor just because fat Geordie told him to.

'I am neither a judge, nor a lord,' boomed Bassett, 'you will address me as mister and nothing else. Good God he thought, the man's bonkers.

'Yes sir, I mean mister,' he tried to smile but ended up

looking like a bad dog in front of his master. You stupid snivelling bastard thought Jack.

Bassett looked up at the ceiling in dismay and carried on.

'The fact is, I am obliged to accept Mr Ridley's statement as true, there were two other witnesses who agree with mister Ridley, or should I say agreed as one has suffered a tragic accident and the other has disappeared, but nevertheless they have made their mark on paper as to what happened. The mines inspector has also stated that the tragedy of the children is outside of the mine's responsibility and no blame can be attached to the men who were merely carrying out their duty as instructed by the mine owners and through me as their deputy. After considering all the information that I have, I have decided that you are to be given your papers immediately.'

Jack was slowly shaking his head from side to side, Brophy merely stared at Bassett in amazement and then rose from his seat.

'Is that it?' his voice booming across the room in its slow laconic Cumberland drawl, 'so you're judge, jury and executioner without hearing our side of the story, you should be ashamed of yourself.'

Bassett remained seated.

'How dare you speak to me in that manner,' there was an angry edge to his voice, 'just remember who you're talking to boy.'

'I know fine well who I'm talking to, mister Bassett,' he sneered as he emphasized the name, 'you're the man who's supposed to look after his men and you're not doing a good job of it, that's the bastard who did it, not us.'

'Shut up, now,' shouted Bassett, 'I'll have no foul language in my office, you hear?' he demanded. But Brophy wasn't going to shut up, he had lost his job and had nothing to lose.

'You,' he snarled, pointing his finger at Bassett, 'are covering that murderers arse, and that makes you no better than him,' he looked to Jack for support but could see from his resigned expression that he would get no help there.

'Get out of my office now.'

'My bloody pleasure,' retaliated Brophy and stormed out of the room, his caustic glance at Cyril on the way out causing the little man to wince in fear. Brophy tore off his slippers and threw them at the office door.

Jack had stood up to leave.

'Well?' said Bassett.

Jack looked at him and shook his head, he spoke quietly 'You're wrong Mr Bassett, you truly are, the wrongdoer is beside you and one day he will pay the price for what he has done.'

'You can't talk to me like that Walker,' said Ridley. 'I always said you were a troublemaker and now I'm proved right,' he was bobbing about excitedly, a smile creasing the scars on his face, his eye twinkled with glee. 'The Lord is on my side, I've been saved to sort the likes of you out.'

Got him, thought Seth. It was better that he should never see the man again, better for both of them. He stared hard at Jack, his expression almost gentle. Jack saw the look and was taken aback. Was that pity or compassion he had seen for an instant, more likely guilt he thought as he stared back at Seth.

'That's enough,' said Bassett.

Jack turned to leave.

'Jack, a moment please.' Seth, go and check how the shaft sinking is progressing.'

The man hesitated.

'Now Seth,'

Seth looked annoyed, something was going to be said that he wouldn't hear. Never mind, Cyril would tell him everything that was said, or else, he winked at the little man as he left. Cyril shuddered in disgust then stood up and put his ear to the door.

Bassett sat quietly for a moment as though sorting out the words in his head, he knew what he wanted to say but had to be careful how he said it, it wouldn't do to let the men think he was soft, and also he had to take into consideration that the man sitting before him was lower working class, whilst he was, what? he thought, I wonder where I am in the pecking order. He knew he was working class but he was management, no, he was the bloody manager, he must be upper working class. He'd never really thought about it before and admittedly it did give him a sense of superiority. He immediately pushed the word and the feeling away, what a pompous arse I am. He laughed inwardly at a vision of himself attending the annual grouse shoot at lord what's his names farm, he would never be accepted, so stop putting on airs and graces. A cough brought him back from his, what? Dreams? Fantasy? Did he really want to be accepted? Bollocks he thought and looked at Jack across from his desk. A simple face, no, an easy face, even though he had lost his wife the man looked at ease with his lot. Nevertheless he looked like the kind of man you would rather have on your side if there was trouble, his tousled hair and happy face, yes that was it, the man couldn't help looking happy even if he wasn't, but he was a tough customer. Bassett had seen his tallies and the man probably shifted more coal than anyone else in the pit and now he was losing him because of that pipsqueak Ridley.

'Did you want me mister Bassett?'

'Err, yes, look Jack, I know what's happened and I am

governed by the rules and like all of us have to do what our bosses tell us,' why did he feel uncomfortable under the man's piercing gaze, he never took his eyes off him.

'I want to say how sorry I am about your wife,' Jack's eyes and head dropped a little and Bassett knew he had broken the man's guard, he felt on top again, or was it superior, never mind, he reached into the drawer in his desk then handed Jack an envelope.

'Thanks Mr Bassett, but as far as doing what our bosses tell us then we'll have to differ. I do what's right, not just to please others and you might remember where you came from yourself and ask if you've done the right thing today.'

Bassett almost apologised but stopped himself, he spoke harshly.

'I've got a job to do and that's the way it is Jack.'

'Aye, but for what price, mister Bassett, sir?'

Jack opened the envelope and scanned the contents only managing to figure out a few words.

George was about to ask the question when Jack cut in.

'I can read, not good, but enough, not all of us sign with a cross, and I'd like to thank you for this, theirs many who'd just forget and get on with it, but you're not like the rest and I'm sorry for what I said.'

'There's a price to be paid for advancement Jack, I didn't

know that but now I've got no choice and sometimes wish I was where you are, but that's as maybe and it's not going to happen, I like the luxuries that I have and surely you can't blame me for that,' it was a statement not a question. 'But you have a chance now, you're not forced to stay at the bottom of the pitheap Jack, you're a clever lad and can move on and why shouldn't you? We have a lot in common Jack, you remind me of me.'

'Aye well Mr Bassett, let's hope I don't end up like you then.'

George looked Jack in the eye and realised that they could never be equal, he was now one of them, not part of the community, something above ,but perhaps not respected which saddened him and there wasn't a damn thing he could do about it. Would he give up his lifestyle? Not a chance. The gap was there and it had to be accepted.

'All right Jack you've said your piece and I've said mine, so let's get on with our lives, you're finished here and we will probably not meet again.' He nodded to the door.

'Oh, by the way Jack.'

'Yes?'

'Learn your letters, you won't get anywhere unless you do that.'

Jack touched his finger to his forehead and left, cursing

himself for what he had just done, he wasn't a serf.

Cyril saw the anger in Jack and said nothing, bowing his head pretending to look at some papers. Jack took off his slippers and threw them at the man.

'You crawling arse licking little shite,' he said as Cyril ducked behind his desk. The door slammed and the clerk watched in case the man returned, but he heard his footsteps clattering down the stairs and slowly relaxed.

CHAPTER ELEVEN

Jack left the office building, his head full of hate, disgust and sadness. His Ada wouldn't have been very happy with what had just happened. His mood fell into despair when he thought of her, oh God how it ached to be without her. What the hell was the point of everything, he asked himself.

He was wallowing in self-pity now, the meeting forgotten when out of the corner of his eye he spotted a commotion across the pit yard. The new man, what was his name again? Yes that was it, Brophy. Why was he racing across the yard? It could only be an accident, he started running. A group of miners were gathered around the new sinking. Shaft sinkers were a tough lot but their job was incredibly dangerous and something had happened. A man was lying on the ground covered in mud and dirt. Jack's natural authority took over.

'What's happened?' he shouted above the noise. One

man turned towards him.

'There's a young'un trapped down there,' he cried, jabbing a finger down the shaft.

'How deep,' shouted Jack.'

'Thirty five fathoms,' came the answer.

Jack ran to the edge looking down into the hole, two hundred and ten feet was a long way down he thought. By now other miners were watching what he was doing.

'Somebody hook that cradle across the shaft,' he gestured to the huge kibble, an iron bucket that hung over the drop, used for shifting the spoil and carrying the sinkers up and down the shaft.

A thin wiry man thrust a long pole with a metal hook on the end to pull the bucket across, he was wearing the typical sinkers hat, made from canvass like a sou'wester with a long flap at the back which offered slight protection against falling rocks.

'You must be daft son, the kid hasn't got a chance down there, all you'll be doing is risking your neck to bring up what's left of him.'

Jack paused for a moment.

'Kid? How old is he for hell's sake?'

'Turned eighteen,' was the answer.

'And you're just going to bloody leave him there, what if

he's alive? said Jack, suddenly annoyed.

'You,' he pointed at another miner, 'a short shovel and a lamp and sharpish,' the man ran to get the gear.

'Make that two lad,' a slow Cumberland drawl rasped out.

He turned to see Brophy beside him, they looked into each other's eyes, Jack's showed resentment at Brophy's determination but nodded slightly, any help would be accepted.

He climbed into the huge bucket holding out his hands for the tools, Brophy followed.

'Let go,' called Jack.

The bucket swayed crazily over the black void, a gasp from Brophy gave little satisfaction to Jack, as he was trying to hide his fear as well, as he dangled over the chasm below their feet. Any man who said he wasn't afraid at times like this was either a liar or crackers. He looked at Brophy noticing the huge hands and the great shoulders for the first time, the lad would have a chance with a man like that he thought, if they could get there in time.

The bucket gradually slowed and settled.

'A rope dammit,' said Jack.

One of the men rushed away and quickly returned with one of the many coils of rope that were scattered around the pit yard.

Jack grabbed the end of the coil judging the length and deciding it was long enough, Brophy quickly realised why and called out.

'One for stop, two for up, three, lower us slowly, four, get us out as soon as you bloody well can.'

'Let us down,' called Jack.

The bucket hung from a davit that crossed the mouth of the shaft, a small steam engine with a tiny version of a pit wheel held a steel cable that fastened to the bucket with a big iron staple.

The banksman who was in charge of the top of the shaft held up his hand.

'Hold on there lad, this is my shaft. You don't have to tell me how to do my job and divvent get perplexed aboot it mind.'

Jack and Brophy both nodded to the banksman in respect. It wouldn't do to try and take over another man's job.

The banksman returned the nod in acceptance and released the brake. The bucket disappeared from sight, dropping at an alarming rate of sixteen feet a second, Jack would never get rid of the gut churning sensation no matter how many times he went underground. He glanced at Brophy, the man's features showed no emotion. Then total blackness enveloped them.

They were in a different world, the world of the miner, the underground savage as some considered them. But not many men would step into their shoes, they considered their situation as just part of the working day. They were intent on the job in hand, and that was to save a terrified boy from certain death.

They sat quietly as the bucket descended, both men intent on lighting their carbide lamps. A carbide lamp was no good in a gassy mine but the sinker had assured them that he had not discovered gas in the new shaft. Jack unscrewed the valve that allowed water to drop onto the carbide rock in the lower container and waited a moment, there, the stink of rotten eggs as the reaction created the flammable gas. He opened a small wooden box containing Swan White Pine Vestas, a new type of match light that when drawn along a strip of grit paper, would burst into flames and the wax impregnated wood kept it burning long enough to light the lamp. He scraped the match on the side of the box and applied the flame to the lamp, the rotten egg smell faded as the gas ignited, giving the best light of any of the mining lamps around. The large reflector that was six inches across lit up the surrounding area. A faint light by anyone who lived on the surface, but to a miner it was the closest thing to daylight they would see underground. Brophy's lamp was burning steadily now and they adjusted the flame by reducing the water supply to prolong the life of the carbide stones. They looked at each other and nodded, there was no need to say anything, both men knew instinctively what they had to do.

The bucket slowed, the banksman up top had the wheel marked so that he knew exactly when to ease off the speed. Brophy tugged the rope once and the bucket stopped. They were swaying slightly but began to steady as the downward movement stopped. Brophy put a finger to his lips, Jack nodded. They listened intently, trying to penetrate the creaks and groans of the earth as though she was angry at the intrusion of these men.

'Is that a light?' a faint voice groaned, 'who is it?'

Jack immediately pointed his lamp down into the blackness, scanning the shaft, it was only sixteen feet wide so they should find the boy soon enough.

'Got him,' he whispered to Brophy, 'three pulls, and,' he waited as the bucket gently dropped, 'and one pull.'

The canvas bucket rested on the rock, both men jumped out and shone their lamps on the boy, the timber shoring was groaning and one wall was bellying out and water was pouring through the gaps in the timber. The men glanced at each other, they didn't have much time.

'What's your name son,' Jack was kneeling beside the lad. A pair of terrified eyes, strikingly bright in the darkness shone into the lamp.

'I thought I was done for mister,' his teeth gleamed through his black face.

'You're not safe yet kid,' said Brophy, 'you've got to do exactly what we tell you, right?'

Both men started digging, the boy was buried up to his waist, his frantic efforts to get free had torn most of his fingernails to bloody shreds and tears had left lines down his blackened face. He had been carrying chalk, his job was to mark the depth of the shaft, and had left a message on a piece of scrap timber, God has decided that it is my time, it said. Jack grabbed it and gave it to the lad.

'Dig,' he said, 'God will have to wait son, now get cracking.'

'You didn't tell us your name,' said Brophy, a grim smile cracking his face, showing a confidence that he didn't feel.

'Jimmy,' the boy grunted, as he hacked at the filth that held him trapped.

Maybe, just maybe I'll get out of this, he thought, his mam needed his pay, his Dad had died in a pitfall and she depended on Jimmy to keep a roof over their heads. The thought gave him a new vigour to his actions that didn't go unnoticed but the shaft was in danger of collapsing in on itself as water began to pour through the wider gaps between the timbers.

'Please, please,' gasped Jimmy, 'don't leave me to die.'

A look of terror in his eyes as he saw what was happening. The shaft wall was only inches from the men, it was about to collapse onto them.

'Steady son, you've got to be brave,' Jack glanced at Brophy as he said it and Jimmy noticed. His cries turned to screams of abject fear.

'Shut up boy, 'said Brophy as he slapped him hard across the face.'

'Jack, get this rope under his arms and tie him tight. Jack quickly obeyed, Brophy was in the bucket and urging Jack to get in.

'We're getting you out of here,' cried Jack as Brophy quickly tugged the rope four times. They started to rise, the rope around Jimmy held, the hole they had dug around the boy had left only his legs trapped in the filth. As the bucket increased its speed, it plucked the boy out of his grave and they rode to the surface, Jack hanging on to the outside of the bucket as the shaft collapsed about them.

'Hang on son,' shouted Brophy over the edge, 'you're going to be all right.'

The water was gushing into the shaft but the bucket was rising swiftly, they could hear the wooden shoring being sucked into the inferno as the shaft collapsed around them. Jimmy was shouting at the top of his voice but the men couldn't hear what he was saying. Suddenly they were in the light and the bucket stopped. The davit was swung to the side and Brophy jumped out calling to the others.

'Get the bloody thing higher, the kid is hanging underneath the damned thing,' he shouted.

As it was winched higher Jack grabbed Brophy's hand and was heaved over the edge of the shaft and to safety. The miners grabbed the canvas bucket and manhandled it to one side while others grabbed the rope and dragged it up. A tousled head appeared and then a black face, the eyes wide with terror. The lad was still shouting incoherently, Brophy knelt down beside him.

'Jimmy son, what the hell are you blabbering about, you're eighteen and have to act like a man, what are you crying for?' Brophy had noticed the tears running down the boys cheeks.

Jimmy calmed down at the insult to his manhood and muttered something to Brophy.

Brophy stood up with a smile on his face.

'Is Mrs Hutton here?' he shouted to the villagers who had gathered at the pit. A woman in a pinny and headscarf shoved her way through the crowd.

'I'm here,' the woman said.

'C'mon get your boy lass, he's fine now.'

'I'm not a boy mister, you said it yoursell,' putting on as manly an expression as he could after his ordeal.

'The thing is Mrs Hutton, 'said Brophy.

'Call me Ethel son, you've just saved my lad's life,' she said.

'Aye, that's as maybe, err Ethel, but the thing is,' he raised his voice so that everyone could hear. 'Jimmy's new boots that you bought him from the Co-op have been sucked off his feet and he's scared stiff about what you're going to say to him when you find out.'

'Come here you silly bugger,' she said to her son, her voice quivering. 'What do I care about boots when I've got you, you daft sod, come here,' whereupon she wrapped her arms about him and nearly suffocated the boy in her enormous bosom. Jimmy fought for air as the crowd erupted into laughter.

Next morning Jimmy's Mother was stirring porridge when she heard a slight sound in the back yard, she smiled to herself.

'Jimmy, are you ever going to get you're lazy backside out of that bed?' her voice booming through the house.

'Aye mam I'm coming,' he answered. She just didn't understand how a man felt, how a man had to hide his feelings and act proper, but she was only a woman even if she was his mam. He stretched and clenched his fists, bending them backwards and cracking the knuckles.

'I've told you not to do that boy; you'll pay for it in the future, and your Dad was just the same.'

'Aye and he didn't listen to you either did he, and I'm not a boy.'

Ethel smiled sadly at the thought of her dead husband, killed long ago by a rock fall underground, and now she had nearly lost her little boy. She didn't want him to go back but was there a choice?

'You're porridge is on the table and I'm waiting to start son.'

He didn't mind son it was better than boy and he jumped out of bed and pulled on his linings. He liked to wear the pitman's long shorts in the house, he ran into the sitting room.

'Afore you start pet, I heard a noise out the backend go and have a look will you?'

Jimmy cocked his head, she never said things like that.

'Aye right if you say so,' he answered brightly, the trauma of two days ago had gone as though it had never happened. He went to the back door.

Oh how he bounces back, the joy of youth, immortality,

fitness and a clean fresh outlook on life. She knew it would soon change after a few years underground but let him enjoy life for now.

'Are you still there son?' she called with a smile on her face.

She got up from her chair and stepped into the scullery, Jimmy was sitting on the step by the back door, there were tears running down his cheeks as he caressed the soft leather of a pair of boots that were sitting on the step. He looked up at his mam.

'Thank you,' he said, I thought you would be vexed over me losing the other pair, they were brand new mam, don't tell anybody you saw me crying mind will you?'

'Don't be daft lad,' she pulled him to his feet, 'It wasn't just me you daft bugger, everybody put money into the kitty for you. You made such a fuss about losing the last pair that everybody felt,' she stopped short of saying sorry for you and quickly changed it to, 'concerned about how you cared for your mam and decided that you should have a new pair of boots. They've been made by Charlie Watts and he's even put your name on them.'

'No,' he said in disbelief. He knew Charlie was the best cobbler and shoemaker in the area. 'He made them for me?'

'Aye lad, if you have a look on the side of each boot you'll see.'

Jimmy picked up the boots and saw his name impressed into the soft leather of each boot, he shook his head slowly.

'Come here she said, 'you're not too big to give your mam a cuddle, and don't worry, I'll say nowt about you being a cry baby.'

Jimmy blushed a little but wrapped his arms about his mother, she didn't let him see the little tear that popped from her eye. She pushed him away and looked at him sternly, once it frightened him but now he just smiled.

'Mind you, look after them lad, pork rind to keep them soft, segs in the soles, there's still some of your Dad's in the shed, and black cherry blossom every day. You've got a lot of folk to say thank you to my lad, especially those two men that saved my bonny bairn.'

He blushed again. 'Stop it mam, I know what to do, right?'

'Aye lad, I'm just your mam,' and smiled at her son. Her face shed twenty years and Jimmy saw for the first time the pretty woman behind the sadness.

'You're not just any mam, mam, you're my mam and I'm going to look after you forever, you hear?'

She smiled again and turned to the sink and began to peel the potatoes for the stew that night. Jimmy was still admiring his boots when he heard her singing happily in the scullery, he turned his head and wondered about her past for the first time in his life.

CHAPTER TWELVE

Jack was content, the lad was safe and he felt as though he had discovered a purpose in his life. What if he could do this all the time, help people, well, miners, imagine being able to save the poor buggers trapped underground as the air was crushed out of their lungs by tons of rock crushing down on them. What about the kids who bled to death after being hit by a tub, common enough but there was no one there to help or stem the life giving blood as it seeped into the unforgiving earth hundreds of feet underground while they cried for their mothers. He was at Madge's, she had insisted. Both he and Brophy sat in separate tin baths filled with hot water in front of the fire. He sat in the tub unashamed, she had seen everything he had and he wasn't embarrassed, why should he be, although it was different with Brophy. He hummed and harred about taking his clothes off and Madge had been forced to leave the room while he hurriedly stripped off, casting sidelong glances at the door as though she would step back in, then sploshed into the tub and covered his manhood with a flannel, a six inch square piece of cotton for washing down with, Jack looked across and laughed out loud.

A bloody flannel's no good for you man, it's not going to hide that thing you need a cart to carry it around.'

'Shut up will you and keep your voice down.'

At that moment there was a knock and Madge walked in.

'Is that better?' she asked, 'do you want some more water? The kettle's just warming up pet,' she said, looking at Brophy.

Her eyes wandered over the man and she raised an eyebrow, a little smile on her face.

'Now I know why they call it Cumberland sausage,' she said.

Brophy's face looked as though it had been scalded as he looked for something to cover himself with.

'Divvent worry pet, it does me heart good to see a man with a, well, you know what I mean,' she said, looking up at Jack as he stood and wrapped a towel around his waist.

Brophy didn't miss the look between them but was more concerned about his nakedness.

'We'll leave you to it,' she said, and they both left the

room.

Brophy wasn't daft where women were concerned and carried on giving himself a good wash down, ignoring the creak of the iron bedstead in the next room.

* * *

'Are you lads going to sit around all night,' said Madge as she opened the front door leading into the garden, where both men were sitting on a bench made from old railway sleepers. They had been enjoying the break in the weather, the rain had stopped and it was one of those rare English summer evenings, the sun low in the sky, casting its light over gold and yellow clouds that were scattered across the sky, the warm air resting gently on the green fields stretching into the distance, the trees a lush green after all the rain, the pit heaps smouldered in the sun, little tendrils of steam floating upwards from the slag, the whinny bushes bright green with their dazzling yellow flowers, clinging to the sides of the heaps. It was odd thought Jack that you only saw those bushes on pit heaps, why nowhere else? No matter, better minds than his could figure that one out. The pit wheels stuck up into the air in the distance, the ring of pits it was called, no matter where you went the view would always remind you of where you were, no chance of a romantic vision, but that was nonsense, he was a collier and that was that,. He was vaguely aware of voices.

'Are you bloody deaf lad,' a woman's voice called and for a moment he turned expecting to see his Ada, but it was Madge, he hid the look of pain.

'You must have been miles away bonny lad,' she said gently, she had seen the tiny look of disappointment that had crossed his face but pretended not to notice. 'I said, there's a club full of men at the end of the street who want to show you their gratitude for what you did today.'

'I haven't got much money spare pet,' he said, giving Brophy a sidelong glance at the same time, they hadn't said a word to each other since the rescue but a kind of companionship sat between them. Jack was trying to come to terms with this, in fact he was trying to come to terms with a hell of a lot of things at the minute.

'After today I'm going to need every penny I've got.'

'You don't need any money you daft bugger.'

'I won't take charity off any man.'

'You took it off me, didn't you?'

'That's different, you're not a man.'

'I've got a few bob Jack,' said Brophy, mind you'll have to pay me back as soon as you get paid.'

'It might be a long time afore I get paid mate.'

'I'll worry about that later, are you coming?' Brophy stood up and Jack reluctantly followed.

Jack turned to Madge. 'Listen pet, I got a letter off Geordie this afternoon but I don't know what it's about like,' he lowered his head as he stumbled over the next words, 'it's, well, I've never really learnt me words properly, if you see what I mean and I thought that maybe you would,' he fell silent.

'I'll sort it for you flower, we'll talk about it in the morning.'

Jack glared at Brophy daring him to say anything but he was already heading off down the garden path to the gate.

'Aye right then, I'll be off,' he said nervously.

She could have hugged him, but there were plenty nosey parkers peeping from behind curtains watching what was going on, so she simply smiled and then winked, which startled Jack because he had never seen a woman do that before, he followed Brophy down the path.

The club was heaving, built by the pit owners for the welfare of the miners and their families, it had reading rooms with a library, schoolrooms for those who wished to learn more, a meeting room and a huge ballroom with a stage at one end where harvest festivals, Easter and Christmas could be celebrated in style with barn dances and parties. Wedding receptions were grand affairs, the trestle tables covered in cotton tablecloths laden with home baked pastries and pickles, but it was the bar that saw the most business. A happy pitman would work better and there was nothing better for the common man than to down a cool pint of beer after work. Any excuse for a booze up was entertained, but here the miners were no different to the rest of the British nation.

Jack and Brophy entered the club and were stopped by the doorman at his desk. He was wearing a cap that had probably been made for the old queen's coronation and the face underneath looked just as old.

'Are ye members,' he growled and then took a pull from his pint, 'yul not get in if you're not mind.'

'You know fine well I'm a member,' said Jack.

'Aye that's as maybe, but what aboot him?' He pointed with his pint glass almost empty now, then looked at his tips tray in front of him.

Jack sighed and took a shilling out of his pocket and dropped it in the tray.

The doorman rapped his now empty glass on the table and soon the barman arrived with a foaming pint of beer.

'You'll never go to heaven you bloody sod, do you know that,' said Jack to the doorman.

'A divvent want to gan to heaven son, they divvent have any beer there, and me names not bloody sod if you want to get through there,' he pointed with his chin.

'Right, sorry, thank you Mr Johnston, can we go now?'

'No you cannat, are you going to sign him in as a guest or not?'

Jack leaned over and put his mark on the guest book, the doorman looked across at him and winked.

'I'll write it out proper for you shall I?'

'Please your bloody self,' Jack's eyes wore an angry glint as he said it, he whispered to the doorman.

'Can we go now? Mr bloody sod Johnston.'

Startled, the doorman pushed his chair back, he knew that look and decided that he had tormented the man long enough, and anyway he didn't like the look of that big bugger that was with him, he wasn't tall but he carried a lot of clout in that body and he wouldn't want to be on the receiving end. He stretched his neck and flexed his shoulders.

'Aye gan on be off with you.'

Once upon a time thought the doorman, I would have took both of you on, but that was then, the pit had sapped him of his strength, he was worn out and knew it, confined to the sorting sheds with bairns and old women, but never mind, there was nowt to go home for, his missus was worn out and all she did was nag. He was content at the club and anyway his next pint was about to arrive.

'Are you a member?'

Jack raised his eyes to the ceiling and Brophy smiled to himself thinking that the old bugger had total control over who came and went in the club.

They pushed open the bar door, the sign above proclaiming 'Men Only', not that any woman would want to go into a men's bar anyway, but it put things in their place, the bar was a man's domain and a woman, any woman was barred from the place, Jack wondered if the Queen would be refused admission, probably, he thought, if that cantankerous bugger was on the door.

As they entered, the clack of dominoes hitting the table died away, so did the banter, the cheerful chatter of men with a drink in their bellies waiting to have their glasses refilled at the bar slowly died away, the tobacco smoke drifted in the air clinging to the ceiling like a rain cloud, the room stank of sweat and leather and stale beer and stale smoke and coal, always the smell of coal. The men stepped back forming a corridor for Jack and Brophy to get to the bar where the steward was standing behind it, two brimming glasses of beer on the counter. As they walked past the men they were greeted with a slight nod or a finger raised to touch the peak of a cap. An older man stepped out.

'What fettle son?' he asked of Brophy who looked at

Jack with a look of puzzlement on his face.

'I'll tell you later lad,' said Jack and answered the man with a 'Canny man.'

'That was my sisters bairn you pulled oot today, so am thankin you from the bottom of me heart and will you allow me to buy you a pint.'

'I'll not take charity mind,' said Jack, 'but I'll gladly accept you're offer.'

With that the bar erupted as the men clapped Jack and Brophy on the back, shook their hands and told them what heroes they were. All night long their little round table, which the steward had brought from the snug, copper covered and usually only used by pit officials, was never empty of brimming pints of foaming beer. Brophy was enjoying himself as the alcohol filtered into his bloodstream, he felt warm and comfortable and wanted a woman. Not much chance in here, he thought, but the beer was good, then he remembered what the man had said.

'Jack? His voice louder with the drink and just a hint of a slur, 'what did that fella mean before?'

Jack snapped out of his thoughts of his wife, he hoped she was proud of him and he hoped she would understand about going to bed with another woman.

'What? Oh that you daft bugger, you talk a different

language over there in Cumberland don't you? Fettle means are you well and you answer canny man, which means I'm fine, alright?

'Brophy nodded.

'Nobody's ever said anything like that to me before,' he smiled and downed the last half of his glass of beer. Immediately another appeared on the table.

'Have that on me lad, with my thanks.'

They lost all sense of time, it was like a New Year's Eve party, but the two of them gradually subsided into a weird world of drunkenness.

'A miner came across to them and studied their faces.

'Aye lads they're blotto. Steward, bring out the bottle.'

The steward proudly lifted a bottle of finest single malt whisky on to the bar, it was his pride and joy, only to be used on special occasions. He had cases of the stuff in the cellar and what the label said didn't necessarily mean that was what was in the bottle, but never mind, it was still good stuff.

He came out from behind the bar, an honour in itself and poured two generous measures into glasses at the table.

'This is from all of us lads, now drink it down and don't offend us mind,' he cast an emphasised wink around the room.

Jack looked up, his mouth slack and managed to mutter a slurred,

'Wha?'

Brophy raised his head, a stupid grin on his face and picked up his glass, drank the contents and slid off his stool onto the floor where he began to snore loudly.

Jack looked down at him and said, 'Oh.'

He concentrated on the position of the glass and reached out his hand and missed, the steward grinned and guided it to Jack's hand. Jack picked up the glass and with one last effort tilted it up as he leaned back and fell off his stool onto the floor, half of the whisky running down his face as he drifted off into oblivion.

Everyone cheered and drank to the health of the two men and then left them snoring contentedly on the floor of the club.

The steward rang the big ships bell behind the bar.

'Time please,' he hollered.

Jack heard the sound in the distance and felt arms lifting him to his feet, he staggered at first then managed to stay upright.

'You all right lad?' said a voice, Jack turned his glazed eyes to the speaker and not trusting himself to speak just nodded. Brophy was standing now, a stupid grin on his face, they were both led to the door and pointed in the direction of home and they started to walk, hanging on to each other for support, a cheer went up behind them as the miners spilled into the street waving to the two men.

A light drizzle cooled Jack off as he tried to get his bearings and then he staggered up the lane, Brophy hanging on for dear life, who was that standing there, he thought. They stumbled on when a voice stopped them.

'I've never seen anyone in such a state, you should be ashamed of yourselves, call yourselves men, get in here now the pair of you.'

Grateful not to have to walk any further they veered towards the voice and stood looking at Madge, or was there two of her thought Jack, as he shook his head which only made his vision even more blurred. Anyway he knew what to say, he formed the words in his mind clearly enough, he was going to thank her but he would stay at his own house tonight thank you all the same. What came out of his mouth was a slurred jumble of meaningless slobber so he gave up, smiled, and went inside, he sat on the settee, lay back and began to snore, Madge shook her head and pulled off his boots, Brophy had curled up on the floor behind the settee, she did the same for him and went to bed, trying to ignore the male harmony going on in the living room as she drifted off to sleep.

CHAPTER THIRTEEN

It was dark and it was raining again. A canopy of cloud hid the moon. Perfect conditions for the three men who approached the high wall at the end of the back lane. On the other side of that wall was George Bassett's house. The twenty four courses of locally manufactured bricks stopped prying eyes and also served as a reminder that those within were different to those outside. There was no broken glass embedded in cement along the top, as it was unthinkable that anyone would consider climbing over. But that was exactly what the three men intended to do. The biggest of the three stood with his back against the brickwork and cupped his hands. No one had spoken, they each knew exactly what to do. One of the other men placed a foot into the cupped hands and was hoisted upwards. He grabbed the top of the wall and pulled himself up and lay flat along the top. It was double bricked so there was just room enough. The second man followed him and they reached down to grab the hands of the biggest man. It was hard work pulling him up, the pit blacksmith was six feet tall, a heavy and hugely muscled individual, but the other men, though not as big, had years of hard graft under their belts and were strong enough to do the job. As soon as the blacksmith was on the top he turned and lowered himself into the garden, dropping the last two feet. The others followed, their feet being guided by the blacksmith's hands onto his shoulders and then lowered onto the ground. A curt nod to each other and they made their way across the lawns to a clump of bushes near the house. Someone was there, they dropped flat onto the wet grass. They heard the wood sliding in the grooves as the sash window snapped shut, the sound loud in the night air.

George went back to his desk, the rain had been coming through the window and the house was damp enough to start with. He sat down and took a soft linen cloth out of one of the drawers, he had touched the surface of his desk and left a smudge. He was polishing the wood when the glass of one of the window panes crashed inwards, a brick clattered onto the desk scraping a gouge in the lovingly polished oak, a sliver of glass rolled under the brick as it toppled onto the inset leather writing pad tearing the green beautifully tooled leather. George Bassett remained sitting in his captain's chair, a look of absolute shock and disbelief on his face. His heart was racing as he slowly rose and edged towards the broken window, his mind a turmoil of questions, why, who, what? He peered into the darkness but he knew it was only reaction, he had no chance of seeing anybody out there, especially since the drizzle had started. His comfortable world had been overturned in an instant. He glanced back into the room as his wife entered, clasping her hand to her mouth when she saw what had happened.

'George, look at the leather.'

For a moment he wondered if she would have felt the same if the glass was sticking out of his neck, probably not, he thought, she was more concerned about how things looked. It wouldn't do to have her friends around for afternoon tea with her husband writhing on the floor with a jagged lump of glass sticking out of him, the blood would ruin the carpet, the bitch.

'It's all right lass, I'm not hurt,' she didn't miss the sarcasm in his voice but ignored it anyway. He noticed a scrap of cloth in the hollow of the brick tied with string. His wife followed his eyes and reached across to untie the string, she opened the cloth and found a note inside. There wasn't any emotion on her face as she read the words on the paper. She handed it to George who slowly sank back into the chair as he read the words scratched in pencil.

'MURDERER.'

'Good God.'

'George, please, don't blaspheme.'

'Sorry lass, but what do I do with this?' he waved the paper at her.

'I didn't even know what was happening down at the drift, how can they say I murdered their bairns when I wasn't there,' he said

Ethel had hoped the matter had been forgotten about by now, but here it was raising its ugly head again, it really didn't do her reputation any good.

She was the daughter of a blacksmith, but since her elevation to the upper working class she had avoided her parents as she saw them as a burden on her way to the middle class that she yearned for. Dragged up by the scruff of her neck she wasn't going to let a bunch of common pitmen get in her way, or underground savages as she commonly called them, in private of course and never to George. She remembered all too well the life of poverty and squalor she had endured and had no intention of going back there, she would have to guide her husband through this and make sure that he didn't slip back into his old ways and become part of the rabble again. She knew what he was like, a couple of whiskies and he would start reminiscing about how he was part of them. A load of codswallop, but she would remind him of what he had and what he had achieved, he wasn't like them, he was better and anyway, she needed him, or at least his position, to move up the social ladder. She had a moment's thought about where George would fit in once she had achieved her ambition, obviously he would have to go. Of course she loved him, well, once she did, when he was a strapping miner, his muscles bulging out of his shirt just like the lad who delivered her groceries. She had already offered him a job as gardener and relished the look of understanding in his eyes. She was still good looking and her body attractive to younger men, especially the size of her breasts, which she delighted in showing off with her low cut gowns, to the frustrated husbands and jealous wives at their dinner parties. They still might consider her common, but by God she would show them. The lad had stood trying to look straight ahead but couldn't help his eyes drifting down to her cleavage and he kept flushing with embarrassment when she caught him looking, but she merely widened her eyes and carried on.

'I'm sure it will be sorted out George,' she said mechanically, as she returned to the present.

She reached for his decanter of whisky and poured him a generous measure of his favourite malt.

'Here, have a drink and then we'll talk about it.'

She knew full well that as soon as he hit the bottle any sensible conversation would end and he would eventually stagger up to bed. A shame really, she thought, he had been a fine figure of a man, now he couldn't even see his dick for the fat gut hanging over it. Well, shame for him, his loss, as she imagined the grocery lad with his clothes off, a shiver ran through her body as she left fat Geordie to his devices.

The three men had climbed back over the wall. The back lane was quiet apart from the footsteps of the man they had targeted for their next attack.

'Down, both of you,' said the blacksmith.

All three of them sank into the shadows of an alleyway as Seth walked past. Only a slight sway now and again showed he had had too much to drink. He was smiling happily to himself, the whore had been good tonight, she always left the light off, he could pretend he was normal which he was, well almost, apart from the livid scar tissue on his face that puckered up around his eye socket. But tonight he was wearing his best glass eye, his going out eye as he liked to call it and imagined that he was like anyone else, but it wasn't just the missing eye and the scars that made Seth different, he was mad. Mad in an intelligent way because he knew it, or thought he did but the good Lord had saved him from the disaster and he knew he was special, but she was good all the same. A surge of anger raced through him, she should be bloody well good, the bitch, he paid her enough. He flexed his shoulders and his thoughts turned to Jack Walker, he was sorted now and it was best for them never to set eyes on each other again. That other bastard who had been there had got his just desserts. Argue with Seth Ridley? Huh, the useless shite.

Tommy swung the pick axe handle and walloped Seth across the back of the head, the overman spun round and then collapsed on the path as his world went black.

'You've killed the bastard Tommy.'

'Shut your face Ralph,' said the blacksmith. 'You were the one who said if he saw us they would have our guts for garters, we all agreed to pay the sod back. If you're going to chicken out now then bugger off.'

Tommy rested the pick handle by his side.

'He would have got away with it, did you want that?' he hissed, 'and anyway, there's no chance of him identifying us now is there?'

He thrust his face into Ralph's and challenged him with his eyes, bright with fear now that he thought he had killed the man.

Ralph backed off, he wasn't afraid of the man but what he said was right, anyway he thought, what's done is done, he turned to the other man.

'Don't just stand there gawping, pull the bugger into the alley,' his voice edged with taut nerves.

They dragged Seth by his coat collar, his boot segs screeching over the brick path causing sparks to fly, Tommy raised his eyes, didn't they know how to do anything? He hadn't meant to kill the bugger. His breathing slowed as his heart stopped racing. He had almost certainly killed the man, how the hell did anyone come to terms with that, he thought. Anyway it served the bastard right, it was his daughter who was lying in the cold earth, but it didn't make him feel any better. What was that?

'Stop,' called out Nathan.

'What?'

'I said stop, didn't you hear that anybody?' He bent over the body, yes there it was again, a rasping sound as Seth tried to draw breath. He was alive.

'Prop him up against the wall and let's get the hell out of here,' whispered Tommy, 'and if anybody says owt there'll be hell to pay, do you understand? We're in this together, it was our bairns that died and it was all due to him.'

His face turned into a contorted grimace of hate as he stabbed his finger at the shape which was now groaning. They left, and the rain pitter pattered onto Seth's clothes until he was soaked through to the skin, a trickle of blood ran down the gutter into the street from the wound on his head, diluted by the rain.

* * *

It was that diluted blood that attracted the attention of the village Bobby. After twenty years in the force Arthur Asquith didn't miss much and there was something just not quite right about the colour of the rainwater running down the street, even though his mind was on other matters. His missus wasn't coping very well and he couldn't help thinking about how little Aggie used to run to the door when she heard him coming down the street, the bright smile and her eyes full of adoration for her daddy.

He didn't sound the alarm with his police whistle, because he was the only Bobby in the village, he followed the blood but stopped short at the alley listening for sounds. He heard a man groaning and pushed aside his cape to pull out his truncheon, eighteen inches of hickory polished to perfection. He cautiously edged along the wall of the alley. A man was propped against the wall of an outhouse, the rain trickling through a cracked gutter onto his head, it was obvious he needed help. Arthur peered closer and then recognised who the man was. A surge of hatred welled up in his gut. Here was the man who was responsible for Aggie's death. The man who had forced his daughter to gasp for air as the water gushed down her throat as he had imagined night after night, waking up suddenly as though he could save her, his hands reaching out until his wife, disturbed by the movements, would wake and they would lie together, holding hands, staring at the ceiling. And they would cry. One good belt on the head would finish the bugger off, thought Arthur and he was tempted, very, very tempted to do just that. But, at the back of his mind there was the thought that it was wrong, and he had been reared to believe that two wrongs don't make a right. It was his job to uphold the law and he lowered the raised truncheon, not realising that he had lifted it above his head, and hooked it back onto his belt. He could just leave, the bastard would surely die, he turned to walk away and then stopped. It was wrong. He opened the high wooden gate to the back yard and hammered on the back door of the house. A light appeared in the window, a hand holding a candle, and then a face snarling angrily.

'What the hell do you want,' growled a male voice.

'Open the door, it's the police.'

The candle waved about until the owner could see who it was. The door was opened and a small wiry man looked up at the policeman.

'Sorry Arthur, it's just that I'm on first shift and you

know how we all get a bit ratty, what's up?'

'There's a man outside your back wall and he's hurt, I need to get him inside.'

'What's happened to him?'

'It looks like he's been attacked.'

'What, round here, you must be mistaken.'

'Are you trying to tell me how to do my job? Frank Shoesmith'

Arthur drew himself up to his full height, at six feet three inches he peered down at the pitman knowing full well that underground he could never match the little man he loomed over but it always did the trick. Arthur's moustache and whiskers always gave him a military look like an RSM which was what he had been when he was fighting the Boers.

'Sorry Arthur, I meant no offence, fetch the man in, can he walk?' he added as an afterthought.

'No. I need your help.'

Frank followed the policeman out into the back lane, he saw the man propped against the wall but didn't recognise him in the dark, all he wanted to do was get out of the rain and back into bed. He helped Arthur pull him through the back yard into the scullery, pushing the door closed behind him. Seth was groaning and swearing.

'Stop your language, you're not down the pit now, d'you

hear, my wife won't tolerate it and neither will I,' said Frank, then a look of astonishment crossed his face as he recognized the man lying on the scullery floor.

'You get this bag of shite out of my house, now, if you don't, I'll kill the bastard meself, why didn't you just leave him, you would have done everybody a favour, dammit even your own bairn is dead thanks to him, what the hell are you playing at?'

A look of terrible anguish flowed across Arthur's face, immediately Frank realised what he had done.

'Arthur, look, I'm so sorry, I was angry, I shouldn't have said what I did, it's just, well, you know what I mean.'

The policeman simply nodded, his wet helmet was dripping onto the floor forming a little puddle on the stone slabs, and for a moment the only sound was the pat, pat as the water hit the floor.

Frank's wife came into the room, a shrew of a woman, she was carrying dry towels and an old blanket, she immediately got to work on Seth.

'What are you doing lass?' Frank looked at her in amazement.' You'll stop now and do as your told woman, in my house I make the rules.'

She stopped what she was doing and stood upright, tiny in comparison to the two men, and then she flew off the handle.

'Your house?' she shouted, her voice loud and resonant and it was amazing that it came from such a small frame.

'Who the hell do you think you are Frank Shoesmith? It's my house and I run it,' her voice was getting louder. 'That's why your dinner's on the table when you get in from work. Who do you think cleans your bloody dirty boots every damned day?'

'Sorry pet, I didn't mean it.' Frank threw his arms into the air and plonked down onto a wooden chair in defeat.

His wife glared at him and then at Arthur, who involuntary took a step backwards as she stared at the puddle on the floor.

'Right,' she said 'let's get this poor bugger sorted, I'll not have anybody saying this isn't a charitable house, whoever it might be I'm tending to.'

CHAPTER FOURTEEN

Jack was lying in bed looking up at the ceiling, it hadn't been distempered for a few years and bits of the whitewash were flaking. There was the ever present odour of mould, but it was the same in every home in the village. The driest houses were at the top end of the street, but it was the way the homes were constructed that was the real problem. The walls were built with a single skin of breeze blocks and then rendered with mortar and pebbles but the water still found its way in, particularly through the poor foundations. The windows were made from steel frames with small panes of glass six inches square, he remembered how Ada hated having to clean them. He became depressed at the thought, would she forgive him for being unfaithful he wondered. Like as not he would soon be with her anyway, miners didn't tend to live that long, wouldn't it be wonderful to hold her hand again and see her sparkling eyes.

But it wasn't going to happen so he might as well forget that for now. He was as God fearing as any man but recently his beliefs had been shattered and he was beginning to wonder if it was all claptrap. God certainly had never helped poor Jack Walker and that was certain. He rolled out of the bed, the old springs protesting as they changed position. He didn't feel too bad after the previous night but couldn't remember how he had got here, no doubt there would be a reckoning so he better tread carefully.

The door burst open, Madge was about to say something but instead stopped and eyed his naked body up and down.

'You're a bad lass, woman, you've seen it all before so stop staring.'

'Oh dear, a bit grumpy are we? It's different when you fancy a bit isn't it.'

'Aye but I never knew what a sex maniac you were before.'

'I can't help what I am, and I don't hear any complaints Jack Walker. Anyway you need to get your clothes on more's the pity, the candy men are outside your house.'

Jack grabbed his trousers and pulled them on as he made his way to the netty, if he didn't do that first he would burst, maybe it would help to stop his head and bladder aching.

'Nice backside,' called Madge as he left the room finally

hitching up the back of his trousers.

That's better he thought, as he pittled through the hole in the wooden planks onto the ashes in the netty, the pain was going from his belly, the ashes stank now, a sort of sulphurous tang like the fumes off those new fangled motor carriages. He went back inside the house and splashed cold water over his face from the scullery sink. As he was drying his face Madge passed him the salt cellar. He dipped his fingers back in the water then sprinkled salt over the first two and rubbed his teeth vigorously, gagging at the taste. An enamel mug of tea appeared in front of him and he gulped it down, he pulled his shirt on and fastened the buttons. He clenched his hands then reversed them and cracked the joints, the sound like pistol shots.

'Will you not do that Jack,' said Madge cringing at the sound.

He simply smiled and pulled his boots on lacing them up quickly. Brophy had appeared, rubbing his eyes and scratching his head.

'What's up?'

'Nowt for you to get concerned about,' said Jack,

Brophy nodded and went back to bed.

'You don't do anything stupid Jack, I know what you're like.'

'Don't fuss lass, I haven't got the strength to misbehave

this morning.'

He left the house and climbed the three steps from the backyard to the back lane, at least the rain had eased off for now. There was already a small crowd gathered outside ready to support him, but more likely wanting to find out what was going to happen next between him and the hated candy men. Well, they were going to be disappointed.

As he approached he could see the gaudy striped suits and bowler hats worn by the candy men. Rainbow colours on a white cotton background, they saw him coming and stood in front of his gate. Jack noticed that they were an inch or so taller than his own five feet nine inches, but that didn't bother him, it was the size of the men. They were almost as broad as they were tall and he bet there wasn't an ounce of spare fat on either of the brutes.

'Are you Jack Walker?' said one of them, his thick Irish brogue difficult to understand.

'Who's asking?'

The candy men raised their eyes, with a look of here we go again attitude.

'Look boy, you can make this as hard as you want or you can make it easy, my name is mister Harmless and this is my twin brother mister Harmless and we are harmless, unless you cause trouble, isn't that right Alastair,' he said, turning to look at his brother.

'That is indeed correct Callum.'

Alastair smiled at the small crowd maybe expecting a chuckle but was met with only a stony silence. There was nothing anyone could do, Jack had lost his job and the house belonged to the pit and the owners had issued an eviction notice. Callum Harmless raised the piece of paper in his hands and read the notice, it never differed in content, flowery words that simply meant that Jack was out on the street, he had one hour to collect his goods and leave.

'Irish bastards,' someone called out followed by a low rumble of anger from the growing crowd.

'We're only doing our job,' said the candy men in unison, 'so watch your lip.'

'Aye, a job that nobody else will do except you immigrants,' said Jack.

He was referring to the thousands of families that had come from Ireland, to settle in northern England. Offers of a happy and prosperous life with guaranteed work had attracted many Irish families to leave their homeland. When coalminers went on strike the Irish were brought in, which caused antagonism and violence among the two peoples. The Irish were Catholics and had their own meeting places and only socialised amongst themselves. They carried out the work that others wouldn't do and were tolerated, but the candy men were hated and despised for what they did.

The crowd was getting angry now and the Harmless brothers were standing back to back.

'We're going to the miner's hall and will be back in an hour to carry out our lawful duty, we don't want any trouble,' said Alastair Harmless and began to walk away with his brother while the crowd shouted abuse at them.

Jack opened his back door, stepped in and closed it behind him. He stood looking around, did he really want anything from this place. It was all a reminder of sad times. He collected some clothing and shaving gear and the hairbrush Ada had bought him last Christmas, it was made from fake turtle shell and genuine pigs bristle, at least that was what she had said. He smiled at the memory and the look of pleasure on her face when she had presented it to him. He shoved everything into a blanket and tied the ends together then sat down on the old armchair. He took a long look around him, this part of his life was over and like it or not it was time to move on. He must have sat for a long time for there was a heavy knock at the door. They were back, he slung the blanket over his shoulder and lifted the door latch.

'Mister Walker?'

'Mister Harmless,' he answered.

'Now you don't have to be rushing off like this you know. I mean we can let you stay longer if you wish, at a cost of course, like if you have anything of reasonable value or maybe some money? Of course it'll go no further than us if you know what I mean,' he smiled broadly and winked at Jack.

'Out of my way you bastard,' said Jack as he barged forward. Alastair Harmless brought a knee up into Jack's groin and as he doubled over Callum brought his fist down on Jack's head. Jack fell through the doorway and into the back yard.

'I told you he would be trouble didn't I Callum.'

'You did indeed Alastair.'

Alastair's face twisted in rage and fury as he booted Jack in the ribs, he smiled as he heard the bone crack. They locked the door with a short piece of chain and a padlock. They each grabbed one of Jack's legs and dragged him into the back lane, his head bouncing on the lip of each step.

There were three men waiting for them.

'That's far enough you bastards,' said Tommy the blacksmith, 'let loose of him now before I kick the shit out of you.'

'Ha, would that be on your own now,' said Callum Harmless as he eyed up the muscles on the man.

'He's not on his own though is he?' Said Ralph, looking across at Nathan who nodded.

The Harmless twins loosened their grip on Jack's legs which clattered onto the ground.

'You didn't have to do that,' snarled Tommy, his face now only inches from Callum's.

'You know you can't do anything boyo, so get out of our way.'

Tommy reluctantly stepped to one side while Ralph and Nathan lifted Jack into a sitting position.

'Top of the morning to you all,' called out Alistair, the twins tilting their bowler hats at a jaunty angle and walking away as the relentless rain started to patter down again.

CHAPTER FIFTEEN

Ralph was gently shaking Jack when he felt a hand on his shoulder.

'Leave him to me now pet,' said Madge.

Ralph looked up and nodded. A trickle of blood was running from Jack's mouth and Madge wiped it away with the corner of her dress.

'Jack, wake up man, you'll catch your death,' she whispered into his ear.

A few moments later Jack raised a hand to his mouth and his eyes opened. He frowned when he realised he was sitting on the ground, then understood why as his senses returned. Brophy had now appeared and helped Jack to his feet.

'The drama's over now people, you can all go home and gossip about it,' said Madge, a hint of sarcasm in her voice. She turned to Tommy and his mates.

'Thanks for your help men, it's much appreciated.'

They touched the peaks of their caps in response.

'Let's get him home Brophy,' said Madge.

He nodded.

'How?' he said.

'A man with your build should be able to manage that.'

Brophy lifted Jack to his feet intending to put him over his shoulder, but a sharp gasp of pain from Jack stopped him.

'Hold him there,' said Madge, 'I'll bring the hand cart.'

She ran off and soon came back with a two wheeled cart that she kept in her back yard.

'Let's lift him in, but gently,' she said.

'Jack, this is going to hurt you more than me,' said Brophy.

Jack just nodded.

Brophy put one arm behind Jack's legs and the other around his back and lifted him cradle fashion into the cart, ignoring the injured man's cries of agony. The solid tyres of the cart didn't make it any easier, as Brophy did his best to keep to the smoothest parts of the road. When he was back at home he lifted Jack out of the cart. Madge opened doors in front of him as he carried Jack into the house.

'Lie him on the bed,' said Madge as she began to pull off Jack's clothing. 'Grab some blankets will you, we need to get him warm as quick as possible.' Brophy dashed away.

Madge began to open Jack's shirt front when he gave a cry of pain, she stopped immediately and gently probed his ribs, his responding gasp showed her which rib it was and that it must be broken. Brophy returned with a heap of blankets.

'I need some Comphrey from the garden.'

Brophy turned his nose up, he was fully aware of the herb and also the incredible stink it gave off when used as a poultice.

'I'll get it,' he said.

Madge stood a black pot of water on the range and stoked the coals, opening a side vent with a hooked poker to allow the flames into the space. The heat soon had the pan steaming and as Brophy passed her the herb she tore the huge leaves into pieces and dropped them in the pot. The room soon took on a smell of rotten vegetables mixed with sour vinegar that stung the back of the nose and throat.

'Jesus woman how do you stand the smell of that stuff?' spluttered Brophy as he made for the door.

'Get back here you soft clart and carry this into the bedroom.'

His nose wrinkled in disgust but he did as he was told.

Madge tore a strip from an old cotton sheet and spread it on the dresser. While Brophy held the pot she scooped out lumps of the stuff with a wooden spoon and spread it onto the cotton. When it had cooled enough Brophy lifted Jack's body upright while Madge stuck the claggy stinking mess over the broken rib, Jack was crying out in pain. Then she wound more strips of cotton around him tightly and they lay him back down gently.

She stood up and listened to Jack's breathing, his short gasps gradually slowing as he lapsed back into unconsciousness. She cleaned the wound on his head and rubbed butter on it to ease the swelling. Quietly they left the room where Brophy gingerly sniffed the air and decided he preferred the rain rather than the stink.

'Where the hell do you think you're going now?' said Madge.

'To get some fresh air,' he responded.

'Here, take this,' she handed him a brown clay flagon and a shilling, 'get it filled up with brown ale will you.'

Brophy looked at her in horror.

'There's no woman going to pay for my beer and that's final. How dare you even think I would take it, what kind of man d'you think I am?' he was getting more and more agitated as he talked.

Madge waited until his tirade was over before she said anything.

'It's a good job you stopped, I thought you were about to blow your boots off, are you going or not? It's not for you anyway, it's for me.'

He took the money and jug and stormed off.

Later that evening as the fire was dying down to glowing embers Madge was sitting on the old couch dozing, Brophy had fallen asleep beside her. After accepting some of the brown ale under protest of course, he had slowly drifted off into sleep. Bless him she thought he has a heart of gold and would do anything to get Jack to accept him. She leaned back into the cushion, the smell of horsehair stuffing and coal smoke making her feel comfortable and safe. She closed her eyes as sleep demanded its entrance. The fire crackled and sputtered as it died down and finally the orange glow turned to red and gently faded into black as the fire went out and she lay her head on Brophy's arm.

Jack responded well over the next few days and soon he was helping with the household chores, Madge's daily helpings of homemade broth had done him the world of good and it was only a month later that he decided he was back to normal. Madge had found the letter from the manager in his wet clothing and had ironed it dry before it ended up as pulp. She handed it to Jack one morning and he realised he had forgotten about it. He looked at the dried paper and handed it to Madge.

'Read it for me please.'

'She was about to say something then decided against it, she read the letter aloud for Jack.

A new rescue team was being set up at Bradley Colliery near Consett further north, the letter suggested that Jack would be an ideal candidate as he was hard working and honest and had a tendency towards the men's safety. Even though his dismissal from the pit was a black mark against him, the sender would consider it a favour if he gave the man a job on receipt of the letter. It was signed G Bassett, colliery manager.

'I can read some words you know, it's just that I'm not that good at it yet,' he said quietly.

'Well we can easily put that right can't we?'

'All the same it was pretty damned decent of the man to do that for me.'

It was the end of July and would go down as the wettest month of that year and it was only the weather that stopped Jack from moving on, and Madge of course. She seemed to be very attached to him he thought, but she was that kind of woman. Caring, loving, kind, and very demanding in the bedroom, but he supposed she would soon fill that gap when the time came, many a time he had noticed the way she looked at Brophy. But she had spent every day teaching him how to read and write properly, he already had the basics and was a willing learner and now considered himself capable of putting words on paper, slowly perhaps but better than most. He finally decided that it was time to go. He sat that evening at the scullery table quietly eating his favourite meal of rabbit stew. He never asked where the rabbit came from, he just presumed it would be from yet another friend of hers.

'It's alright you know Jack,' said Madge.

He looked up to see her face set in a gentle smile, a look of acceptance but not sadness. She knew, he thought, she damned well knew what he was going to say before he opened his mouth. The aroma from the stew proved too much and before he answered he took another mouthful of the meltingly tender meat, mixed with vegetables and herbs from her garden.

'Nice?'

He nodded.

'I must be mad pet but I'm going after that job up north, but you already know that don't you?'

She inclined her head slightly, her deep brown hair falling across her face, a face that had seen much pain and passion but still had that irresistible something that he just couldn't put his finger on. She raised her eyebrows waiting for more.

'Damn you woman, I think I bloody well love you,' he clashed his spoon down, 'in a different way,' he added gently.

'I know Jack, and don't worry pet, I've enjoyed every moment and I know you have to move on. We've had our time and it's over now and I'll always remember you, and don't worry about me, something always seems to turn up,' she licked her lips with the tip of her tongue, which reminded Jack of a feline, sensual, sleek and sly and he shivered. He nodded and finished his stew. She nodded at his dish.

'I've packed what's left in a water bottle for you, I know how you like it, and there's a loaf of bread with some jam to keep you going. It shouldn't take you more than three days to get there, the other bottle has a drop of rum in it to help you sleep. You'll find everything else packed in an old army haversack that I had. He was about to speak but she put her forefinger on his lips and beckoned towards the bedroom with her eyes. He turned off the gas lights, only the light of the fire showed him the way.

CHAPTER SIXTEEN

Jack pulled the heavy canvas cape over his head and on to his shoulders. It was only five o'clock in the morning but he was almost ready to leave. Everything was under the cape to keep the rain off. The house was quiet, the acrid smell of ashes mixed with rain dripping down the chimney gave the house an unpleasant smell, but every house would be the same and he hardly noticed it. He took a last look around and opened the back door. Well this is it, he thought. He stepped outside and climbed the steps to the back lane, he had said his goodbyes to Madge last night, she would soon have someone else to fill her bed, lucky sod, he thought. He pulled a canvas hood out of the pocket in his cape and jammed it over his cap. Then set off without looking back.

It was clean in the mornings, the air was fresh and sweet, the persistent rain had turned into a drizzle, the cloud a single mass of dull grey from one horizon to the other. It looked like it was in for the day. Jack wondered if it would ever stop, he was pretty fed up with it now, but he was pretty fed up with everything, why the hell he should have to go traipsing north to get a job when all he had done was try to help. Ada was dead, he had lost his job, why should things get any better just because he was running away. It must be the weather that was making him feel like this, a bit of sunshine cheers everyone up. He cast a cynical glance at the sky, not much chance of that, he thought. He gritted his teeth, a look of grim determination on his face and set off on his journey to Consett, fifty miles up north.

An hour later Brophy burst into Madge's room.

'Where's he gone,' it was a demand not a question.

She had been sitting quietly, dressed in her petticoat, sipping tea from an enamel mug, the steam from the bitter leaves swirling around her face. It eased the eyes, something that concerned her these days, she'd noticed the crow's feet getting deeper, but what could she expect after the silent tears when she had felt Jack stir and ease out of bed. She knew she wasn't the hard and efficient woman that was her reputation, she loved like any other person but always lost them, maybe it was just the way it was meant to be.

'He's gone William.'

Brophy frowned at the unusual use of his first name.

'Where the hell has he gone woman?'

Madge simply ignored him, he angrily grabbed her arm and spun her round.

'I said,' then he stopped, seeing the tears in her eyes.

'I'm sorry love, it's just that, well I didn't realise he was that important.'

'How dare you,' she said, a flash of her quick temper sparkling for a moment in her eyes, but fading like a fire that wouldn't catch.

'Do you really think that I'm just a tart William Brophy, something to mess about with then ditch? I've got feelings believe it or not, and you can pack your bags and get out as soon as you can,' her temper had exploded and Brophy was in the firing line, but she suddenly sagged like an empty coal bag and began to weep. He brought a blanket from the bedroom and wrapped it around her shoulders.

'There you go love, it's damp in here and you could catch your death,' he said quietly and if he would admit it to himself, a bit embarrassed. He'd never been involved like this before, his relationships with women were confined to the bed and he was happy with that and yet, somehow this woman stirred something in him and it wasn't just physical.

'I can't let him go by himself, I've got to prove to him

that it wasn't me that harmed those kids and that I tried.'

'I think he already knows that William. Remember, he's lost his wife, his baby and now his job. He hasn't got a lot going for him and for a man like Jack that's not good enough. He needs a purpose in life and maybe he now has that chance.'

'What do you mean?'

'Didn't he let you read his letter?'

'Well yes, sort of, but, well I just didn't have the time to read it, all right?'

Madge heard the shame in his voice.

'There's not many that know their letters William, it's nowt to be ashamed of you know.'

He smiled sheepishly and she dropped the subject.

'Come on lad, if you're going after him you better get cracking. You can borrow the handcart for your gear, but I want it back mind, I'll give you a hand to get sorted.'

By the time Brophy was ready to leave Jack had two hours lead on him. Madge had packed him some thick potted beef sandwiches and filled his water bottle with cold tea.

She came to the door with him, he pulled down his cap and pulled his canvas cape around him, she had told him the direction Jack would take, indeed it was the only road to Consett anyway.

'Don't you forget where that hand cart lives William

Brophy,' she said quietly.

He turned to her, her voice had startled him, it was soft and gentle and seductively smooth.

'What's wrong?' she asked.

'I'll bring this hand cart back to you if it's the last thing I ever do, I think I'm going to miss you Madge.'

Drops of rain fell onto her hair and ran down her forehead causing her to wipe her eyes.

'What's wrong pet?' said Brophy thinking she was crying.

'Nothing, it's just the rain.'

He pulled her towards him and suddenly kissed her, not with lust but with a feeling that he would have to try and find out about. She returned the kiss, a surge of hope ran through her body.

'I will be back for you Madge, that is, if you want me back?' he was staring into her eyes.

Madge nodded slowly.

'I would like that William, I really would.'

He headed down the bank looking back to see her until the rain blotted her out, but not from his mind. He set off now with a spring in his step, all of a sudden the world was a good place to be in and he began to jog along closing the gap between himself and Jack.

Madge turned and went back into the house, she sat by

the fire for a while, the tears dry now, the rain a good excuse. She wondered why she had shed tears anyway, he wouldn't come back, they never did. But maybe this time it might be different. She stared into the flames, hoping that she was right.

Jack looked up at the sky, he would need to find shelter soon, it was mid-afternoon and he was going to be like a drowned rat if he didn't find somewhere quickly. The canvas gear was fine but nobody had yet found a way to stop the bloody rain trickling down his neck. He was so concerned with trying to keep dry that he didn't see the two men hiding in the hawthorn bushes by the side of the road.

One of them wore an agricultural smock and a sheepskin around his shoulders. He looked down at the other man, a thin wiry and hard faced farmhand.

'We'll catch him on the bend on the edge of north field, he'll never know what hit him, he's bound to be carrying money Fred,' said the shorter man.

'If he's carrying money then why the hell is he walking in this bloody weather Sammy?'

Fred glowered at him and raised his hand as though to hit the smaller man.

'You try that boy and your balls will be off the first time you fall asleep,' Fred sneered at him while turning a wicked looking knife in his hands, the razor sharp edge gleaming as he jabbed the point at Sammy's chest.

'Shit, pack it in will you? All right I'm sorry, let's just get on with the job and put that bloody thing away.'

Sammy was fully aware of Fred's reputation with that knife of his and backed off. It had been a bad year for them both, the crops were failing due to the weather and farms were laying off men as there was no work, not even for an experienced gelder like Fred. He shivered at the thought of that knife getting close to his manhood. They were both out of work, without families, and the situation was getting desperate. They needed food and here was a provider walking past them, oblivious to what was going to happen to him.

'Come on,' said the big man,' as he eased back into the undergrowth and stepped out into the field behind him. They both padded along the flattened hay and reached the north field, Fred was drenched, wearing only a serge jacket and a pair of old Harris Tweed trousers tied up with string, he looked as though he had fallen in a horse trough but it never seemed to bother him.

Jack was just turning the corner past the field, a thick glade of trees obscuring most of the hazy light. The branches were almost touching the ground with the weight of water on them. He stopped, he had heard something. Suddenly two men jumped out of the bushes. Jack was taken completely by surprise and had only a second to notice the murky shapes in the rain, then his world went black.

'You stupid bastard,' cried Fred, 'you didn't have to hit him that hard, the poor buggers dead.'

'Well he won't be able to recognise us then will he,' said Sammy nervously. A cow or a sheep was one thing, but a man?

He knelt down and started tearing Jack's clothing off, searching for money. Suddenly Jack grabbed his wrist, more a reflex than anything else, Sammy picked up his club again ready to whack the man into oblivion, but Fred grabbed his arm.

'Maybe I should slit the bugger's throat, we can chuck him in the pond, a couple of rocks tied to his feet, who would ever find out.'

'Wait, I've found something, here cut the hem of that coat, there, Sammy smiled in satisfaction as he pulled out a bag and shook it hearing the clink of coins.

'I reckon that should keep us going for a while,' he grinned.

Fred smiled in anticipation.

'Can I finish him off?' he said, his eyes gleamed with the chance to see another creature die at his hands, he was excited at the thought.

'Please yourself, but get on with it.'

Kneeling down Fred turned the knife towards Jack, the

belly or the throat he wondered, but it didn't matter the man wouldn't feel it anyway. He raised the knife into the air.

Suddenly a man was running towards them, roaring at them, Fred hissed like a cat being disturbed with its prey, then jumped up and ran. Sammy looked up in time to see a heavily built stocky man bearing down on him. He jumped up and ran after Fred.

Brophy wasn't bothered about the two men, he would recognize the big one anywhere, even in the gloom the wide staring bright blue eyes with a touch of madness in them would always stick in his memory.

He bent over Jack, he was breathing. He grabbed him by his arms and dragged him through the mud to the side of the road, then hoisted him into the handcart, shoving his own possessions to one side to make room for him. He threw Jack's canvas cape over him and grabbed the handles of the cart, pulling it behind him. He had to find shelter, dusk was coming on fast and he didn't want to be outside in these conditions. He struggled on, the road was now a sea of mud that stuck to his boots threatening to suck them off his feet. The rain was running down the inside of his cape, the air stank of wet cow pats and rotting hay. It was getting darker and still he couldn't find shelter. The scraggy bushes offered no respite and the drizzle turned to rain and began to pelt down again. He never thought he would ever find himself in this position. He had been following Jack but now had no idea which way to turn as he stood at the crossroads that had appeared before him, he was in the middle of nowhere and it was rapidly getting dark, his eyes flitted about at every rustle in the hedges. Something squawked up ahead of him, those two men could still be stalking him, what the hell should he do. He would try and wake Jack, he would sort things out, but he dismissed the thought as stupid. To the left lay open fields, a signpost stood upright on the corner, only one cross piece remained, hanging drunkenly, the name on it worn away and pointing to the clarts at his feet. There was woodland straight ahead and in desperation Brophy headed towards them, at least the trees would afford some relief and perhaps he could rig a hasty shelter for the night.

'I'll get us through this Jack, then you'll see what kind of man I am. Can you see that light Jack, in the distance?'

CHAPTER SEVENTEEN

George Bassett sat at his desk in the manager's office of the colliery waiting for the engineer's progress report. He didn't particularly like the engineer but as an agent of the owners it was best to keep on the right side of the man. He heard shouts of alarm from down in the pit yard. Now what's wrong? he thought. He stood up and went to the window to see what the hue and cry was about. A winch had snapped and a huge drum of steel cable was wreaking havoc in the pit yard. The damned thing seemed to defy all the laws of nature as it bounced backwards and forwards, scattering the miners who were diving for cover. One man was lying on his back, blood pooling around his head. No-one attempted to help him. The drum was losing its inertia and finally rolled to a halt. George stared at the fallen man wondering if he should go and help, but a deputy was running across the yard towards the man. George turned away. It was happening all the time, his pit was being sabotaged by its own miners. He didn't have to give an explanation about the drowning but the men were now holding him and Seth Ridley personally responsible for what had happened. His conscience was clear, whether Ridley's was, well that was another matter altogether. There had been constant breakdowns and holdups whenever Ridley was on his shift and he had narrowly escaped several accidents that had been undoubtedly rigged. George remembered his last inspection of the village. He had ridden around on horseback as he always did, but was met by a stony silence. In fact anyone he had spoken to had the unbelievable audacity to turn their back on him. He had asked Madge if she new what was wrong, when she was carrying out the office cleaning. He remembered her answer.

'You know as well as I do mister Bassett, and I'll tell you something, the community is angry and there's no forgiveness in them. You've been there yourself as we both know, and you also know there's only one way out.' She nodded brusquely and carried on polishing the bookcase.

George thrust out his jaw.

'I'll be damned if I have to give up for something I didn't do,' he said.

Madge turned, anger in her eyes, his manner raising her hackles.

'So why don't you tell them that?' she said, her voice as cold as water from a stand pipe.

'I can't.'

'Then you will be damned, George Bassett.'

He was quite startled at the angriness in her voice, she couldn't talk to him like that, she was only the bloody cleaner God dammit. He was about to put her in her place when there was a knock at his door.

Cyril opened the door and tried to look important, but instead looked ridiculous.

'Yes Cyril,' said George, trying to keep the annoyance out of his voice.

'The engineer has arrived mister Bassett.'

'Then please ask him to come in,' he nearly added, stupid bugger, but bit his tongue.

William Cartwright swept into the room, a bundle of drawings and plans threatening to spill from his arms. He managed with his left hand to sweep off his immaculate bowler hat and nodded curtly.

'Mister Bassett,' he said, as though George was just something that interfered with his work.

'Mister Cartwright,' said George loftily,' there was no way he would let this jumped up upstart take control in his office.

'I am here to discuss the progress of the new deep mine,' Cartwright answered in a manner that would show who was in charge here.

George looked down at the man, he looked varnished, he thought, even the fold down collar was perfect on each side, his waistcoat and watch chain were immaculate and his tie was a masterpiece in knotmanship. Arsehole, he thought.

'Certainly mister Cartwright, please take a seat,' he lowered his eyes to check that the engineer had taken his shoes off and smiled when he saw that the immaculate man was wearing the office slippers.

Cartwright noticed the action and admitted to himself that maybe he did look a little silly wearing the stupid things, but, needs must.

'We have a problem sir,' he said.

George sat and said nothing.

'We are behind in our progress sir, and his lordship is becoming concerned about all the delays and breakdowns,' he raised an eyebrow at the last word, offering it more as a question to George. He carried on.

'As you may or may not know, I report directly to his lordship on matters of finance and he, well,' Cartwright looked George in the eye, 'is somewhat concerned about how the effects of the tragic accident, not that it is in any way his responsibility I might add, is affecting the progress of the new colliery.'

Well, here it was thought George, his stomach churning, his mouth dry as he realised that this was the beginning of the end for him.

'So what happens next?' he said, his voice husky and quieter than usual. Cartwright had seen his shoulders sag a little and knew he had control. He sat back in his chair and smiled at George.

'His lordship is on his way here to have a talk with you.'

'What, now?' shouted George, the anger returning to his voice.

'You've known this all along and yet you saved it to the last, you pile of shite, you're lucky I don't kick your arse all the way downstairs, you back stabbing bastard.'

He turned away from the shocked expression on Cartwright's face and stared out of the window onto the pit yard, just in time to see a magnificent motor car turn into the gateway.

The fact that it was a Rolls Royce Phaeton didn't mean anything to George, it was who was sitting at the wheel that made him uneasy. Bloody hell, he thought, it's the gaffer. He was referring to lord Ravenhill, the man who owned most of the land in the area, whose father had had the foresight not to sell off parcels of it to enterprising prospectors but instead offered short term leases with thirty percent of the coal profits going to the Ravenhill family. It had made them fabulously rich. George turned to his desk, his nervous fingers adjusting an already perfectly adjusted tie, then sat waiting, flicking bits of imaginary dust from his desk.

At forty three Charlie Ravenshill was enjoying life, he bounded up the stairs and burst into the outer office with a beaming smile. Cyril shot out of his chair muttering grovelly sounds which Charlie ignored. Madge was polishing the filing cabinet and gasped when she saw who it was. Their eyes met and just for a moment lingered awhile. Madge gave a slight curtsey and lowered her eyes. Charlie opened his mouth to say something and then changed his mind. Instead he raised his riding crop to his hat and opened the door to George's office. Madge left the room quickly.

'George, good to see you again, no don't get up. Cartwright leave us please,' waving the man away. The door closed leaving the two men alone. Charlie was wearing his red hunting jacket and black hat, his goggles pushed up onto his forehead, the rainwater from his wet clothes dripping onto George's precious carpet.

'Fifty miles an hour, can you believe it, even more with a little coaxing,' he laughed as he brought his riding crop down onto George's desk, the pain almost physical in George's face.

'Only ten built last year but the colour was a bit feminine you know, pink not a man's colour, so I had the whole damned lot painted again. But let's get down to business, the fact is this damned unpleasant business with the children has upset the men a bit and things aren't going right, which I'm sure you will agree.'

'I think I can still sort it out given time your lordship.'

'Yes but that's the problem you see, we don't have the time do we?' he followed the words with a disarming smile.

You don't fool me sitting there in your pretty clothes, you're here to finish me you bastard, thought George, his stomach churning and gurgling loudly as the acids of fear crept in.

'Well you've obviously already decided my Lord, so I would respectfully ask you to let me have your decision but also remind you that I wasn't involved in the tragedy.'

'All in good time,' said Charlie, as his eyes lingered on the decanter of whisky on George's desk.

'Would you care for refreshment my Lord?'

'Delightful.'

George placed two glasses on the tray and pulled out the stopper of the decanter, he poured the golden liquid into the glasses and went to replace the stopper but noticed his lordship still staring at the glass. He sighed inwardly and poured again until Charlie waved his hand.

Charlie stood up and went to the window, he rapped on the glass with his riding crop.

'Sporty isn't she?' The crowd of miners gathered around the motor looked up and hurriedly moved away.

George obediently looked out of the window, the warming whisky easing his rumbling gut, he needed to fart but held it in.

'Two seater, open to the air and look at the size of those wheels man. Lovely colour as well what? Royal blue quite dashing don't you think? It's almost like a proper carriage but without having to stare at horses arses all the time. But come on let's get things sorted.'

He sat down and to the horror of George, leaned back and put his feet up on the desk and he wasn't even wearing slippers.

'We are bringing a new manager in.'

The news hit George like a bombshell, I'm finished, he thought.

'And we're moving you to another of our coalmines. You see George, experience like yours is too good to throw away. We need men like you and the damned unfortunate events recently have forced our hand.

George wondered who we were but said nothing and hoped his lordship had not heard the wind escaping from his backside.

'You can take that wretch of an overman with you or simply sack the blighter, but that's up to you. It's a new pit so there's no shame in going there but we want results,' his voice had hardened now. 'We are expecting a lot from you George, we could have dismissed you but you have another chance, so do not let me down,' he stared hard at George who understood exactly what he meant.

'Questions?' His face had relaxed into its youthful posture again but his nose wrinkled at the obnoxious pong that seemed to hang in the air.

'Well?' he said jumping up, anxious to get away from the smell.

'Can I take my staff?'

'Take who the hell you want,' he answered as he threw down an envelope.

'Your instructions and directions are in there, you have one week.'

George downed his whisky when Charlie had left. He poured himself another glass and put the remains of the gaffer's whisky into his. He cocked his leg and farted luxuriously while sipping his whisky, his gut settling down as he sat in the gasses of his bowels.

He picked up the envelope and began to waft the air around him, he would open it shortly after another glass, he thought.

Lord Ravenshill was at the top of the stairs when he heard his name whispered. He turned just as Madge stepped from behind the broom cupboard door.

'Margaret,' he said, his eyes taking in the still youthful figure of the woman.

'Charles,' whispered Madge, 'it's so good to see you, how are you?' Her eyes sparkled with pleasure as he reached out his hand. She took it and stood on her tiptoes kissing him before he realised. He put his arm around her, a sudden surge of desire coursing through his body, he felt the same from Margaret and suddenly released her.

'Phew,' he said, 'we could have caught fire there,' he smiled sheepishly, the lord gone and only the man standing in front of her.

'How's Edward?' she asked.

'He's fine Margaret, a strapping young man and doing well.'

'It's been eighteen years now and still I dream of us and our son and what might have been.'

Charles hung his head for a moment.

'There was nothing we could do about it as well you know. We are from different classes, it would never have worked, we would both have been condemned by our own class and I hate myself and society for not doing what I really wanted to do. So many wasted years, I still love you and always will, the baby's arrival was unfortunate.'

'How can you say that Charles, you're talking about our son and nothing will ever change that apart from you're barren wife who my son calls mother,' tears had welled up into her eyes.

'She's dead Margaret, consumption, two years ago and no there is no one else.'

'I'm so sorry, I didn't know, please forgive me.'

'There's nothing to forgive Margaret, the world is changing and the old attitudes with it. If it had happened now then things might have been different. Oh yes there would have been gossip but who gives a damn. The manager is being moved, why don't you go with him? I'll sort out a home for you. You know I'll always look after you.'

'What's the point of doing that?'

'You would be closer to your son Margaret.'

She gave a little gasp , 'You mean, I could see him?'

'Think about it Margaret, maybe I've made promises I can't keep, but I've said enough for now. I might be rich but I have dreams as well as you.'

He looked about him then kissed her full on the lips, a long and lingering kiss, releasing the love between them that had been trapped in a secret corner inside themselves. A lock of his black hair fell forward across his forehead as they parted, she twirled her finger around it.

'Remember how you always loved me to do that?'

Lord Ravenhill turned, and with a wink at Madge ran down the stairs.

'Madge?' called George, 'I need you in here now, and bring your cleaning gear.'

She passed Cyril on the way.

'What's the matter with him?' she said,' he sounds as though he's been chewing a bluebottle.'

CHAPTER EIGHTEEN

It was in the early hours of August the third 1906 that Brophy saw the light in the woods, he headed towards it. It had to be shelter. He crashed through the undergrowth, all concern gone, he was wet, cold and miserable, he was dragging a wounded man through woods, he was thirsty and ravenous. He let out a roar as a sapling sprang back and slapped him in the face. He grabbed it in a frenzy of anger and frustration, but even a man of Brophy's strength couldn't budge it, he let go and stood for a moment, his anger subsiding, his breath coming out in ragged gasps.

There was a crashing in the undergrowth, what the hell was that? His mother had told him about the fairies and pixies that lived in these places and the monsters that devoured people, leaving no trace of their victims. Rubbish, he thought, but his eyes were bright with fear now as the wind blew the trees backwards and forwards, shrieking and howling in the branches. A sudden gust blew a heap of old leaves up into the air and Brophy watched, terrified, as they climbed up and floated back down in a spiral. He ran, as fast as he had ever run before, there were demons in these woods, Jack's body was bouncing up and down in the cart as he tore through the undergrowth, then Brophy burst into a clearing. The wind wasn't too bad here and everybody knew that the creatures of the woods would never venture from the trees. He relaxed a little, protected from the rain by the trees behind him. There was a building of sorts in front of him, it looked to be made up from all sorts of scrap timber and corrugated iron. The light he had seen shone through an opening partly covered by an old potato sack. He turned to look at Jack, he was still unconscious. He gently put the handles of the hand cart onto the ground and crept forward. He found a doorway and peered inside. It was empty, no matter he thought, it was shelter and if he respected the owner's goods then he would be welcome as in any house in the north. He went back for Jack and pulled the cart through the doorway. As he entered he noticed a wooden panel to his left, instinct told him it was a door and he picked it up and put it over the entrance, it was a snug fit.

The savage weather was blocked out and everything became quieter and calmer, he was aware of the water dripping off him and immediately turned his attention to Jack. He hauled the sodden form out of the cart and carried the man to a pile of hay, gently lowering him into the stooks, Jack groaned and his eyelids started to open, but then he settled down again. Must have been a hell of a clout thought Brophy.

The hay was dry and warm, Brophy pulled off Jacks clothes leaving him in his vest and long johns which were only damp. Looking about him he saw a pile of blankets near a stove that was burning brightly, he covered Jack with the warm blankets. Jack curled up and began to snore loudly.

Brophy raised his eyes to the roof in annoyance, but a wonderful aroma circled around him. Bloody hell he thought, rabbit stew, and indeed it was. A black kettle hung suspended over the stove filled with a bubbling stew. On an upturned tea chest sat two bowls and two spoons all made from wood. You would think we were expected, thought Brophy. He banished the idea and helped himself to a bowl of stew, the aroma irresistible. After a guilty look around he called out.

'Hello?' no answer so he tucked into the glorious food.

Jack was quiet now and Brophy attended to his wound, there wasn't much he could do for now but when Jack began mumbling Brophy grabbed the other bowl and poured stock into it then spooned some into Jack's mouth, he swallowed greedily. Brophy spooned more into him until Jack began to retch and then settled him back into the hay. He needed a pittle, he opened the door and nervously moved a few yards from the shelter and unbuttoned his flies. That's better he thought as he relieved himself, and then an owl shrieked past him. He gawked into the sky and decided enough was enough and hightailed it back into the shelter. He closed the doorway, stripped off his clothes, leaving only his linings on, his underpants being the only part of him that wasn't totally drenched and lay down beside Jack, pulling some of the blankets across himself. The warmth of the hay and the dryness of the coarse wool blankets had their effect and soon the dwelling was filled with the snores, grunts and farts of the two men as they sank into oblivion.

Brophy woke the next morning as rays of sunlight slanted through the sacking curtains and a shaft of light shone through a gap in the entrance, the rainbow colours beautiful as they spread across the coffin in the middle of the floor. The rain was still pattering on the corrugated roof. It's the only bloody place where you can get four seasons in one day he thought. The stove was still lit and an enamel mug sat on the top of it, steam drifting up into the air from the contents. He felt rested for the first time since setting off, he had already checked Jack's condition as soon as he woke and as far as he could tell the man was in a deep sleep.

Suddenly he stopped in his tracks, what the hell was a

coffin doing in the centre of the floor, he slowly turned his head to prove that he hadn't imagined it. It was there all right, maybe they were in the grip of a woodland troll and the food and tea was a way of sweetening him up before he was eaten alive. His imagination was interrupted as the coffin lid began to lift.

'Agh,' cried Brophy and ran to huddle beside Jack in the warm hay.

The lid continued to lift, two bony arms pushed it to one side where it landed with a thump. Brophy shrieked out loud as his eyes darted around the building for a way of escape. A leg raised itself out of the coffin and a huge fart followed. Brophy knew all about the gasses of the dead, his uncle Eddie had been propped in the corner of his auntie's house during his send off. The bloody man had stood in his coffin and farted all evening, indeed many thought he was still alive until one of his brothers had tugged the dead man's belt and he had fell out of his coffin, much to the dismay of his wife, who thought he might be alive but thank God she had thought, the bastards dead. The tradition of touching a dead man to show you had no ill will towards him was ancient and still practised in the coalfields, but that night had seen a constant flow of visitors, obviously he wasn't liked.

His thoughts had lasted no more than a second or two and he realised that this was a visitor from the other side, wherever that was, he thought.

Slowly, the figure raised itself from the coffin, sitting upright, its eyes staring straight into Brophy's. It stretched its arms the shoulder bones crackling like a fire in the grate. The creature's left hand scrabbled around in the coffin and finding what it was looking for placed the top hat on its head. It opened its mouth in a huge yawn, the ancient jaws snapping like wood on a fire. Brophy simply stared, too late to run he just stared.

It opened its mouth again showing a few old teeth in its head, but this time it spoke. Brophy nearly died as the words penetrated his muddled brain.

'Why haven't you drank your tea Brophy? I didn't make it for fun you know,' his accent pure Northwest Durham.

Brophy huddled even further into the hay as though it would offer protection. How did it know his name, he wished his mother was here, she would protect him.

'Who are you? Thank you for the tea, I'm sorry I didn't' ask but I was desperate,' Brophy spluttered nervously.

The man raised a hand.

'Whoa there boy, you're like a horse loosed off its plough, settle down and drink your tea.

Brophy edged to the stove and picked up the enamel mug forgetting that the handle would be scorching hot, he yelped and dropped the mug. The man shook his head.

'That'll be a canny scald lad, come here and let me have a look, aye as I thought,' he selected a bottle from a wooden shelf, opened it and administered some of the brown liquid inside. Immediately Brophy felt relief, the burn cooled and the pain became tolerable.

'What's that? He asked.

The man eyed him, enjoying the moment, after all, he didn't get many visitors.

'Mainly cow shite son with a couple of herbs in it for effect, found it by accident, scalded my hand in boiling water, ran outside, tripped over a log and fell into a cow pat. Wonderful stuff it is, good for fuel, great on potatoes and leeks and good for upset stomachs, it makes you sick, see.' Brophy merely nodded wondering what the other bottles on the shelf contained.

'Here, drink this,' as he offered Brophy more tea.

Brophy gratefully accepted, and took a moment to take in his surroundings.

It was no bigger than an average pitman's house, about fifteen paces long by eight paces wide but the place was stuffed with bric a brac and old bits of wood. The kind of place a man who didn't waste much would keep odds and ends in case they came in handy for something. The corner where Jack lay looked like a barn, even down to the huge scythe propped up in one corner, the whole place was encased in walls of corrugated tin and railway sleepers which gave off a strong creosote smell throughout. Rainwater still plopped into buckets on the earthenware floor from the dozens of holes in the roof.

'Just can't seem to keep it out son, that's the only dry place in this weather,' he cocked a glance at the coffin on the floor and Brophy began to understand.

'Anyway, at my age it keeps the draughts out as well and if I pop my clogs then I'm already set up to meet my maker eh,' he cackled loudly. 'The name's Tommy Thompson, folks know me as the hermit of Allansford.' He was interrupted by coughing and spluttering coming from Jack.

'Get him on his side William,' Brophy hesitated for a second. He even knows my first name.

'Ask me later son, just get on with it.'

Jack was choking as they turned him onto his left side, a dribble of bile from his mouth dripped onto the hay. Tommy scrutinized it.

'It's green,' he muttered, an edge of concern in his voice. 'Get him covered with those blankets son, the hay will warm him from underneath, he's developing a fever.'

'Shouldn't I go for a doctor?'

'What for? They can't do anything that I can't and probably less if the truth be told. Stoke that stove lad and get that pan of water boiling.

'Good, right let's go, we need a poultice.'

Tommy pulled a canvas cape over his shoulders and made for the door with Brophy close behind. Outside the sun was attempting to burn off the low mist around them, the world smelled damp and foisty. Tommy was grabbing some huge leaves from a plant that stood as high as a man.

'Hold these lad,' he didn't wait for an answer but dashed into the undergrowth where he crawled on his hands and knees cursing and muttering loudly until at last a triumphant yell showed he had found whatever it was he was looking for. He reappeared, his legs and hands covered in clarts but he was brandishing a clump of leaves with bulbs hanging from them.

'Back to the hut lad.'

Inside, the water was boiling on the stove and Jack was shouting and tearing the blankets off himself. Tommy scrambled over to him and stared for a moment.

'Chuck that stuff into the pan William and quick about it.'

Soon a sulphurous stink rose from the pan along with an odd smell of bitter onions.

'What's in that?' asked Brophy, wrinkling his nose in disgust.

'Dead nettles, wild rhubarb and garlic lad, now stop

asking questions, pass me that bottle behind you, yes, that's the one, the blue striped one, hurry up, and wash your hands sharpish, those rhubarb leaves are poisonous.

Tommy sprinkled some of the grey dried contents of the bottle into the soup.

'No it's not dried spiders or anything like that, they're just herbs.'

'How the hell do you know what I'm thinking?'

'Later son, later. When you get to my age you get a feeling for things, maybe you'll find out one day,' Tommy laughed at the expression on Brophy's face.

'Right lad, let's get cracking. Strain the soup into the bucket beside you, using that old garden sieve over there on the wall and chuck what's left away.'

When Brophy had finished, Tommy grabbed a wooden spoon and stirred the contents, which turned into an obnoxious and evil smelling paste. Brophy was gagging as he carried the bucket across to Jack where Tommy immediately began to spread the stuff over Jack's heaving chest.

'Turn him back onto his side lad.' Tommy examined the wound. A huge bruise spread from his neck and across his shoulders.

'Must have been a hell of a clout, he could be bleeding inside, get some more of the poultice over his neck and shoulders, the poor bugger must be in deep shock.' There was anxiety in the man's voice.

Brophy put a hand on Tommy's shoulder, the hermit turned his head to look at the hand and then into Brophy's eyes, he saw something he had not seen for a long time.

'I'll do my best lad,' he said quietly.

'That's all I ask.'

That evening Tommy and Brophy sat with a bowl of rabbit stew outside the house and quietly ate their evening meal, followed by a mug of the fiercest homemade alcoholic beverage that Brophy had ever tasted, it left him gasping for breath while Tommy merely smacked his lips with satisfaction.

Jack was sound asleep, his temperature high but the next twenty four hours would decide his fate. There was nothing else they could do but wait.

It started to drizzle so they went inside, Tommy to his coffin and Brophy beside Jack, the one man he wanted to be his friend, and maybe he would let him be just that. That's if he survived. ·

'Tommy?'

'Yes son'

What are you all about, I mean, why do you live here and?' Tommy cut him off.

'Later son, later.'

CHAPTER NINETEEN

Seth was sitting on his cracket under the overhang of the pit prop stacking area, there had been hundreds of pine logs delivered to the pit. They were chopped up into chocks and props. Every miner had a cracket, a homemade low stool used underground at bait times and as a useful bench to sit on when hacking out the coal. Every year there were cracket competitions and some were works of art. Seth's wasn't. His was a simple affair, a four sided stool with a flat piece of timber across the top, fourteen inches high, twelve inches wide and eighteen inches long. It was a tool and in Seth's opinion did not need any fancy attachments. The stacking area had become so overloaded that an overhang had been constructed to carry the extra weight. An earth bank provided access and the props were rolled down onto the overhang to be stored. Two huge timbers held up the deck of wood above him and it provided a little respite from the rain. Seth cast a rueful eye up at the sky, sometimes it was hard to wonder why God made it rain like this, he supposed a mere mortal man could never understand why things happened. Like the attack on himself. The cowards had waited in the dark and then clobbered him, but the Lord had protected him yet again. He pushed up the dirty brown leather eye patch and scratched at the empty socket of his left eye, flicking away the dried mucus on the end of his fingers before he started on his bait. He thought about his meeting with Bassett.

'They're going to kill you Seth, mark my words, and me as well if they get the chance.'

He had then told him about the transfer and he remembered jumping up, fear on his face at being left alone.

'Don't worry,' Bassett had said, 'you're coming with me.'

Seth stuck his finger in his mug of tea, the carbide lamp had warmed it up tolerably well, the piece of mucus he had missed slowly dissolved into the liquid. He took a bite out of his sandwich, two thick slices of stotty cake slathered with pork fat and jelly, then washed it down with his tea.

The bastards had tried to kill him all right and he knew that if he stayed he would meet his death due to some convenient accident. Maybe crushed by runaway tubs, a convenient rock fall or nudged over the edge of the shaft. They were everyday events and he would be jotted down in a deputy's book and that would be the end of it. The horrible scars on the left of his face were twitching as Seth grew angry. The bastards, he thought, one day he would get them all, the Lord had told him, especially the ones who had attacked him. The village bobby had made investigations but nothing had turned up, he was probably in it with them. He cast his gaze over to the group of men across the pit yard also sheltering as they had their bait. All of them, he thought, they're all out to get me. A gleam of madness shone in his eye as he imagined pointing his yardstick at them and seeing them burst into flames. The wrath of God, he thought and laughed out loud spraying sticky crumbs down his immaculate waistcoat, but today he didn't notice.

The men stared back, Seth's power had gone, he had no authority above ground, the miners were being directed by others now in their haste to get the new pit open. He had offered advice to those others but they merely glanced or totally ignored him. He was an underground savage and to be honest about it he hated the surface, people could see him. He preferred the damp noisy darkness where he had supreme power and control. Well it would happen again, where he would be in his natural element.

The railway line in front of Seth led down to the huge steel hoppers that stood on iron girders. The coal would be transported along the line to the hoppers and dropped into the waiting railway waggons underneath. Two of the miners opposite Seth had moved away from the group and were manhandling a tub of coal from a siding onto the railway. Seth noticed them but took no notice.

The other miners had stopped talking and were watching the tub. Seth noticed the silence and followed the men's gaze. The two men were walking away from the tub which was gaining speed down the slight gradient.

Hold on, thought Seth, what the hell were they up to, they shouldn't walk away like that. He was about to call out to the men when he noticed the thick rope lying over the rails, he couldn't see that it was fastened to one of the metal bolts holding the line in place. It was only when the tub, which had picked up speed and flashed past his good eye that he realised what was about to happen. In an instant he saw what had been done. The other end of the rope was tied around the base of one of the timber supports, covered with wood shavings but he spotted the knot at the base of the timber.

The hook on the front of the tub dangled below the height of the line and the rope was snarled round the tub. The rope snapped tight and pulled the timber support away. Seth, forgetting about his bait, flung himself to the right, rolling twice then jumping up into the shelter of the earth bank. His waistcoat and immaculate boots were covered in wet coal dust from the small pieces of slag that formed the surface of the pit yard. Three tons of props smashed to the ground as the overhang collapsed, he had escaped by the skin of his teeth, his rage exploded. He stormed over to the miners.

'You bastards nearly killed me, what the hell are you up to?'

One man stood up, brave now that Seth had lost his power.

'We're up to what you just said, Ridley, but it's a shame about the nearly.'

'I'll see you out of a job for that remark Ralph Shaw.'

'You'll do no such thing you pile of shite, you killed my daughter you bastard and one day I'll get you. We know you're being transferred, but that don't make you safe.'

Seth saw the anger in the man and for the first time since his accident he felt fear. He said nothing, he walked away, he wouldn't be coming back, he ignored the taunts and heckling as he walked through the pit gates and went home to pack his belongings, his time here was finished.

The next morning he stood in the drizzle, on the platform of the train station. Fat Geordie was there with his wife. He didn't acknowledge Seth, they were travelling first class and it wouldn't do to speak to a third class passenger. He could hear the chuff, chuff of the locomotive as it approached the bend in the line. As its huge snout appeared a great gout of black smoke and steam coughed into the air, hurling the rain out of the way as it reached into the sky. The engine driver slowed the Class R tender loco as it pulled into the station, he pulled the cord twice and two loud shrieks filled the air to announce the arrival of the huge beast. The four giant wheels rolled past Seth, the pistons driving them slowly coming to a stop. Small gouts of steam hissed from valves in the guts of the engine, its great black tank reared above him. The train ground to a halt, it was gasping and heaving after the pull up the long incline. The first class carriages were nearest the platform for the ease of its passengers. Seth's third class carriage was at the rear of the train. He looked both ways, wary of a last attempt to get him, but the platform was clear and he hurried to the rear lugging his baggage with him. He reached up and pulled opened the carriage door and hauled himself up into the carriage compartment .The smell of polished wood gave the carriage a warm rich smell, the brass fittings on the doors gleaming. He slung his baggage into the net above the seats and sat down, there was already another passenger in the carriage. Seth glanced at him, a lad probably just about twenty he thought, nothing to worry about there then, he was still wet behind the ears. He simply ignored the lad and sat down. The seats were sprung and cloth covered, basic but comfortable for third class. He noticed the oil lamps were still sputtering above the seats, the flame giving only the faintest of lights. The carriage was of the clerestory roofed type without a corridor, a long way from the express trains that ran on the main lines, draughty, bumpy, but at two shillings what could you expect, he thought. He leaned back in the seat and began to relax. As the train slowly pulled out of the station following the stationmaster's blast on his whistle, Seth pulled out a clay pipe and tamped fresh tobacco into it from his leather pouch. He lit it with a match which he threw out of the pull down window and puffed contentedly, the smoke drifting up into the already yellowed ceiling. He settled down to the regular clikety clack of the train as it crossed the joints of the tracks. He had made it, he thought, a new life, a new start. He decided he would be tougher on the men he was to control, obviously he had been too soft with the buggers. Seth knew he was right, he had asked God and the answer was brought to him by an angel when he was asleep. His scarred and blinded face twitched spasmodically, hideously. One day they would all pay the price. Seth knew it, he threw his clay pipe out of the window and spat on the floor ignoring the no spitting or swearing notice on the carriage wall. He began to drift off into sleep. The young man looked at Seth in disgust and closed his eyes. He was looking forward to being George Bassett's gardener, his wife had even paid for his train fare. He was thinking about her as he too fell into a light sleep.

CHAPTER TWENTY

Jack was sitting upright, his back against an old cast iron
bed frame. He was still unsure about what had happened. He
remembered the sound of someone behind him, then the pain,
then nothing. One thing he did know, he was bloody hungry.
He stared at Brophy who was stirring some kind of stew in a
black kettle over the fire and was willing him to bring some of
the stuff across to him. He couldn't remember ever feeling so
hungry. Tommy Thompson, or the hermit of Allansford as he
was known, had nursed Jack back to health and it was a favour
that Jack would never forget. He had spent his time talking with
the wise old man, and before he realised it he had opened the
can of worms from his past and told Tommy about the death of
his father, something that he had never told anyone. He had
told him about the beatings and the inner hate he had felt, and
had soon drifted off into the past when he was a boy of thirteen

again. He carried on with his story.

His father had taken him underground for the first time. The old deep workings were empty now but the shaft still dropped four hundred feet down to the bottom, a deadly fall for the unwary. The drift tunnel stretched away into darkness, the sounds of the miners in the new coal seams faint in the distance. His father had grabbed him by the scruff of the neck and swung him towards the bottomless black hole of the shaft. Jack hung on to his father, frozen with fear.

'You ever tell anybody what goes on at home you little shit, then you're over the edge, get it?'

He jerked Jack savagely so that he was actually teetering on the edge. Jack's hands were so sweaty with fear he thought he might lose his grip on his father's clothing, he knew he would do it, so just nodded.

'Better boy, much better.'

He pulled Jack back from the brink and spun around as he heard boots clumping towards them. It was one of the last things he ever did. His left foot skidded over the edge of the shaft, his outstretched arms flailing wildly as he tried to regain his balance.

'Grab me boy,' his eyes and voice imploring.

Jack suddenly took a step backwards. He would never forget the look of sheer horror on the face of the father he was murdering, as the man frantically scrabbled at the air and then fell into the shaft. He screamed all the way down, then his voice was instantly silenced when he hit the bottom. Jack stood and stared in disbelief at what he had done, he had wanted it to happen, he knew it was wrong, but he didn't feel guilty, he didn't know what the feeling was. He knew he was a murderer and would be hanged for it, but at least his mother would now be safe.

'Go on,' urged Tommy gently, 'I can see there's more.'

Jack looked at him and nodded slowly then carried on with his story. It was easy to slip into the nightmare again, he had done it so many times before. He went on to tell Tommy about the footsteps that were still approaching. It was the deputy on shift, a kindly man who was well respected.

'Sit down son,' the deputy had said,' I saw everything that happened.'

'Are you going to arrest me mister?'

'No son, but you deserve a medal for what you did. I know he is, well, was your dad, but with all respect lad, he got what he deserved and a lot of men would be willing to shake your hand. Most of us knew what he was like, he used to brag about it when he was drunk, the way he treated you and your mam, so the less said about the matter the better eh lad?'

Jack had nodded silently, his eyes widening in fear as the

deputy reached into his pocket and took out a notebook, he pulled a stub of pencil from his top pocket and licked the end of the lead and began to write.

'Shaft accident lad, happens all the time, he tripped and fell over the edge, it'll be reported son and nowt more will be said, I was the only witness you see, won't even get in the local paper, so let's get you sorted.'

The deputy beckoned to Jack and headed off along the tunnel, suddenly he stopped and returned to the edge of the shaft, he crossed himself.

'May God forgive you for your sins, because no bugger else will.' He winked down at Jack.

'Catholic son, I'm a catholic, come away now,' he said and retraced his steps along the tunnel.

Jack returned to the present to see Tommy looking into his eyes.

'Better for that Jack?'

Jack nodded and a slight smile crossed his face, 'Thanks Tommy.'

'It's all right lad, I know there's more, so whenever you want to tell me just say.'

It was a week later when Jack pulled the letter from Bassett out of its envelope, he had almost forgotten about it, even though it was the reason for his journey. If he had had any money, then he would be at his destination by now using the train system, but he was skint and there was nothing he could do about it. He recalled the events that had led up to the attack. When Brophy had asked him about it Jack couldn't remember much, but he did remember Brophy's words.

'Yes but I remember them and the faces I saw that night are in here,' said Brophy as he tapped the side of his head.

Jack didn't fancy being in those men's shoes if they was ever spotted again.

He was fit again at least, all the rabbit stew and salads he'd eaten made him think he would turn into a rabbit but it had done the trick and he was almost ready to leave. Tommy was sitting outside in the afternoon sun, the rain had stopped and the trees and grass were steaming in the heat as the sun evaporated the rain. It was still damp but there was a fresh clean smell in the air. He was drawing a map for the men as Jack sat down beside him and handed him the letter. Tommy put down his pencil and took the letter moving it away then closer again to his eyes.

'I'm sorry Tommy, I just expected you to be, well handy with words if you know what I mean.'

'What the hell do you mean, you cheeky bloody whippersnapper. I can read as good as anybody but it doesn't mean I can see the damned words does it,' it wasn't a question.

'Sorry.'

'Stop saying sorry boy you'll find out what it's like to be sorry one day when you're as old as me.'

'Here, I'll read it out, your opinion would be appreciated.'

Tommy nodded slowly, satisfied that honour had been served and that his opinion was required.

'Don't read it word for word lad, just give me the gist.'

'All right. it suggests that I would be suitable for a job at the Bradley main pit as rescue officer, if the manager approves, but to consider the fact that there have been no volunteers as yet and that I am out of work at the moment due to recent events that will be familiar to the manager.'

'Go on son.'

'It says that I should set up a rescue team to oversee any accidents or disasters that might occur. The job is temporary with a view to a permanent post if it is a success. I would be classed as a pit official with suitable accommodation as befits a post of that type.'

'Hm it's obvious nobody wants the job, but beggars cannot be choosers can they? And you don't want to look a gift horse in the mouth and turn away, my advice is take it. Here's a map on how to get there.'

'How did you know?' Jack shook his head in amazement

and decided to shut up when Tommy ignored him.

'It'll take you four hours to get there, if you go up Allansford bank through Castleside up into the iron works through Consett and down to Leadgate. From there it's straight down the Roman road to the bottom, turn right past the wooden Coop, past the institute, turn left at Bradley cottages and the pit is at the top of the hill. Can't miss it son, course you could have done the whole lot on the train when you left Blackhall Rocks and saved yourself a lot of effort.'

'I didn't have the money and you know that, anyway I would never have met you, would I.'

'Aye there is that son, mebbee it was just meant to be eh. You come back and see me , I'll be waiting.'

'I haven't gone yet, have I?'

'Gears all ready lad,' Tommy glanced over his shoulder where Brophy was readying their packs. 'Did it last night see, while you were snoring like a trooper. Pleased to see the back of you, you noisy bugger, and that other one, spends his nights farting he does. He should practice with it, he could play tunes at the local fair.'

Tommy stood at the edge of his beloved Allansford Woods and watched the two men trudge up the steep bank to Castleside. They turned to look back but the woods were all they saw. Jack frowned and looked at Brophy who shrugged his shoulders.

I'm sure you'll be back to see him,' he said.

'How do you know that?'

'I'm your friend aren't I?'

Jack turned to Brophy, a glance passed between them, it was enough.

'Aye, I suppose you are, marra.'

'You what?' Brophy frowned as though he had misheard Jack.

'Marra, a friend, you know, somebody on the same shift down the pit,' Jacks face split into a wide grin until Brophy put his arm around his shoulders and almost squeezed the life out of him.

'I didn't mean that friendly, you great daft bugger.'

Brophy grinned and they carried on up the hill.

CHAPTER TWENTY ONE

The giant water coolers of Consett Iron Company loomed in the distance when they reached the crest of the steep hill. Arteries of steel seemed to reach everywhere, connecting everything together. Huge Bessemer steel converters opened their giant maws eagerly swallowing the tons of iron ore being fed to them, occasionally belching great clouds of red dust up into the air. The clang of giant hammers and presses deafened the workers inside. Some men pulled barrows of new steel, red hot from the furnaces. These men were easily distinguishable by their huge protruding chests and unusually long arms, a legacy of years doing the same job. There was a constant turnaround of locomotives bringing in ore and taking away steel along the maze of railway lines inside the works.

The site was a cacophony of noise mixed with red dust. Jack and Brophy walked through this hellish scene and on to

Consett town, pleased to see the back of the works. New bungalows were being built at Villa Real just outside of Consett for the ever expanding coalmines in the area. They trudged past, weary now, Jack casting a wary glance now and then at the sky which was starting to cloud over. By the time they reached the small village of Leadgate a fine drizzle was falling, but in the distance, on the other side of the small valley they could see their destination. They glanced at each other and carried on down Watling Street, the old Roman road. The time for talking was past, they just wanted to get to their journey's end. An hour later they walked through the gates of Bradley pit and straight to the main office. They rested outside for a while, breathing in the familiar smell of coal dust. The great wheels were turning on their huge steel gantries towering sixty feet into the air, the noise of machinery surrounding the two men, at last, it felt as though they were home.

They entered the offices and climbed the stairs. At the top was the usual half glass door, Jack looked down, almost expecting to see a pair of old slippers but there was nothing. He knocked and opened the door into the clerk's office. He glanced round and suddenly swept the cap from his head, nudging Brophy at the same time. A woman was sitting behind the desk.

'Hello missus,' said Jack 'is the clerk about please?'

'And why shouldn't I be the person you want,' she had a

soft and pleasant voice with an edge of authority to it.

'Well, er, you're a woman aren't you?' said Brophy.

'And?'

'He didn't mean owt by it missus, it's just that, well, we're not used to seeing a woman sitting where you are.'

'Well what a shame for you,' she smiled. Bloody hell thought Jack, she's got better teeth than a pit pony, damned pretty as well.

'So what's your business?' she said, standing up and moving around the desk.

'We're here to see the manager,' said Jack, his eyes appraising her from top to toe, Brophy was doing the same as Jack heard a quiet 'cor' behind him.

'Appointment?' raising an eyebrow as she eyed them both up and down.

'No, but I've got a letter for him from the manager of my last pit,' said Jack.

'I'll ask if he'll see you,' a smile was playing around her lips.

She seemed to glide across the floor, thought Jack, as she rapped on the door with the back of her hand, then disappeared into the office behind.

'Bloody hell Jack, I wouldn't mind a bit of that, tasty as a suet pudding eh!'

Jack frowned at the comparison and shook his head.

'Aye, she is at that, but keep your hands to yourself you dirty bugger, chance is she's the managers wife.'

'Proper teaser though, isn't she?'

'Pack it in man, is that all you think about?'

'Aye, most of the time.'

They both turned as the door opened. He's right though, thought Jack.

'Mr Harris will see you now,' a flicker of amusement on her face. They both turned as she closed the door behind her, just in time to catch a glimpse of a curvy backside.

'Forget it,' a deep voice boomed, 'she's the assistant manager's wife and wouldn't have time for the likes of you two.'

A man was standing by the window, a fat cigar clamped between his yellow stained teeth, his long grey beard a relic of another era. He raised himself to his full height as he approached the two men but he still had to tilt his head back to look up at them. Jack and Brophy glanced at each other, the action noticed by the pit manager.

'Listen you two,' he jabbed his cigar up at them then clamped it firmly back between his teeth.

'I've learned to live with my height so you two will do the same,' his voice had a deep resonance to it which was unusual in a man of his stature.

'Right?' he boomed.

Both Jack and Brophy nodded silently, after all this was the man who might give them work.

'My name's mister Harris, that's mister and don't forget it, now why are you here?' he stepped behind his desk and sat down showing only his head and shoulders. A slight flicker of amusement crossed Brophy's face.

'Think it's funny do you arsehole.'

'No sir,' said Brophy.

'Like I said son, its mister, not sir or your honour, don't do it again. Right?'

Brophy nodded silently.

'Well, what the hell do you want?'

'We're looking for work mister,' said Jack.

'Names?'

'Jack Walker and Bill Brophy,' Jack held his head up and thought, well, it's now or never lad.

Mr Harris frowned, where had he heard those names before, then the penny dropped.

'You two were involved in those kids getting killed, bloody trouble makers the pair of you.'

'We tried to help those kids mister, we didn't cause the trouble, anyway I was asked to give you this letter,' Jack pulled the crumpled envelope out of his pocket and handed it over.

Harris looked at it suspiciously, slit it open with a Scottish dirk, a tiny dagger that he had brought back from Scotland. He loved its sharp tip and was fascinated that such a small thing could cause death, then he read the contents of the letter, his face giving away nothing.

'Sit down,' he said.

'The men did as they were told and sat on two ladder back chairs against the wall.

'So you want to volunteer for the mines rescue team, alright you've got the job.'

The two men looked startled, why was it so easy.

'You can use the old wood shed in the pit yard for your office and can live there for now, it's got a netty and a stand pipe, the rest is up to you.'

'What about the other volunteers' mister?' said Jack.

'There aren't any, except you two that is,' he smiled at them, 'five bob a week until you get yourselves organized and then we'll see.'

'We can't survive on that,' piped up Brophy.

'Please yourself. It's all you're gonna get for now, so take it or leave it, you can always use the tommy shop.' He was referring to the overpriced stores that were owned by the pit where credit was given at inflated rates. They were hated by the miners but sometimes it was the only way to survive.

'We'll take it,' said Jack.

'Good, you can start straight away, the sheds at the top of the pit yard, I'm moving on anyway so somebody else can sort you out. He's having a break in Durham and will be here next week.'

'Who is he mister? If you don't mind me asking,' said Jack.

'Oh I think you might know him,' he handed the letter back.

'In fact you can give old Geordie his letter back when you see him.' He grinned broadly and clamped his cigar back between his yellow teeth, the laugh that followed caused him to cough and splutter and hawk up a dollop of phlegm that he spat into the coal fire behind him.

'Right, that's it, familiarise yourselves with the pit and its surroundings and report back to me at two-o-clock tomorrow, off you go.'

The men left the office leaving Harris shaking his head slowly, the stupid buggers, he thought, they haven't got a clue what they are letting themselves in for. He shrugged his shoulders, so what, it wasn't his problem, he was off to take over fat Geordie's pit and put things right again.

* * *

Deep beneath them Nathan Rewcastle sat contentedly smoking his roly, as usual he had sneaked the tobacco in by hiding it in the crack of his backside. He didn't agree with all the nonsense about gas exploding because of a naked flame, after all his time down the pit he knew where the dangers were, he could sense gas or sniff it out.

'You're doing it again, you silly old fart, why can't you chew it like everybody else,' said one of the miners.

'Bugger you, arsehole, when I want your opinion I'll ask for it.' He stood up, struck another match, stretched out his arm and carefully presented the flame to a recess in the wall. A sudden whoosh and the recess burst into flame immediately dying out as he pulled the match back.

'There's nowt to be frightened about,' he said as the other men flung themselves to the ground.

'I don't know what all the fuss is about, having to carry these bloody safety lamps, give me a good carbide lamp any day at least it gives off a bit of light.'

The safety lamp while being safe as its name suggested gave off a very faint light and was very unpopular with veterans of the mines.

'For Christ's sake Nathan, one of these days you'll blow the whole bloody lot of us to kingdom come, you're not funny so pack it in,' shouted one of the men.

'Or what?' was the response.

'Forget it, you'll be on the surface soon anyway.'

Nathan was looking forward to the end of the month, at last he had been given a surface job. At seventy he was beginning to ache a bit when he'd finished his shift and lighter duties would suit him fine and get him away from the bunch of nancies he was working with.

'Come on you lot,' said the shift deputy, ' let's have you back to work you lazy bastards, bloody sit there all day long if you had the chance,' nobody mentioned Nathans escapade to the deputy, a man didn't drop his work marra in it, whatever the reason

CHAPTER TWENTY TWO

Jack and Brophy hardly noticed the woman on the way
out, much to her annoyance. She had watched them leave, the
taller one with the hazel eyes and unmanageable hair, he was
well, nice, sort of, there was just something about him, a power
that her own husband didn't have, not that she would ever find
out. She dipped the pen in the inkwell and started to write out
the miners wages on their chitties. She had heard the
conversation, her ear at the door, he was leaving at last, she was
free, no longer would she have to please him just to keep her
husband in a job, but not yet she thought as she heard the
manager call from his office. He called in a voice that he
thought was sexy but was merely the slimy purr that she had
become used to.

'Ruth, I'm waiting,' the repulsive voice purred.

She sighed and stood up, a look of disgust crossing her

face. She knocked on his door.

'Come.'

She entered and looked down at her manager who was lying stretched out on a brown leather settee. Already he was erect and throbbing with lust, his huge belly hanging over his little dick as he played with it. She began to remove her clothes as usual then it would follow the same pattern, she would walk backwards and forwards naked, except for her shoes, while he ogled her.

She was loosening the buttons on her blouse, her full breasts bringing a gasp from the manager. Suddenly she stopped.

'Keep going Ruth, if you want that useless husband of yours to keep his job as assistant manager, you better not disappoint me lass,' he leered up at her, beads of sweat forming on his forehead. He was panting noisily as he masturbated himself, his gasps rising to a crescendo.

'You're leaving,' she hissed, the realisation of what she had just said filled her with joy, a happiness she had never felt for a long time. She knew exactly what she was going to do. Never again would she let anyone put her in this position.

'I heard you talking to those men you dirty bastard and I don't have to do this anymore, you bag of shite.'

She snatched up his dirk from the desk and rammed it

against the quivering white flesh of his belly.

He looked up at her and was afraid, he knew that she would kill him if she could get away with it.

'Don't pet, it was only ever a bit of fun, now wasn't it? I've never laid a hand on you,' his voice was a whisper, pleading.

'Please don't kill me,' he whined, his lips trembling as he tried to pull a cushion over his nakedness.

'You're going to die, look at you,' she sneered, 'you look like a fat slug.' Then she pushed the knife further into the soft yielding flesh.

He squealed like a stuck pig when the point of the knife pierced his flesh.

'Please, please no,' he squeaked, the look of utter hatred in her face made him realise he was about to die. Suddenly the pressure eased and she flung the knife to the floor.

'You will die, you dirty bastard, but it won't be by my hand. She left him lying there. She dressed and went home. She wouldn't be back until he was gone.

* * *

'What do you think of that Jack?' said Brophy, 'I mean, how does somebody like that get a position of power?'

'I suppose it's who you know, but it's a start at least, but

I wonder if Geordie will keep us on, we'll just have to wait and see.'

'Aye, but how long has the job been open, and why are we the only two?'

'Who knows, let's get to that shed and settle down a bit, have you got any food left?'

'Aye, I've still got that sausage off Tommy and some tea left in my bottle.'

'Well I've got some bread, so let's go and have a banquet marra.'

The shed turned out to be a brick building with a good roof. It was also where the carpenter used to live while the miner's bungalows were being built. There were a couple of old striped mattresses lying against a wall and a set of cast iron bed springs. There was even a stove in the corner.

'Brophy, if you get that bed sorted out I'll get some coal and kindling from somewhere and we'll settle down for the night.'

Being surrounded by coal and wood it didn't take Jack long to get the stove blazing away. Brophy had the bed sorted, the two mattresses side by side on the floor, the springs were useless. They sat by the stove eating their meal, Brophy constantly examining pieces of the sausage.

'What d'you think is in it Jack?'

'How the hell would I know, anyway I don't want to think about it, it tastes sort of funny but it's all we've got so enjoy it.'

'Hm,' was Brophy's only response.

It was getting dark outside, they stoked up the stove and lay down on the bed pulling their travel blankets over them. Jack looked up at the window, the moon was rising and the grubby glass was spotted with drops of rain, it's back again he thought and pulled the blanket up around his shoulders.

'Are you asleep yet?' he asked.

Brophy responded with a huge fart and started snoring like a trooper.

Jack closed his eyes and pulled the blanket over his head to hide the noise and drifted off to sleep, the glow of the coals in the stove gradually fading until they slowly turned black, the grey ashes dropping through the grate underneath to be collected for use in the netty the next day.

Outside, the pit still worked, the great wheels towered sixty feet into the air turning constantly as they sent cages up and down the deep shaft. Bradley pit was big. The main shaft was sixteen hundred feet deep. A tall brick building straddled the shaft, known as the heapstead, inside were railway lines running up to the mouth of the shaft where coal tubs were brought to the surface and empties returned. The coal tubs were hauled onto a small weighbridge where the overseer or keeker as he was known would check for any stone in the tub, a miner could be fined if too much was found. The coal was then tipped down a chute and onto the picking belts where women, children and old men picked out the slag under the watchful eye of the keeker who even had a window in the floor of his office, where he could keep an eye out for anyone slacking at their work.

The second shaft was still being sunk but the miners, eager to earn wages, were prepared to take the risk of working underground and earn some money. The second shaft allowed circulation of air but more importantly provided an alternative escape route in the event of an accident. It was a legal requirement but both workers and owners were content to relax the rules, after all it would soon be finished and nothing would happen in the next month or two.

Sixteen hundred feet underground a fourteen year old boy was crushed to death by a runaway tub, his screams of agony shocking those who were nearby. His mangled and pulped organs squirted out between his legs and from his mouth in a bloody broth. As he leaned forward shrieking for his mother, for God, for help, he vomited onto the coal in the tub, his screams cut short as a jet of blood erupted from his nose and mouth. His head sagged forward in death as others came to help too late.

A face worker lost both his legs when the floor of the tiny sixteen inch tunnel he was working in heaved upwards, the jagged outcrop severing both legs. Some would say he was lucky, as he died from loss of blood before the pain hit him.

The shot firers had been on the night shift which ended at twenty past two in the early hours of the morning. They had planted their shot. The explosions, small, but sounding huge in the confined space brought down the rock around the seam of coal. A dangerous job requiring skill and a large dose of courage, for it was always possible that the explosions could ignite gas with terrifying and fatal results. As they rode to the surface another cage was dropping the fore shift into the pit. Five men and two boys, whose job was to clear away the rubble leaving the coalface open to the hewers or face workers. On the way down the cage had lurched to one side as if it was coming off its shoes, the metal clamps that gripped the rails running down the shaft allowing cages to pass each other without danger of collision.

The men had joked nervously about how the two boys were terrified on their first journey underground.

One of the miners, more experienced than the others held up his hand for silence.

'The cage isn't running true, I reckon there's something wrong with it,' he said, his eyes showing his fear.

CHAPTER TWENTY THREE

The thin watery rays of sunshine gave a little light in the room as Jack returned from a deep and peaceful sleep. He slowly opened his eyes and had to think hard about where he was. Gradually his brain brought all his memories back and he slowly sat up rubbing his sleep gummed eyes. He stretched his powerful arms and clenched his fists together reversing them and putting pressure on his finger joints, a comfortable crackle followed.

'Do you have to do that Jack? A voice muttered from under a blanket.

'It wakes me up properly, and anyway it feels good, so get lost.'

'It doesn't bloody well sound good, you'll pay for it in later years mind, I'm telling you.'

'Huh, later years? How many men get that far? I'm going

to the netty, see you shortly,'

Jack stood up with the blanket around him and went outside to the toilet.

Later the two men were standing outside their spartan accommodation looking down the pit yard. The ground seemed to be covered in random railway lines of different sizes, it looked like total chaos but everything had been carefully planned. The big steam locomotives would ride up the wider tracks to fill their waggons with coal from the two great storage hoppers that stood on iron legs. Each waggon was driven underneath filled and then shunted into a siding by the pit locomotives as another waggon took its place. When all twenty were filled the big locomotive would take on water from the tower and have its tender filled with coal for fuel for the journey. Then with a blast on its whistle the locomotive would bellow out its usual great cloud of black smoke and slowly chuff its way out of the pit yard, gradually picking up speed as the huge steam engine gained power.

Jack and Brophy watched one of the trains disappear round a bend, only the smoke showed where it was. It would pick up the main line to Newcastle where the coal would be sent via coal barges to the ports of Britain.

The great pit wheels were turning as usual, the heavy steel cable disappearing through the roof of the heapstead where the cages relentlessly carried men, coal and equipment up and down the shaft. Deep below five men and two boys were almost at the end of their shift, looking forward to a wash in a tin bath full of hot water, followed by a hot meal at home.

'Heapstead first?' said Jack.

'Aye if you like, but what about something to eat .'

'How much money have you got?' said Jack.

Brophy just shook his head.

'So, its heapstead then, isn't it?'

They walked past the blacksmiths shop and the engine shed that was used for repairs on the shunters and approached the lamp cabin. The term cabin was a relic of the past but still used as the cabin was actually a big brick building with a door at both ends. This was where every miner had to report before entering the heapstead. Behind a long counter stretching the length of the room were row upon row of pit lamps. The deputy in charge would light the lamps before passing them on to the miners. A tally would be handed to the miner, one of a pair, the other placed on a hook until the pitman returned. If he didn't he could be identified by his tally. In some cases that was the only identifiable bit left after an explosion.

They entered and Jack spoke to the deputy behind the counter.

'Hello, we are the new rescue volunteers, can we go into

the heapstead to see what's what?'

The deputy glowered at them.

'Nobody telt me aboot rescue people, no you cannit gan in till somebody tells me aboot the pair of you.'

He turned away and ignored them.

Brophy squared his huge shoulders and barged past Jack, the cheeky bugger wasn't going to talk to them like dirt, he thought. Before he had a chance to say anything the far door opened and a wiry man walked straight up to the pair of them.

'You two must be the new body collectors are you?' His comment aroused a few chuckles from the men in the cabin.

'Rescuers,' roared Brophy angrily, 'and anybody who calls us otherwise will get a knuckle sandwich,' he raised his meaty fist in the direction of the other men. The chuckles stopped, nobody fancied his chances with the man standing by the counter.

'What do you want with us?' he said, as he faced the newcomer.

'Mister Harris says you're to move into eighteen First Street, the keys are under the coal scuttle, not that the door's locked mind, a bit pointless because nobody's got owt to pinch have they?' His wide smile and creased face diffused the situation. 'I'm banksman and just finished so I'll show you where it is if you like.'

Jack nodded and they left the lamp cabin.

'I'm Charlie Whittles, have been since I was born, been banksman in pits for nigh on twenty five years now,' said the man as he offered his outstretched hand to both men who shook in turn.

Jack studied the man, a worn and creased face with startling blue eyes looked back, lean and tough, this was a veteran of the pits, hard and dedicated at work, kind and generous outside.

'I live in number seventeen and would be pleased if you would come inside my home and meet my wife. It's baking day and there'll be enough to feed the street.'

Brophy and Jack stopped in their tracks but before they could say anything Charlie held up a hand.

'I'm not offering you charity boys, I'm just asking you to partake of my wife's good cooking, the whole village has tasted her pies at some time or other, so please don't take offence.'

'We'll gladly accept your offer of hospitality Mr Whittles,' said Brophy hurriedly, before his stubborn friend had a chance to refuse. He just hoped nobody could hear the heavy rumblings in his stomach, the thought of food made him lick his lips in anticipation.

They could smell the aroma of fresh bread and pastry long before they reached the bungalow. The very thought of living next door made Jack's mouth water, while Brophy's belly was rumbling so loudly they could all hear it.

'I can't help it, it's just the way I'm made,' he said.

'Our lass will soon settle that down son when we get inside, but I suppose you'll want to see your new place first. When you're finished just come to the back door, if you don't know where it is just follow your nose,' said Charlie with a laugh.

They stopped outside the bungalow, Charlie grabbed the sneck and opened the gate, three steps led down into the small back yard. To the left were two outhouses, the coalhouse and the netty. Charlie turned right and opened the back door.

'It's only me pet, I've brought us some guests.'

'Fetch them in pet, you know anyone is welcome in this house, with your say so of course,' she added.

It wouldn't do to let anyone think that she was in charge and not Charlie, even though he was happy with her running the house.

'This is wor lass, lads, if you would kindly introduce yourselves.'

'Me names not wor lass it's Lindy.'

Lindy was a tiny woman, but she was a perfect match for the wiry Charlie. She gazed at her husband and Jack was startled to see nothing but love and devotion in her eyes and even more so when Charlie's eyes lit up with pleasure at seeing her.

An hour later both men made their way back to the pit with full bellies, Lindy's meat and potato pie followed by bacon and egg tart had been enough to satisfy any man and yet she had insisted on serving up a bowl of homemade broth as well.

'Phew,' said Brophy, rubbing his big hand over his belly, 'that was something wasn't it?'

'Aye you're right there lad,' smiled Jack, 'did you see those stotty cakes cooling on the wall outside? The smell of the yeast was bloody wonderful.'

'So that's what they're called.'

Jack was referring to the loaves of bread that were well known in the north east of England, the loaf was circular, about two inches thick and had an open stretchy texture.

'So what do you think of the bungalow then Jack?'

'It's a hell of a lot better than what we've had lately, it's even got some furniture in it, so I'm not complaining. Anyway we've still got a couple of hours spare before we see the manager so let's check out the heapstead again.'

They entered through the high double doors of the building and made their way over to the shaft mouth. A man in a suit was standing talking to the banksman of the shift, his hair was slicked down in the fashion of the upper working class of the area, his collar starched to perfection. A tie, neatly knotted was at the exact centre of his shirt and two inches from the top of his collar. He was in the process of pulling out a good quality pocket watch from his waistcoat pocket when he noticed Jack and Brophy approaching. He was obviously a man of some importance, thought Jack.

Underground five men and two boys waited for the cage to take them up to the surface. It had been a particularly hard shift as the shot firers had brought down a lot of rock that had to be shifted and they were all eager to get home and relax after a hot bath. Only the gleam of their teeth and the whites of their eyes shone in the darkness, all exposed skin was soot black with coal dust.

'Stand back,' roared the deputy as the cage suddenly appeared, filling the open shaft in front of them.

'Right, in you get,' he roared again and the miners stepped into the cage.

'Gear and arms and legs inside. Is that you're dick sticking out son? You'll lose it just like that, ' as he snapped his fingers in the air. 'And that's before you ever get the chance to use it.'

The men in the cage burst out with exaggerated laughs, as though they had never heard the deputy say that before.

The boy looked down and blushed under the coal dust when he realised he was being had. The deputy winked at him as the others chuckled around him. He pulled an iron lever twice, known as a rapper, the rap was repeated at the surface. The cage whooshed away at sixteen feet a second, it wouldn't take long to climb the sixteen hundred feet to the bank head where the banksman would hurry them out as the hewers took their place.

Jack was crossing the rails in the heapstead to introduce himself to the suited man when he stopped. Something wasn't quite right, the sounds were wrong, something was different, he looked up. The heavy steel cable that the cage was suspended on was resisting the pit wheels, that was the noise. Suddenly he leaped forward and grabbed the banksman by the arm.

'Look,' was all he said.

The banksman grabbed the rapper and pulled it once, the signal was repeated in the engine room where the engine man stopped the powerful equipment instantly. But it was too late.

CHAPTER TWENTY FOUR

There was silence. Later Jack would swear to himself that he stood for a long time before anything happened, the world had stopped turning. The heavy steel cable that was attached to the cages was taut for only a moment then it seemed to relax, had the engineman reversed the huge engine giving some slack to the cable? Jack almost breathed a sigh of relief, then the cable lazily recoiled. The end appeared above the shaft, the heavy steel bracket that held it to the cage hung from the end. It swung around the bankhead and clobbered the banksman who had just come on shift, the blow probably broke his skull but no one would ever really know because the momentum of the blow hurled him over the edge of the shaft. If he was lucky he was dead, if not then pray to God that he didn't regain consciousness as he fell to the ground hundreds of feet below. Jack had wondered sometimes if a man had time to contemplate his own death as he hurtled to a terrifying end during a shaft accident. The cable slammed into one of the upright girders stretching up to the roof, the heavy bracket shattered and fell around them. The cable, released from its heavy burden fell to the floor and gracefully coiled itself around the head and shoulders of the suited man and then yanked him up into the roof of the building before it uncoiled and he fell with a wet slap onto the rails near the shaft. Jack and Brophy ran across to him. Already the light of life was leaving his eyes but he was trying to say something. Jack knelt down and put his ear to the man's bloody lips. He then turned towards the remains of the man's face and said. 'Yes, I promise.'

Jack was certain he saw a faint smile cross the man's lips then blood spurted from his mouth and his head lolled to one side revealing the horrific gash in his neck where more blood was steadily pumping from his body. He shuddered then died. Jack took a deep breath and stood up. He looked at Brophy who saw the sadness in Jack's face, but there was something else as well, it was compassion for the dead man. That was when Brophy realised that all Jack wanted to do was save lives, but this time had failed.

'What did he say Jack,' said Brophy quietly. Jack shook his head slowly and walked away a few paces his head down. Then he turned.

'He asked me to look after his wife Brophy.'

The heapstead was filling with men. A miner had noticed that the great wheels had stopped for too long, there had to be something wrong.

'What's up?' called a deputy as he approached Jack and Brophy, 'good God,' he whispered as he saw the bloody remains lying on the floor. It wasn't anything he hadn't seen before but it still shocked.

'Get an ambulance up here, sharpish,' he shouted to no one in particular.

Two men ran back out of the heapstead doors and down to the village where Billy Guest had a flatbed cart drawn by an old nag which acted as the local ambulance.

Jack looked at the deputy, 'Why isn't there an ambulance in the pit?'

The deputy merely shrugged his shoulders.

'Jack,' said Brophy, 'we're supposed to be the rescue team aren't we.'

Jack nodded.

'So why aren't we trying to rescue people.'

'Shit, right you men he shouted above the noise, I want a bosun's chair rigged over this shaft as quick as you like and enough rope to get me to the first level.'

'I did a stint in the merchant navy,' called out a man.

'Well get it organised then,' the authority in Jack's voice surprised himself but the man just nodded and started giving out instructions to his companions.

'There better be room for two Jack.'

Jack nodded, 'Thanks Brophy let's get cracking then,' he smiled slightly which was all Brophy asked for.

In ten minutes both men were hanging over the shaft, the bottom was sixteen hundred feet below them. Jack tried not to think about it but it was all Brophy thought about.

'Bloody hell Jack, it's a hell of a long way down there, what if?'

'Don't even say it Brophy, let's just get on with the job, there'll be time later to dwell on it.'

Jack hoped it was true.

A signal system had been set up via tugs on a separate rope held by Jack as they were lowered.

'Are you ready?' asked Jack, trying not to show his fear.

'Lower away,' said Brophy as he nodded to his companion.

Suddenly they were dropped into an alien world, the circle of light above them rapidly shrinking, the voices above died to a murmur. All that could be heard was the rapid breathing of the two men and the creak of the rope as the knots tightened up.

Both men had carbide lamps because the open flame in the big reflector gave off more light than a safety lamp. It was reckoned to be a safe pit so the risk of a gas explosion was very small, at least at this depth.

They swung their lamps around the shaft, Jack noticed a repair to the rails that held the cage in place, later he thought, men's lives were more important at the minute.

They passed by the two hundred and fifty feet marker that was chalked on the shaft wall, when Brophy called out in alarm.

'Jack, there's a cage wedged across the shaft,' his voice boomed and bounced off the walls of the confined space.

Jack gave the signal to slow down and they were gently lowered to the roof of the cage. He tugged the rope again, with the command to stop.

Brophy leaned over the edge and peered inside, the open side of the cage was facing down into the void. He edged back and knelt beside Jack.

'There's nobody in it, but somebody tried to hang on, look,' he said and pointed to the criss-crossed wire wall. Someone had been hanging onto the grid with both hands but had finally let go leaving chunks of ruined and bloody flesh stuck to the cage.

'Can you imagine it Jack, what they must have thought.'

'Christ Brophy, will you shut it, I don't even want to think about it at the moment,' he instantly relented, 'I'm sorry mate it's just that, well we've never done owt like this before.'

They stared hard at each other an instant of understanding between them, that both knew had strengthened the bond of their relationship.

'Are you ready?' Brophy nodded. Jack gave the signal and they began to drop further into the bowels of the earth.

They soon discovered the second cage thirty feet below, on its journey to the shaft bottom, there were two bodies lying on top of it, one was stretched across the mounting bracket, his back broken, the other was face down on top of the first body. Jack gave the signal to slow down and then to stop as their feet touched the top of the cage. Brophy rolled the body of a boy over on to his back, he was incredibly gentle for a man of his strength, he hung his head in sadness as he looked down at the victim. The boy's nose had been smashed and a tooth was sticking through his top lip, his face a mass of drying blood. An arm lay at a strange angle showing that it was badly broken. Jack saw the look in Brophy's eyes.

'It wasn't your fault Bill,' it was the first time he had used his Christian name.

'It's just so wrong Jack, the lad hasn't had a chance at life.'

Jack clapped Brophy on the back, it was like hitting a railway sleeper.

'Come on, at least we can get them back to the surface.'

'Are we just body collectors Jack?'

Jack's eyes flickered towards the boy's body, a frown creasing his brow. He held up a hand for silence. Brophy cast the light from his lamp over the boy's bloody face, was that movement or just muscle relaxing, he thought.

Suddenly the boy started gasping for breath, his eyes scrunched up in the lamp's glare.

'Bloody hell, he's suffocating on his own blood Bill, get him turned onto his side.'

Brophy picked the lad up and gently turned him on his side holding him like a mother would hold her baby.

'Come on son, you're safe now,' said Brophy, as he cleared the blood and spittle from the boy's mouth, 'you just hang on tight for a minute, this might hurt a bit.' The boy's eyes widened in fear but Brophy had already pulled the tooth out of his lip and then pulled him into his chest his arms wrapped around the lad. The boy began to weep.

'Shush lad you'll be fine now,' Jack lifted his lamp in time to see a huge tear rolling down the man's face.

'Bill,' he said quietly, 'take him up top and get an engineer and the pit smithy down here, I'll wait until they get here. Brophy got into the bosun's chair and Jack signalled for them to be taken up. He sat with his legs dangling over the edge of the cage and just for a moment his thoughts went back to his father's death. He wondered how it had felt, did he have time to know that he was about to die as he hurtled down the shaft. Four men and one boy had fallen over thirteen hundred feet to their deaths, how long did that take he wondered, the poor bastards.

It wasn't long before he noticed the faint shine of a lamp in the shaft, it was Brophy again.

'You can't lift him yourself Jack,' he said pointing to the man's body. They manhandled the corpse into the bosun's chair, Jack pulled off the man's belt and placed it under the body's arms then wrapped it around the chair rope to secure him. He signalled the surface with three tugs and the chair began to rise swiftly leaving the two men sitting on the cage.

'There's a senior deputy up top now, he says to stay on the top of the cage and it will be lowered to the next level, the second shaft is linked to that level now, it's a mile walk to the shaft and the shaft engineers and the blacksmith will sort out the damage in the meantime.' Jack nodded, he supposed the other five victims would be dragged out of the shafts sump and tidied up before being taken to the surface.

'Aye let's go then, I suppose we've missed our

appointment with the manager.'

'We've missed our appointment alright Jack, the buggers gone, the new man's arrived to take over hasn't he,' there was an edge of nervousness in his voice which made Jack lean closer to Brophy as he brought his lamp up and stared at the black face opposite him.

'You're not telling me everything you big bugger, come on let's have it afore I throw you over the edge.'

'That'll be the day mate.'

They smiled at each other then burst out laughing, the tension releasing after recent events.

'Come on then?' said Jack.

'Fat Geordie's arrived.

'Bugger,' said Jack.

CHAPTER TWENTY FIVE

It was dusk when Jack and Brophy finally arrived at the surface, they were both hungry, tired and bone weary and were looking forward to their beds. Several people raised a hand or touched their caps in respect but said nothing, noting how tired the two men looked.

When they arrived at their modest bungalow they noticed the oil lamps burning inside. They weren't alarmed, it just seemed unusual that anyone would do that. Nobody locked their doors, it was inconceivable that anybody would break in to a home with evil intent it just wasn't done, so who was it?

As Brophy opened the door he was assailed by the aroma of meat pudding.

'Jack, can you smell that?'

'Aye, bloody lovely Bill, it smells just like the pudding that,' he shut up.

Brophy's eyes widened in surprise, or was it hope thought Jack.

'You best go in first Bill, I'm just going to see if it was Charlie and Lindy next door that did it.'

Brophy wasn't listening, he just grunted and went in the house. Jack hoped the man wouldn't be disappointed and that she would be there. He knew he had an affection for the woman himself, but it was Brophy who had turned her head in the long run. He knew he had been a convenient vessel for her passion but he didn't mind. She had been there at the right time for him.

He knocked on the banksman's door, opened it and called out.

'It's Jack, can I come in?'

Immediately the contented face of Lindy Whittles appeared.

'Jack, come in pet it's good to see you, where's that big brute of a friend of yours?'

'He's next door missus Whittle.'

'You call me Lindy son, now how about a bit of pie while you're here?'

Jack was beckoned into the living room where Charlie was sitting in his rocking chair happily puffing away on a clay pipe, the sweet smell of tobacco and the acrid sulphuric smell of coal smoke gave the room a warm cosy feel. The fire in the range was dying down and showed only glowing embers in the grate. Jack thought it was like a furnace in the room.

Charlie nodded in greeting.

'You get used to the heat son, got no choice have I when she's baking all the time,' he winked as Lindy gave him a disapproving glare which turned into a mischievous grin.

'You're a cheeky little bugger Charlie Whittles, I don't hear you complaining at tea times, anyway, mind your manners and offer our guest a seat and a beer.'

'Sorry Jack, I'm forgetting myself, I would ask you to accept my apology.'

Jack held up his hand.

'No need for that please, but I will accept your kind offer of a beer.'

Lindy was delighted, she knew the way to a man's heart was through his stomach and she took pride in making her husband and his acquaintances content.

As Jack poured the thick black stout out of the bottle into a tankard, Charlie pulled a poker out of the fire, its end glowing red.

'Here you go son.'

Jack took the poker and sunk the red end into his stout taking care not to let it bubble over on to the floor.

'You cannot beat a bit of iron son, it'll do you the world of good, cheers marra.'

'Cheers,' said Jack.

He felt honoured that he had been called marra, only friends called each other by that name which was used between men of the same shift underground. It showed respect and reliance on each other and was indeed a compliment.

He could tell that Lindy was eager to say something, but sat back in the offered fireside chair and contentedly ate his bacon and egg pie, washed down with a good stout. The warmth of the room and the atmosphere sent him drifting off into a dream where Ada was waiting for him. He had to go to her and ran across the meadow where she was waiting, a beautiful smile on her lovely lips.

Charlie took the tankard from Jack's hand and looked at Lindy his eyebrow raised.

'Let him rest pet, he deserves it,' she said.

Next door in number eighteen First Street, Brophy had gone into the living room and sat at the little table by the window, and waited for Jack. The main bedroom door opened and he jumped up, his face a picture as Madge walked into the room. She wore a simple milkmaids dress, cut low across her breasts and held together with a loosely tied cord. Her hair was fastened at the back with a ribbon in a curious style, almost like a horse's tail of some kind, but it gave her face a fresh and appealing look. She was still a good looking woman, thought Brophy. She smiled, showing her teeth which were still good, unusual at her age thought Brophy again. He stood gawping at her.

'Well, you great oaf, are you going to say something? Or just stand there like a wallflower.'

'Madge,' was all he could say.

'Aye, it is me you daft bugger, where's my handcart, it's obvious that you weren't bringing it back so I thought I'd better come and get it.'

'It's out the back pet, just waiting for me to fetch it.'

'Sit down man, you've obviously lost your wits, don't you understand why I'm really here you silly bugger.'

Brophy thought for a moment.

'Your cart?'

'I've missed you Bill,' she whispered.

Finally common sense penetrated Brophy's head as realisation dawned on him.

He looked across the table as she poured two mugs of ale, passing one to him, he took a huge gulp and set the mug down. She was still looking at him.

'Madge, I don't know how to say this properly.'

Her face suddenly lost the glow of happiness to be

replaced by doubt, had she been wrong? Maybe she was just dreaming, the silly imaginings of a lonely woman. She lowered her head and sipped at her ale.

'I've missed you as well,' blurted out Brophy, 'in fact I've thought about nowt else flower,' he grinned at her.

She looked up, her eyes bright again.

'Honestly Bill?'

'Aye lass, honestly.'

'What if I said I would like to stay?'

'Then you would make me a very happy man pet.'

'I mean forever Bill,' her voice was quiet and nervous now.

He looked at her for a moment, the realisation of what she was hinting at tearing his emotions apart, but he knew what he wanted and she was sitting opposite him right now. He got up and crossed the room to where his kit was stored. He reached inside one of his bags and pulled out a black bottle. He picked up two tea cups from the pantry, sat down at the table again and poured a generous measure of dark navy rum into each cup.

'Remember the first time you had a drop of this?' he said.

She nodded.

'I've never had a drop of it since, it wouldn't taste the

same without you love. I think now's the time to celebrate and if you will have me I would ask you to be my wife.'

He held his breath as she savoured the heady aroma of the rum.

'Delighted,' she said.

* * *

Jack woke up suddenly, the fire was out, only the faint light of a candle glowed on the mantelpiece. The clock continued its monotonous tick tock which had put him to sleep in the first place. It was four- o-clock in the morning, he shouldn't be here, it was taking advantage of a good neighbour's hospitality. He would apologise next time he saw them he thought as he crept out of the house and into his own next door. He quietly slipped into bed and drifted off to sleep again.

The next morning Madge and Brophy were sitting at the table when Jack appeared . Brophy looked bright and alert.

'Morning Jack,' he said.

Jack replied in kind and then turned to Madge.

'It's a pleasure to see you again Madge.' She stood up and gave Jack a cuddle but it was restrained, not like it was before and he knew that his place was now only as a friend and not a lover. He didn't mind, she had looked after him when he was in need and he would always be grateful for that.

'Bill has asked me to marry him Jack and we would like your blessing.'

'With all my heart, both of you,' smiled Jack and embraced both of them, which was difficult with a man as broad as Brophy.

There was a sharp and insistent knocking at the door.

'I'll go,' said Jack.

He opened the back door and looked down to see a broad and familiar smiling face staring back up at him.

CHAPTER TWENTY SIX

Jack's concern about his position was forgotten when he saw who it was that was staring up at him.

'Has that grin not cracked your face yet young'un?' he found himself grinning back.

'No sir, will it like?' the boy's face had gone serious.

'I'm only having a laugh son, don't worry, anyway I remember you lad, we had a slice of toast together once.'

The boy's grin impossibly widened when he realised that Jack remembered him.

'It's me mister Walker.'

'Now, I reckon you would never have remembered my name unless someone had asked you to pass a message on to me, am I right?'

The boy nodded vigorously.

'Now I remember the last time we talked and had a bit

of a session about who was who, so I know that I am me, therefore if you would kindly remind me what your name is.

'I'm Bobby Samms of course, don't you remember?'

Rather than upset the lad Jack played out the game like a bit of tomfoolery.

'Of course I remember, I just wondered if you were me and I was you, or something.'

Bobby frowned and concentrated, eventually he came up with his answer.

'You've just made a funny, haven't you mister Walker?'

'Aye lad, I have at that, come on in I think I can offer you something better than toast this morning.'

They went through into the sitting room where Jack introduced the lad. Madge immediately began making a fuss over the boy and he soon ended up with an enamel mug full of hot sweet tea and a huge slice of cheese and onion pie.

'Is that all right for you pet?' she asked as Bobby swigged the sweet tea, his face smudged with wet pastry.

'It's lovely missus, but why has the tea got such a nice taste?'

'It's sugar, me little flower,' Madge's face was bursting with adoration for the lad.

'What about the message Bobby?' said Jack.

'Oh aye, I forgot about that,' he said, hurriedly wiping

his mouth with the back of his hand, which Madge immediately wiped with a damp flannel.

'Geordie, oops sorry,' he looked around in case he was in trouble, but the faces he saw nodded or winked for him to carry on. He went quiet for a while as he tried to recall the exact words of the message. At last the words fell into place and he recited the message like a piece of school homework.

'Mister Bassett says that you and mister Brophy are to take the next two days off and to go to his office at nine o clock the very next morning after that, to discuss the future of the rescue team. In the er,' he couldn't grasp the word, 'you have to go to the pit office and they'll give you both some money.'

Jack looked at Brophy, surely if they were being paid then the team wasn't to be disbanded before it even started.

'Oh by the way,' said Bobby, 'the money is in appreci-something or other for what you have already done.'

'Well you could have bloody well told us that earlier,' exploded Jack.

'That's the way I had to say it mister,' Bobby cowered like a dog being scolded.

'Leave the bairn alone,' said Madge, her tone demanded no argument.

Jack was about to protest but shut up instead and changed the subject.

'What are you doing here Bobby?' he asked

'Me dad got killed and me mam would have ended up in the workhouse. So mister Bassett brought us with him, saying he needed a messenger boy and that I would get a job in the pit.

Jack didn't ask what had actually happened to the boy's father as the lad appeared to be matter of fact about it.

'So how's your mam these days?' he asked. For the first time the boy's face took on a frightened look.

'Jack, I think the lad is upset,' Madge's voice was softer now.

'Only tell us if you want to,' she said.

'Well, me mam has something called consumption and she is going to die soon.'

They became quiet, the crackle and spit of the coal fire the only sounds in the room.

Brophy spoke first.

'So what will happen to you then?'

The boy shrugged his shoulders.

'Maybe I'll have to go into the workhouse sir,' the look on the boys face showed he had thought about the matter a lot.

'As long as there is breath in my body lad you will do no such thing.' Brophy had stood up now his voice booming. 'There will always be a bed for you in this house my lad and don't you forget it.'

Madge raised a hand to her mouth, Brophy had said exactly what she would have said herself, given the chance.

'Come on son, let's go and have a word with your mam.'

Bobby looked up at the huge bulk of Brophy, then at Jack, who nodded. Brophy took the lad's hand in his and left the house.

'Well, that's that then,' said Madge.

They sat silently for a few moments.

'Does Brophy know about us Madge?'

'Of course he does, he always has done, he's not as daft as he looks Jack.'

'You don't have to tell me that pet, anyway it looks like you're going to have a family after what's just happened.'

'Well that'll suit me fine,' said Madge with a smile on her face.

'I'll see Bassett about finding somewhere else to live, it wouldn't be right for me to stay here.'

Madge looked at Jack closely.

'You're an independent bugger Jack, but you're right all the same.'

'I'll be down the welfare hall if Brophy wants to talk about it,' Jack left, giving Madge a smile as he closed the back door.

He felt let down somehow, but that was purely a selfish thought, as always at times like this his thoughts turned to Ada, what would she have said to him. Why did he suddenly feel alone, Ada always said he was a loner, she was probably right, she usually was. He smiled at her memory then a huge wave of emotion washed through him leaving him drained and miserable. He turned into the little park and sat down on a bench, his head hanging down on his chest as the first tears filled his eyes at the memories of her. It was mid morning and the trees in the park still hung heavy with the recent rains. The sun was burning off the dampness and a thin mist lingered around the plants and grass around the park.

Jack breathed in deeply smelling the freshness around him. It's good to be alive, he thought, and began to pull himself out of the grief he had slipped into. It was easier now, it still hurt like hell but he was beginning to accept the way things were. He looked around to make sure no one had seen his tears then stood up and walked down to the miners' welfare hall. It had a good library and now that he could read better than ever before he intended to study how a coalmine worked.

Jack was entering the library, when back at the pit Nathan Rewcastle had just reached the top of the shaft. One more shift and I'm out of this, he thought.

The banksman was eyeing Nathan warily.

'You been smoking underground again, you old bugger?' he said.

'Somebody stitching me up is there?' replied Nathan, his eyes sweeping around the men from his shift.

'You'll bloody well kill us all Nathan,' spoke up one man. 'You know the rules.'

'Rules,' sneered Nathan, 'there's nowt you can tell me about the pit, anyway you'll all be shot of me shortly, only one more to go.'

'If I find any baccy on you tomorrow, except for chewing,' said the banksman, 'then you'll get the sack.'

Nathan didn't like this particular banksman and never had, too bloody big for his boots he was.

His lip curled in contempt.

'Shite,' was his parting answer as he walked away.

The banksman shook his head slowly.

'Come on you lot,' he shouted, 'don't stand there gaping, bugger off out the way, the sooner he's gone the better for all of us.'

The men voiced their agreement and headed off home to a tin bath full of warm soapy water and then a hot meal to follow.

CHAPTER TWENTY SEVEN

Seth was content. He was rid of those fools now. How the hell could anyone blame him for what had happened to those children. Anyway the mothers will all be knocked up again likely, the dirty bastards. He had to do the right thing, if he had let the door be opened then everyone would have been swept to their deaths, no matter what anyone said to the contrary. It was just like he had said to Jack Walker, they breed like rabbits. He didn't expect Jack's reaction, the man was damned fast he had to give him that. Bassett had no idea how to handle men, the same as he had no idea how to handle those big tits of his wife. He had seen the gardener arrive at their new house and could see what Bassett's missus was up to, maybe he could use that information if the lad ever set his lip up to him, the lucky shite. But never mind, he was sure he could sort things out to his satisfaction. He looked in the mirror and straightened his tie. He always made a point of not looking directly at his destroyed face, he preferred to remember how he used to look. His wife had soon buggered off when she saw his face after the accident. They were all the same, women. All they wanted was self, self, self. They only spread their legs when there was something in it for them, the bitches. He wished the bloody twitch would go away. He wasn't stupid, he knew it was getting worse, the same as his short temper, that was getting worse as well.

Anyway he was overman of the new pit, he knew his job and he knew he was bloody good at it and he was going to show these new miners of his just who was the gaffer. He squared his Tweed waistcoat making sure all the buttons were fastened, then clamped his compressed cardboard pit hat on his head, there was no peak. His puttees were perfect and he could see his face in his boots if he wanted to, which he didn't. He left his house and walked down the lane to the new pit, his yardstick under one arm, shoulders back and the other arm swinging with military precision. God was on his side. He looked a fine figure of a man unless you noticed the torn and scarred face that jerked and twitched every so often.

* * *

Today was the last shift for old Nathan, so he wouldn't

give him a hard time, as long as he behaved himself that is. He knew about his smoking underground but one more day wouldn't matter. Anyway there was still coal to be won out of the first tunnel inbye. It was only ten yards in from the shaft, aye, he thought, I'll stick him in there out of harm's way. There had been a rule in place that only safety lamps could be used because the second shaft hadn't reached the same level yet, but it didn't appear to be a fiery pit to Seth, nevertheless rules were rules. Although if rules were to be obeyed then there shouldn't be anybody underground until the second shaft was finished. That had come into force a few years after the New Hartley pit disaster when the broken arm of a beam engine had fell down the shaft. There had been no way out for the miners' trapped underground, all dead, every last one of them. But a man had to feed his family and the owners never bothered themselves with the day to day running of the pit.

He noticed the candy men leaving the manager's office as he walked towards the heapstead. Look at the buggers he thought, in their stupidly striped suits and matching bowler hats. He hadn't seen those two before, he thought. He steered left and approached the two men who were chattering excitedly about their new found position. Seth stood in their path and the men stopped.

'Canny job you've got there lads eh?' Where you from?'

'Off the farm,' said the bigger man, 'no work you see, now if you don't mind we've got a job to do.'

'You'll go when I tell you,' said Seth, his voice taking on a growl.

'We don't work for you mister,' said the smaller man.

He had a strange look in his eyes, obviously he lived on a short fuse thought Seth, he was picking at his fingernails with a slender sheath knife, it looked sharp, very sharp.

'Take that attitude son and I'll shove that pretty little knife so far up your arse it'll cut your tongue,' Seth was close enough now to spit in the man's face.

The candy man swept the blade up in front of Seth's nose and sneered up at him.

Seth's expression didn't change. He whacked the brass headed yardstick across the man's head felling him instantly.

'Bastard,' he shouted as he swung round to face the bigger man. He could see that the man was not frightened by the little smile of anticipation on his face.

'Cmon then big fella, I'm no match for you am I?' said Seth.

'You asked for it arsehole,' said the man as he crouched slightly, his big fists clenched ready for the pounding that he was going to give this jumped up tosser. He smiled as he swung a left but Seth sidestepped neatly and whacked the man on the knee with his yardstick. The man stopped suddenly, the pain in his knee was unbearable and he couldn't move the bloody thing. His leg collapsed under his weight and he fell to the ground, his good knee supporting him. Seth swung back his yardstick and then sliced it through the air hitting the man on the temple. The man stared upwards for a moment, his eyes rolling up into his head then fell face down in the dirt.

The smaller man was coming to, rubbing his head, he looked up at Seth.

Seth smiled down at him.

'The sooner you know whose boss round here the better boy. Try any of that again and you're dead, got it?'

The man ignored him.

Seth's face began to twitch, his anger rising.

'Got it?' he shrieked.

The miners who had been watching turned their backs, they were getting to know Seth's moods and didn't want to see what happened next. Anyway they were candy men, who gave a damn about them.

The man saw the madness in Seth's eyes and knew he would probably kill him with that bloody stick of his so he nodded.

'That's not good enough boy,' Seth's voice had a dangerous calm about it now, he even smiled.

'You say, yes mister Ridley it won't happen again,' he nodded encouragingly swinging his yardstick in front of the man's face.

'Yes mister Ridley it won't happen again.'

'Good, good, shift that pile of shite and let's all get on with our lives,' he said, pointing at the other man sprawled on the ground.

Seth's laugh was slightly hysterical as he walked away, then he put his stick under his arm and started singing as he headed towards the heapstead and the cage that would carry him deep into the earth where he was in total command.

The candy men stood in a daze, what was going to be a lesson for the pitman had gone horribly wrong. They noticed the men working on the surface grinning at them, distaste also showing on their faces. They wouldn't say anything because one day it could be their families who may be evicted. The job might be well paid but it wasn't going to attract any friends. So what, thought the big man, what you never had you never missed, anyway they had a job to do.

'C'mon,' he said to the small man, 'we've got a job to do.'

'I'm gonna sort that crazy bugger out,' said the small man.

'Aye, but not today Fred, let's go, I think we are gonna

have some fun me lad,' said Sammy.'

They walked through the pit yard gates and turned into the lane leading to official row.

The assistant manager's house was now needed for the new rescue team official and evicting a woman should be a very interesting experience. It was a while since he had taken a woman.

'What's the number?' said Sammy.

'Fourteen North View.'

CHAPTER TWENTY EIGHT

Jack had woken early, he was keen to find out about the meeting with the manager. He had cleaned out the grate and started a new fire. The sticks were dry and lit instantly, the flames greedily consuming the wood. He placed coals on the sticks allowing enough air to circulate and before long the fire was blazing away, the coals glowing red then a bright orange. He hung a kettle of water over the flames and stirred in the oats adding a spoonful of salt. It wasn't long before the water was bubbling and the oats began to thicken. He lifted the kettle off its iron bar and stood it on the range out of the way of the flames. The heat in the cast iron kettle would do the rest without the porridge sticking to the bottom.

He knocked on Brophy's bedroom door, once he would have walked straight in but things were different now and he waited for an answer. He heard a grunt and a man's cough.

'Fires on and porridge is ready you two.'

'Right,' was the reply and Jack went back to the range to organise a billy can of tea, which

he carried along the passage, then opened the front door onto the garden. He liked this time of day, the world seemed at peace with itself. A faint mist hovered over the ground, the damp earth finally drying out, the clouds slowly rolling across the sky like giant marshmallows with great areas of blue in between them. He could feel the heat of the sun as it appeared low on the horizon. The whole scene took on a golden hue, beautiful thought Jack. The pit wheels on the horizon brought him back down to earth. The coal seams were so big that wherever you looked you were guaranteed to see the signs of mankind's efforts to dig it up. The ring of pits it was called locally, it wasn't pretty but a man might as well get used to it because it was always going to be there. Jack stretched his arms and stood up as he heard signs of life behind him and went back in to check the porridge.

'Mornin Jack' said a cheerful voice behind him.

'Mornin,' he replied as Brophy spooned porridge into a bowl. 'We've got about an hour afore the meeting if that's all right.'

Brophy noticed Jack's guarded attitude towards him.

'You all right marra?' he asked.

'Champion, why?'

'Well it's just you seem a bit off like, I mean, can I have a word with you after the meeting?'

'What's wrong with now?'

Brophy raised his eyebrows and held an empty bowl out, Jack nodded and he spooned porridge into the bowl, he offered Jack a spoon and they went outside into the garden, sitting down on the home made bench in front of the greenhouse.

'So what's up?'

'It's not me Jack, it's you, and I know it's about me and Madge, so let's have it.'

Jack stared at the ground for a moment then looked Brophy in the eye.

'I don't really know, I'm pleased for you and maybe I'm a bit jealous.'

Brophy's face turned hard.

'No, no it's not about my relationship with her, that's over and I wouldn't wish you any harm, I just hope that you can live with that if you understand my meaning.'

Brophy was quiet for a moment, then he turned to face his friend.

'Jack, don't let that bother you, it doesn't bother me, in fact it has helped me understand you a bit more, you didn't think Madge wouldn't tell me about you?'

It was Jack's turn to look offended.

'No you daft bugger, she's never told me about owt like that, that's private and I respect both of you too much to want to know.'

'Bill, I'm sad to see you happy, can you understand that? I'm sad because I've lost my wife and now it looks like I might lose both of you, I mean I'm trying to understand why I'm not happy.'

'Isn't it because you've lost Madge as well?' Bill said the words quietly.

The words struck Jack like a mel hammer, he looked at Brophy, there was no malice in the man's face. He nodded.

'Yes, you're right,' he said. 'I have to leave for all our sakes, I'll try to find lodgings after the meeting.'

Brophy nodded in agreement, he hated the tension between them.

'You won't lose us Jack, but only you can sort the rest out, just take it from me I'm here if you want me.'

Brophy stood up and went back into the house. He couldn't help remember when Jack didn't want anything to do with him. It's a funny old world, he thought, you just don't know what's round the next bend.

An hour later they were walking side by side up pit bank.

* * *

Deep underground Seth shouted along the gallery.

'You finished yet Nathan Rewcastle?'

'Nearly,' came the reply.

'Well get a bloody move on, you're holding up the whole pit.'

'Bugger off,' muttered Nathan. He reckoned he would be finished in an hour, he was hewing his last tub of coal.

'Mek sharp young'un am var nigh finished,' the boy loading the coaltub understood, but why should he hurry for the old fart and who cared if he was nearly finished or not. It was all right for him, he would be working up top after today. Nevertheless he answered respectfully.

'Yes mister Rewcastle.'

Nathan picked up a fag next to his bait box and struck a swan vestas, holding it to the end of his cigarette and sucking in the smoke.

'Ah, that's better,' he said out loud to no one in particular.

'You're not supposed to do that,' said the boy, his nose wrinkling with disgust at the smell.

'Shut your mouth, you little bag of shite afore I belt you one.'

The boy turned away muttering under his breath, Nathan ignored him and leaned against the rock wall, his eyes shut as he enjoyed the luxury of his smoke.

Up top Jack and Brophy smiled at each other when they looked down outside Bassett's office.

'Some things don't change do they Jack.'

They pulled off their boots and tugged on a pair of old slippers lying on the floor. They knocked and entered.

'Stay where you are,' commanded a shrill voice.

'Well, well look who we have here, its Cyril isn't it?' said Jack.

'You better do as you're told.'

'Us?' said Brophy leaning across the desk putting on what he hoped was his most frightening expression, 'we'll do anything you say,' his face was an inch away from Cyril's.

'Pack that in now you two.'

Brophy stood up instantly and Jack swung round to face the voice. The voice jerked a thumb.

'In here now. Cyril, no disturbances please.'

'Yes mister Bassett, a smug almost feline look spreading across his face.

The door closed and the three men were alone.

* * *

Sixteen hundred feet beneath them Seth Ridley was striding along the motherway to where the bulk of the shift was, almost a mile inbye. Nathan had finished his fag and hunkered down in the tiny space. He swung his pick at the coalface and unusually it went all the way to the pick handle. He tried to pull it out but it was stuck solid, suddenly the whole face burst outwards. Nathan realised it was a pocket of gas, firedamp. As he fell backwards his feet were scrabbling for a foothold, the metal segs on the bottom of his boots caught on the pan of his shovel and sent sparks flying.

* * *

'Sit down please,' said Bassett. 'I'll not beat about the bush, the owners have agreed that the rescue centre will be here at our pit and that you Jack will be the official that runs it, assisted by you William. You will both be given wages appropriate for the position. You already have a house William.'

'Jack, you now have a house on official row. Work starts on your headquarters today and I need a detailed report of your plans and the people who are going to work with you, by the end of this week. If you're not sure how to do that Jack I'm sure Cyril will help you, when you've apologised to him of course,' a little smile lifted the corners of Bassett's mouth.

'You could also ask the late assistant managers wife to assist you, she could do with an income after her husband's tragic accident. Her name is Ruth Shaw and you'll find her in the welfare hall library most days.'

They left Geordie's office, as they passed by the clerk's desk Jack raised his voice and glared at Cyril. He put on what he thought was his best tough look and shouted.

'Cyril.'

Cyril nearly jumped out of his chair with fright.

'I'm sorry for the way I spoke to you,' and left the office with Brophy behind him.

'I'm going to check out the new place Brophy, so I'll see you later.'

'I'll tag along if you've no objection Jack,' he had noticed the candy men walking down the lane and had a feeling that he might be needed.

The lane was lined by tall lime trees, once the avenue to the grand ballroom of the great house where carriages bearing their elegant passengers would pass through. Now it was mostly dirt, coal dust and slag. The trees once full with leaves at this time of year were drab, the leaves yellowing and falling from the branches, giving up the struggle against pollution. The ballroom had been demolished years ago when coal was discovered beneath it. The galleries below making the ground unstable for such a huge stone building, but it was satisfactory for miners' houses, even pit officials. Cloud was rolling in again from the south west threatening to block out the sun and a light breeze stirred the canopy above the two men as they walked along, their boots crunching underfoot.

Official Row, or to give it its correct name North View, faced the direction in which it had been named but it was a name rarely used. Fifteen houses stood in a row all with back yards and outhouses but bigger and better built than the pit bungalows. The yards were stone paved instead of concreted, the doors sturdier and sash windows fitted instead of the usual small paned steel frames. Inside there was a hallway with three rooms leading off, the kitchen the living room and a best room. The kitchen even had a fitted bath with a lid next to the range. The houses were considered posh to the miners but not outside their reach. If a collier learned his letters and had ambition he could move up to deputy or shot firer, or in rare cases pit manager.

The house Jack was looking for was the last but one, number fourteen. As he approached he shook his head slowly.

'Bloody hell Brophy, who would have thought I would end up in anything as grand as this.'

'Posh isn't it?' said Brophy in a whisper as though they were trespassing. The high back yard gate was slightly ajar and

Jack pushed it gently. It swung open, and he noticed the back door was open, was that voices he could hear? Brophy had dropped into a crouch, a frown on his face. They both realised something was wrong, a woman's voice raised in anger and fear, sounds of a struggle. Jack ran for the door, Brophy close behind him.

The candy men had not even bothered to knock on the door, there was always the chance of finding a woman bathing or dressing. Sammy had found Ruth in her sitting room, she turned suddenly to see the big man standing in the doorway with a leer on his ugly face.

'I suppose you know why I'm here,' he said as he approached her, 'you've got nowt to fear as long as you do as your told,' he smiled in his nicest way, but the look in his eyes told her she was in trouble.

'If you behave yourself then we can let you stay for another month, if you know what I mean.'

His eyes roamed over her body. Suddenly he lashed out and grabbed the housecoat she was wearing, it ripped easily. Her face showed a startled expression as she tried to cover her breasts but it was no good, the man had gone too far now and she knew it. It had been too long and he was going to have her whether she liked it or not.

'Come on darling let's have a little feel.'

'You keep your dirty hands to yourself,' Ruth had tried to sound threatening but she was terrified and her voice shook with fear.

A sudden noise from behind made the man turn. Jack was standing in the doorway.

'You're spoiling my fun you bastard, now bugger off.'

Jack moved towards him.

Sammy smiled, anticipating the thrashing he was going to mete out. He would sort this out first and then finish what he had come for.

The poker came down on his head with all the strength Ruth could summon up. Her housecoat fell to the floor leaving her naked, Sammy fell to the floor without a sound. Jack couldn't help but stare at Ruth's naked body.

She saw his look.

'You're all the same, dirty rotten bastards and I thought you were better than most.'

She sat down on the floor holding the remnants of her clothes around her and burst into tears. Jack grabbed a tablecloth spilling the vase of flowers and wrapped the cloth around her. Some inner instinct made him turn. That instinct saved his life. The knife flashed past his ear and clattered in the fireplace, Fred was already pulling another knife from his belt. A hand grabbed his wrist and twisted it.

'Drop it,' said Brophy.

He dropped the knife and somehow wriggled out of Brophy's grasp. He ran upstairs and clashed a bedroom door behind him. But Brophy had his foot in the door. Without a word he picked up the candy man and heaved him out of the bedroom window, the man's shrieks and howls suddenly cut off when he hit the paving of the back yard.

Downstairs, Jack was concerned about the candy man, a trickle of blood was running from his mouth and his skin was a waxy white. He knelt down and put his face close to the man's mouth, he wasn't breathing. He looked across at Ruth.

'He's dead.'

Brophy came into the room, he looked around and figured out what had happened.

'Dead?'

Jack nodded.

'I bet the other bugger is as well,' said Brophy.

Ruth was still crying.

'Shush woman,' said Jack, 'I've got to think, what the hell do we do now?'

'Let's get him out of the house,' said Brophy.

Jack nodded and grabbed the dead man's feet. Between them they carried the body out to the washroom where they dumped it on the floor. They went back outside. Fred's head was at an impossible angle. They had both seen plenty of accidents to know that his neck was broken. Brophy hoisted the small body over his shoulder and took it to the washroom where he dropped it on top of the other carcass.

'What happens now Jack?' said Brophy.

'They attacked her didn't they? All we did was save her.'

'Did you recognize them Jack?'

'No, why should I?'

'They were the two buggers that clobbered you by the fields.'

Jack nodded slowly.

'It still doesn't make me feel any better, serves the buggers right though. Like I said before we were defending this lady's modesty.'

'Who would believe that in a court Jack, we could get hanged for this,' his voice had a worried edge to it as he realised the enormity of what they had done.

Underground it was a different matter, justice was meted out as required, but on the surface they were liable to the law of the land.

'Look, just shut the door and bolt it, nobody is gonna ask questions yet, we need to go back inside and sort it out between us,' said Jack.

Ruth already had a kettle on the range, the water starting

to boil, she poured three good measures of dark rum into three enamel cups. The water came to the boil, using a rag to lift the hot kettle she poured the water into a teapot and allowed the tea to mash before pouring it into the mugs, followed by milk and two teaspoons of sugar into each one. No one spoke, they waited until the scalding mixture had cooled a little and then began to sip the liquid. A warm glow spread through Jack's body.

'By lass, this is some mug of tea.'

Brophy nodded in agreement.

They talked until late that night, the ample measures of rum making all of them tired. They had agreed that they would have to face the consequences of their actions and inform the local bobby in the morning. They slept where they sat, the flames of the fire growing smaller until only a red glow remained in the grate.

The man quietly entered the back yard, he silently moved over the ground, the only light came from a quarter moon in a sky of broken clouds. The moonlight flickered over his features, the eyes intelligent, the face had seen many years, in fact more years than most people. He was wearing a top hat, a favourite of his. He had seen the events that had happened, he had been out in the fields foraging for wild vegetables and fuel when he had seen the candy men enter the house. He had hidden nearby and watched. It was now time to help, justice wasn't simply an eye for an eye, some deserved to die and those that killed them deserved to live and that was why he was helping them. He knew he would be here tonight, he had felt it yesterday, but not many would understand his gift.

He used the wheelbarrow that was against the wall to carry the bodies one at a time down to the old sandpit, there wasn't a soul about. He knew exactly where to tip the barrow, each body slowly sunk beneath the surface of the quicksand, nobody was quite sure how deep it was, but Tommy Thompson knew it was deep enough for the bodies never to be found. He stood the wheelbarrow against the wall in the yard of the house when he had finished and went into the wash room. He pulled an ancient greatcoat off a nail in the wall, wrapped it around himself and lay down on the floor. It wasn't long before the room was filled with deep snoring as Tommy drifted into sleep.

Jack woke early after a fitful sleep, the other two were waking up as well. He got up out of the chair and peered through the window and across the yard. Everything looked the same and why shouldn't it? he thought. He heard movement behind him, without turning he spoke quietly.

'I suppose we had better get the bobby then.'

'Aye,' said Brophy , he put a hand on Jack's shoulder. 'Jack, look.'

Jack did as he was told and his eyes widened as the wash room door began to open slowly.

'Lord save us,' said Brophy as a booted foot appeared, nothing happened for an eternity. Suddenly a fountain of pittle arched out into the yard and slowly eased off, followed by a grunt of satisfaction. The foot disappeared and the door was pulled shut.

'The buggers are alive,' said Jack and made for the back door with Brophy close behind.

They cautiously approached the wash room, with a nod to Jack, Brophy yanked the door open and Jack rushed inside to face Tommy Thompson the hermit of Allansford.

'Ah Jack you're looking well, and Brophy as well what a surprise, you'll be putting the kettle on then will you? It makes my old bones ache having to lie on the floor.'

Jack and Brophy peered around the room, there was no trace of the candy men.

'All in good time boys, or are you going to let me die of thirst?'

Back in the house they introduced Ruth to Tommy, she looked baffled.

'It's a long story Ruth,' said Jack and raised his eyebrows.

'You'll have plenty time to talk about that,' said Tommy, 'the fact is, they're gone.'

'Gone where?' asked Jack.

'You don't need to know, but you'll never be bothered by those two again.' 'Anyway, there's no need for the police, justice has been done, they were never here, who knows what happened and who cares. I don't suppose anybody will miss them so live with it, it's over.

'But how did you know what was happening mister Thompson?' said Ruth.

'Don't ask,' said Jack, 'he just did.'

Ruth looked as though she was about to speak again, but Brophy gave a shake of the head and she shut up.

Tommy gobbled down the toast Ruth had made him and then noisily gulped down a mug of hot tea. He stood up.

'Thank you for the breakfast Miss,' she inadvertently gave a small curtsy, he bowed and swept his top hat onto his head in an old fashioned graceful manner.

'I'll see you around, just remember when you need me I will be there,' and left.

They looked at each other bemused, Jack smiled at Brophy who shrugged his shoulders and said.

'That's that then.'

'What do you mean, that's that, we've had two dead bodies shoved in the washroom, murdered for want of a better word and that's all you've got to say,' Ruth's voice was rising as she spoke.

'Would you rather face the noose?' said Jack.

She said nothing more.

'One day I'll tell you the whole story, just be assured that we are all right now,' Jack smiled at Ruth.

'What do you mean one day, you seem to forget I'm being evicted.'

'I need to talk to you about that,' said Jack.

'It's time I was going,' said Brophy and left without another word.

'What's going on,' said Ruth.

'Nothing to worry about it's just that when your husband had his accident I was there and he asked me to look after you and I promised him I would.'

She lowered her head but there were no tears.

'Anyway I can't let you be evicted, I'm not asking you for anything, if you know what I mean, but I would like you to look after my home. That is, our home so to speak. Before you answer you can have half the house and there's no obligation. As far as anyone is concerned you're my housekeeper and nothing else.'

CHAPTER TWENTY NINE

Nathan wasn't daft, he saw the gas ignite, he had time to shout at the boy to get out when his world blew apart. He didn't have time to scream as the flesh was burnt from his dismembered body, he was already dead. The boy had enough time to hide behind the coal tub when the explosion threw it against the wall, mashing him against the rock. He had time to see the flames that were going to devour him as the roof of the motherway crashed down around him. The gas could now only go one way and that was up the pit shaft, the workings underground were blocked as the roof collapsed. There were seven men on their way down the shaft when the blast caught the cage they were in. The heat and flames surrounded them. Those men had time to scream for their mothers as they died in agony. The blast hurled the cage up the shaft, tearing away the steel cross girders, the shaft walls collapsing in on them as the cage rode at the top of the explosion.

* * *

'Right,' said George Bassett, relaxing comfortably in his leather chair, 'is everything clear?'

Jack wasn't listening anymore he was wondering where the odd rumbling was coming from. Suddenly the windows began to rattle and the decanter of whisky started moving across the manager's desk. They all stared in horror at the phenomenon and then jumped out of their seats. Only one thing was responsible.

It was the tremor that was felt first, pots and pans slid into a sink, a toasting fork slid down onto a fire grate where it had been standing in the hearth. A woman was peeling potatoes into a bucket, the skins to be boiled up for the chickens, her husband liked mashed potatoes. The handle of the metal bucket began to tremble then rattle. She dropped the knife, her hand going to her mouth, her eyes wide with fright. No, she thought, it can't be, but when the tiny window panes blew inwards and the long sad wail of the disaster siren began, she knew there was no mistake. She ran out of the house and down the street, familiar faces ran with her but nobody spoke. They were running to save their sons and husband. There was already a crowd at the gates of the colliery. Hundreds of them waiting silently to see what happened next.

Jack was downstairs now and running across the pit yard, he saw Brophy close beside him.

The men on their way up after a tough shift were caught on the top of the blast as it travelled up the shaft, the heat starving the air of oxygen, the seven men suffocating as the cage was hurled upwards. It burst out of the top of the shaft and smashed itself to pieces in the workings of the heapstead, the men were thrown against unyielding steel and mashed into unrecognizable lumps of scorched flesh. The blast, now released from its burden burst upwards blowing the roof off the heapstead and throwing dust, smoke and debris a hundred feet into the air. Jack and Brophy were blown off their feet, the men in the heapstead were blasted apart chunks of them landing with a slap like meat on a butchers slab. Suddenly a strange groan began, Jack looked around dazed, where was it coming from? Then he realised it came from the people as they became aware of the enormity of what was happening. Suddenly a huge fireball shot from the mouth of the blasted shaft, it seemed to go on and on into the sky but then stopped, leaving a huge plume of muck in the sky. The bigger bits of slag and coal and dreadful human remains rained down onto the area like pumice from a volcano. The plume spread across the sky turning day into night.

Jack struggled to his feet, instinct told him to run away but there were men inside the building, probably dead but what if some lived? He began to run towards the devastation. He saw Brophy beside him, a grim look of determination on his hard features. The huge double doors of the heapstead were lying flat on the ground, blasted off their monstrous hinges. They entered the building, the darkness making it very hard to see. The creaks and groans of the wounded building were all around them. Brophy held up a hand.

'Jack, I can hear something.'

He pointed towards the shaft mouth, they climbed over twisted girders and broken coal tubs.

'Got him,' said Jack and then stopped in horror.

'God save us Brophy, the poor bastard's still burning and he's alive.'

The blackened shape was writhing in agony, a mewling sound coming from the horribly mutilated face. The man's lips had been burnt off, his white teeth startling.

'Good God Brophy, what the hell do we do with him?'

'Get his tally Jack.'

Jack reached out and tore the medallion from around the man's neck, he looked up just in time to see Brophy swinging a long metal bar. It hit the man on the side of his head, the force of the blow shattering the skull, the mewling stopped.

Jack stared in horror.

'What the hell have you done?'

'I don't need you to tell me what I've done Jack,' Brophy looked down at the body. He looked at Jack, his eyes pleading with him for understanding. Jack nodded.

'I know why Brophy, it's just that it seems like murder,' he said quietly, 'and believe me I know the feeling.'

He stood up and shoved the tally in his pocket, it would match its partner in the lamp room along with the man's name whoever he was.

'What was that you just said Jack?'

'What?'

'You know what it feels like?'

Brophy was studying Jack's face.

'Heat of the moment Brophy that's all, come on there's nothing more we can do here.'

Brophy knew he was hiding something but just nodded.

They ran out of the building heading back towards the manager's office. Bassett was on his way downstairs to meet them.

'One hundred and forty is the estimate, all trapped or dead,' his voice trembled but he kept his self-control, it's time to earn your wages men.'

'You never said how much.'

'Does it matter that much?'

Jack shook his head.

'Brophy, get the team together, we'll meet here if that's all right with you mister Bassett.'

'Do anything you have to Jack, you have my full support, for what it's worth.'

'It's worth a lot,' said Jack.

'What team? said Brophy, 'there's only one, the rest are underground.'

The team had not been properly formed so the members were earning wages until they knew what was going to happen.

'Who is it?' asked Jack.

'That quiet man that just appeared to ask for the job, his name is Ralph Henderson.'

'Then get him,' said Jack abruptly and immediately regretted it, 'sorry marra and please ask for volunteers, will you?'

Brophy nodded and left.

'How deep is the second shaft mister Bassett?'

'I'll get the engineers, they'll tell you everything you want to know.'

Jack suddenly realised he was alone. How did they expect him to rescue all those men, he had never done anything like this before. A feeling of inadequacy swept through him, where do I start. A group of men were hurrying towards him, it was Brophy and the quiet man and about eighteen others. Bugger, pull yourself together, you're in charge of this whether you like it or not, so come on, make Ada proud. He realised that it was only mid-day and yet the sky was overcast with dust making it look like evening, the dust from an explosion that had killed or trapped over a hundred and forty men and boys and it was his job to get them out and he would do his best to do that.

'Brophy, I need the mines inspector, the surveyor and any deputies that are available. Can you see mister Bassettt and sort it out, I want them all here as soon as possible.'

'I'm on to it Jack,' he ran off smiling to himself, that's better he thought, he's back on the job.

Jack turned to the volunteers.

'Any of you deputies?'

Two men raised a hand each.

'Names?'

'I'm Bob Crawford and he's John Shaw,' as he nodded at the other man.

'I need you down the ventilation shaft as quick as you like, have a look at the damage and report to me immediately.'

Jack surprised himself with the force and confidence in his tone, because inside, his guts were churning. Am I doing the right thing, am I expected to save those men and boys, maybe I am just a body collector after all, what experience do I have for this kind of stuff? He was looking down at the ground, it had gone quiet, he looked up and saw the faces of men waiting for their orders.

'Well, what are you waiting for?' The deputies beckoned with their yardsticks, a sign of their rank, and ran off with four men close behind.

That left twelve volunteers.

'The rest of you get you're gear on, lamps from the lamp cabin and picks and shovels, sharpish now.'

'They'll not give us lamps without authorisation mister Walker.'

'Aye you're right.' Jack pulled a notepad out of his top pocket and wrote out the request, he hesitated a moment and signed the note with Mines Rescue Station Officer.

'Take this, and don't call me mister, I'm a pitman just like you and I know you're all as determined as me to get those lads out of there.'

'You'll need Mollies as well,' said Ralph Henderson.'

'Good thinking, you sort that out,'

The man nodded and ran off with the others. Jack stopped for a moment, the man looked familiar, where had he seen him before? No matter, he could think about that later.

Normally pit lamps were lit in the lamp room and sealed

to prevent a miner opening his lamp to light a pipe that had been sneaked underground. Mollies were similar to tallies but instead of carrying one token around the neck so that a miner could be identified after an accident, the rescue team carried three. One was worn around the neck, a yellow enamelled tally was given to the banksman at the head of the shaft and a red one was held in the lamp room.

Brophy had returned, the officials would be there in fifteen minutes.

'It's too long Brophy, don't they realise that men are dying down there?' his voice was edgy.

'Steady Jack, this is the chance to prove ourselves and that a rescue team is necessary. They're doing their best to get here as fast as they can.'

'Yeah, all right, it's just that we've never even been trained properly for the job,' said Jack as he calmed down.

'I don't suppose anybody's had the experience to be able to train anyone, except us maybe,' Brophy shrugged his shoulders as he looked at Jack.

'So we are the experts then, I suppose.'

'Well, it looks like that bunch of officials coming our way, think we are,' said Brophy.

Jack raised his eyebrows as he took note of the men rapidly approaching.

'Well then Bill my friend, then experts we shall be,' Jack squared his shoulders and thrust out his chin.

CHAPTER THIRTY

The two deputies stepped into the emergency cage at the top of the ruined shaft. The banksman checked that all clothing and equipment was inside but the men were experienced, too many times had they seen an arm or hand snapped off through carelessness

'Something you should know,' said the banksman, 'this shaft was done in a hurry, so take it easy, at least you're better off than the poor bastards stuck down there.'

He stepped to the side and pulled the rapper, the signal repeated itself with a loud rap in the engine room and the engine man released the force of the hydraulic engine that raised and lowered the cages. Only a slight hiss was heard as the shining rods began to slide in and out, the metal casing a bright green lovingly polished by the engine man. The cage dropped slowly this time and wasn't connected to the side rails. Six pit lamps were suspended beneath the little cage giving the men time to signal a stop. At fourteen hundred feet they signalled the surface to stop the cage, they had gone as far as they could. Beneath them the shaft was completely blocked with debris. Bob Crawford lifted the small wicker bird cage in his hand and held his pit lamp next to it, the finch was still sitting on its perch.

'No gas,' he said, 'but keep an eye on the bird would you Tom?'

'Aye, no bother,' was the response.

Holding their lamps at arm's length they leaned over the edge.

'Shit,' said Bob, the whole friggin lot's come down, we'll never get through that lot.'

He climbed out of the cage and examined the debris.

'It'll take a month to get this lot out Tom.'

His heavy segged boots scraped on the cage rails as he scrambled back to relative safety. The sound travelled the remaining two hundred feet to the bottom.

'We might as well get back up top, there's nowt else we can do down here,' said Tom.

'Aye your right, that bird still all right?

'Yep.'

'Good let's go then.'

They clambered into the cage and Bob pulled the rapper. Whoosh, the cage surged up the shaft. The men were quiet, deep in their own thoughts, after all it could have been them living out their last few hours in fear and torment. That was if they were alive which was doubtful, not many miners ever got out of a fix that bad.

'Did you hear that?' said a voice in the blackness.

'Aye I did,' a hushed voice answered.

Seth Ridley crawled along the floor.

'Hear what?' he hissed at the men.

'It sounded like tapping on one of the cage rails over there, but it was very faint.'

Seth whirled around and sped across to the pipe.

'And you did nothing you useless bag of shite,' he shrieked as he tore one of his pit boots off and began to beat the pipe with the metal segs on the sole of the boot. He stopped and listened, nothing, he beat on the metal again, nothing, he turned and threw the boot at the two men.

'Bastards, bastards, useless shit faced bastards,' the headache was starting again over his empty eye socket.

He rubbed it violently and sagged against the wall. Everything had happened suddenly, one minute he had been dishing out orders wagging his yardstick about, the men jumping at his command. It had felt good to be in control again and then wham!! The world had collapsed around his ears.

It was strangely quiet in the cavern, even the boys who should have been crying for their mothers were silent. It was dark, a pitch black terrifying hole hundreds of feet below the earth. The last time sunlight had shone where they were trapped was over twenty million years ago.

Seth realised that it was him they were relying on, he was the one to get them out. He felt a surge of pride. He knew it was vanity but he loved it. Then a wave of hatred came over him, if it wasn't for these bastards and others like them, he wouldn't be stuck down here. He decided to ask God for guidance. His empty eye socket began to twitch violently, there, it had to be a message, whatever he did now would be guided by the hand of the Lord. An hysterical giggle broke the silence for a moment, he stood up and banged his head on the roof of the cavern, nobody laughed.

'Gather round, all of you,' he said to the miners, 'I'm going to get you out of here, that useless so called rescue team don't even know if we're alive, but the Lord has spoken to me my children,' his voice had taken on an almost priestly tone.

'The Lord my arse,' shouted a voice in the darkness, 'the man's bloody bonkers, we're not getting out of here we're going to die and the sooner you all accept that the better.'

They were agitated now, this was the truth they all knew,

but did not want to hear. A few voices rang out in agreement.

'You shut you're big mouth Telford, I know your voice and you're a troublemaker, in fact you're the biggest pile of shite I've ever come across and when we get out of here I'm gonna take you down a peg or two.'

Seth's voice was rising in anger and then his temper broke and he began to shriek.

'Don't ever interrupt me when I'm talking to you, any of you, you bastards.'

Silence, then a quiet voice spoke up, it was Henry Robinson, a veteran in his sixties.

'This isn't going to help Seth, if there's a chance of getting out then I reckon he's the best option we've got.'

Most of the men murmured their agreement.

'Right,' said Seth, 'Tom, you get all the lamps together and the food and the water and I want you to ration it the best you can. Telford you collect all the tools you can find.' There was no response.

'For pity's sake answer the man,' said Tom.

'Right I'll do it,' said Telford, there was a collective sigh of relief from the miners.

* * *

Back up top, Jack was in the manager's outer office with Brophy. Cyril was bringing hot tea into the room.

'Thanks Cyril,' said Jack, any animosity between the two forgotten for the moment.

Bassett was there with the pit surveyor, the mining engineer and three deputies who had been off shift.

'How deep is the upcast shaft?' Asked Jack across the table.

A week ago these men wouldn't have even noticed him, they were so far above him in the class riddled society that he lived in. Now they needed him and his new position put him on equal terms.

The surveyor rustled some papers and glanced at the mining engineer.

The mining engineer, a man in his sixties turned to Jack.

'Eight hundred feet, but it's coming on fast.'

The room went quiet.

CHAPTER THIRTY ONE

Jack was quiet, deep in thought, he cracked his knuckles one at a time causing the other men in the room to grimace in distaste, then he turned to Bassett.

'You are in charge of this mine,' there was an angry edge to his voice, 'why wasn't that shaft built properly?'

George Bassett held up a hand, he was startled by the anger in Jack.

'Jack, the shaft was built before I came here,' he said quietly.

'But that's not going to help those poor men and boys down there,' he said looking at each man in turn.

For the first time Jack saw the compassion and pain in the man's face. He cares, he thought, he really cares about those miners.

'I'm sorry mister Bassett, you're right,' he looked straight into the man's eyes and saw him nod slightly.

'You just have to tell me what you want Jack and you'll have it.'

That's the problem thought Jack, I don't really know what I need. But he was going to have to come up with some answers fast.

'I need a team down that shaft to start digging, at least it's a start. Brophy you get on to that now.'

He turned to the pit engineer and surveyor.

'I need you to bring whatever plans and maps you have of the pit and surrounding area.'

They were about to protest at his insolent manner, which didn't go unnoticed by Bassett.

'Just do it,' said Bassett

The engineer and surveyor stood up and left, heading for their offices.

Bassett nodded and walked off to direct runners to get the men Jack wanted, all of a sudden the atmosphere had changed, everyone felt it, they were doing something to save their own folk.

Five minutes later Jack was talking to Brophy at the top of the shaft as men were hurriedly gathering equipment, they would be lowered in kibbles, large man carrying buckets that were normally used for shaft sinkings.

'Jack, the men are back in my office now,' called out Bassett as he hurried towards him.

'Thanks, I'll be there right away.' Jack turned back to Brophy, 'do your best my friend.'

Brophy nodded then turned away roaring out orders as Jack ran to catch up with Bassett just as he reached the pit offices. Upstairs the engineer and surveyor were waiting. The engineer turned to Bassett as he entered. He was a heavy man and still sported a pair of mutton chop whiskers long out of fashion, his black serge suit and waistcoat finished off with a magnificent pocket watch and chain, showed that he was a die-hard Victorian and everything that that society stood for.

He turned to Bassett.

'What is it you want with us?' his voice crackled and his brown tobacco stained teeth told why.

'It's not me you need to talk to, it's Jack here who has the questions,' he noticed the look of superior contempt when the man looked at Jack and decided to settle matters there and then.

'Right, now listen to me the pair of you, yes Jack is a collier, however that may disgust you both, he is in charge of this operation. I know that your term for these men is underground savages, but this particular underground savage is chief mines rescue officer and you will do everything in your power to assist him,' the force of his voice shocked everyone and it was a few moments before anyone spoke.

The surveyor, a man in his thirties wearing a light cotton suit turned to Jack.

'Ask and ye shall be given, I am at your command sir,' giving a slight bow.

Jack didn't pick up on the man's sarcasm.

'I need to see the surveyors report on the mine and also the engineers report,' said Jack.

And what are you going to do with them?' said the engineer raising his bushy eyebrows.

'I'm not going to do anything with them, you know fine well that I'm no expert yet, so you two are going to find me an alternative route into that pit so that I can save those men and boys.'

'You haven't got a chance,' sneered the engineer, but then the surveyor spoke up.

'Then give him a chance, what would we do if we were stuck down there?'

'Humph,' said the engineer.

'At least try,' said Jack.

The surveyor unrolled a huge piece of paper across the desk and the engineer unfolded the plans of the pit. Hours later they were still talking. Most of the stuff the two men were talking about was incomprehensible to Jack, even Bassett looked confused at times, but at last a result was decided.

'It can't be done,' said the engineer hotly.

'Right we have to get some rest, I need to look at these plans again so if you don't mind I'll take them home and return them later,' said Jack.

The engineer didn't look too happy about the proposal but grunted his acceptance.

'Mister Bassett, I'll be back in four hours, any volunteers would be appreciated,' he left the building.

It was raining again as he opened the door to his new home and the wonderful aroma of freshly baked bread. He opened the scullery door to see her standing by the stove stirring a big pot, the bread was cooling on the wooden table.

'Oh,' she said a little startled, 'it's you, do you like rabbit stew? Sit at the table and I'll bring you some,' she didn't wait for a reply from Jack and placed a small basin of the stew in front of him.

'Help yourself to bread, I've only just made it,' she smiled and sat down opposite him to watch him eat.

He sat for a moment doing nothing.

'Go on then, eat it up.'

He got stuck in. When he had finished she brought him a bottle of dark beer, full of flavour and very rich in colour, she poured it into a tankard and then poured a small amount into a glass for herself. Jack had not said a word.

'Well?'

'Lovely lass, I've never tasted better, and thank you.'

'You're very welcome kind sir,' she giggled a little, 'It's a thank you for what you've done for me, and there's plenty more where that came from if you're happy with things,' a flash of mischief lit up her eyes for a moment.

He looked up and she was staring at him, he held her gaze for what felt like eternity and then it was gone. They both looked a little embarrassed for a moment, she wondered if she had gone too far. Jack hoped she hadn't read his mind.

'When are you going back?' she asked quietly.

'As soon as I can, maybe two or three hours, said Jack.'

'I've put a blanket on the settee for you.'

He got up and headed towards the sitting room, he turned at the door.

'Thanks,' he smiled at her and turned away, he was fast asleep in five minutes.

She felt like singing, so she did, she felt normal, and she was, and she felt happy and her movements had a spring to them that hadn't been there for a long time.

CHAPTER THIRTY TWO

Seth had called the men and boys together, he stepped into the middle of them, they were sitting or kneeling. He had the only lit pit lamp now and he waved it to and fro as though to get a better look at them, but inside he imagined himself as some holy bishop waving his chalice and saving souls.

'The Lord has put us in this predicament,' he intoned, ' we are his children and I have been sent to save you, your souls are in my hands and I will lead you through this troubled time either into His hands or back to the surface.'

'Never mind the bullshit Seth, how about our water ration?' called Telford from the darkness.

Seth swung around angrily, staring into the blackness.

'It's you again Telford,' he roared angrily, 'I've told you before, shut your shit filled mouth, you'll get it when I'm ready.'

'We're going to die down here and none of that claptrap

is going to help us,' there were murmurs of agreement, 'we've decided to take the water and what's left of the food and then let God do what he wants with us.'

'Whose we?' hissed Seth, his voice now had an undercurrent of angry hysteria to it.

'Most of us,' said Telford. The men were rising to their feet, they had had enough of Seth's ranting's.

'Hand it over Henry,' said Telford, 'c'mon were all marras down here, we look after each other.'

Henry stared into Telford's eyes.

'Yes, we are all friends down here but that doesn't make you right and you're not getting the water.'

Telford made as if to turn away and then turned back swinging a meaty fist at Henry but all he got was space. Henry had leaped behind him and threw two short punches into Telford's kidneys, the man gasped and fell to his knees.

'Bastard,' he said, 'c'mon you lot grab him,' he spluttered as the pain increased in his sides, it would get worse before it got better he knew, it was like being kicked in the balls. But no one moved. They were not prepared to pass leadership on to a man such as the likes of Telford. He had always been a troublemaker and in the unlikely event that they did get out there wasn't anyone who would want to face the wrath of Seth Ridley. Seth leaned over and looked into Telford's pain filled eyes and smiled.

'Arsehole,' he said, 'mutineers get hung like, for what you did you bastard, down here it's different you friggin pile of shite, this is what you get.' He swung his yardstick, the brass ferrule hit Telford behind the ear and he collapsed onto the ground unconscious.

The boy was fifteen, he had become terrified after listening to the older men talking about how they had no chance of getting out. He didn't want to die, he would never see Mary again, he had been in love with her for at least six months and couldn't bear the idea of never seeing her again. She didn't know this of course but one day he would sum up the courage to tell her. But it was looking as though he would never see daylight again. He had begun to cry, he just couldn't help it, he had tried to be a man but the tears were rolling down his face as he quietly sobbed in the corner. He had felt movement beside him and an arm went around his shoulder. It was his dad.

'C'mon lad, there's better men than you been shedding tears and they are all grown up so there's no shame in it. Anyway, we're here together and when I start missing your mam you can put your arm around my shoulder.'

'I'm sorry for crying dad, it's just that, well I'm scared to die and I'm not scared to tell you, is that wrong?'

'Don't be daft lad, we're all scared to bits and that's

including your old dad. Look, I've got a piece of wood and some chalk why don't we send your mam a note telling her we're together and thinking about her, we'll even sign our names on it, what do you think?'

The lad was wiping his tears away when he felt the draught in his face, he pushed his dad away and called out.

'Shut up, all of you,' called the unbroken voice of the teenager. It went quiet, it must be a brave lad to say that when Seth was angry.

'Who's that?' said Seth.

'I can feel a breeze,' there was total silence.

'Right son, where are you?'

'At the back sir.'

'Keep talking son I'm on my way,' he followed the voice to the back wall of the chamber.

'Are you still there lad?' a hand touched his shoulder, startling him.

'I'm here sir.'

The boy was beside him now.

'I can feel air blowing on my face sir.'

Seth shoved him out of the way and thrust his ruined face against the rock.

'Praise be to the Lord, he has answered my prayers,' whispered Seth.

He opened his Davey lamp then turned and faced the general direction of the men.

'Look lads, at least we're not going to suffocate,' the flame was bent over at an angle. ' it has to be coming from somewhere, we're going to organise round the clock crews to dig our way through, but make sure the supply is not cut off by rock falls or I'll have your balls for garters.'

A murmur of excitement filled the chamber, at last, a faint hope.

He didn't have to tell anyone to move they were already organising themselves into work parties. They had found hope, a chance to fight for life however small that chance was, at least they would try.

CHAPTER THIRTY THREE

Jack hated the hand that was gently shaking his shoulder, it was so persistent and it was waking him up.

'Jack, Jack, wake up, wake up.'

He opened his eyes to see Ruth looking down at him.

'Tommy Thompson is here to see you.'

'The hermit?' said Jack.

He could see she didn't understand and got up from the settee.

'Where's he at?'

'In the parlour, he's looking at those charts and maps you brought with you, I couldn't stop him.'

'That's fine Ruth, don't worry, I'll sort it.'

Tommy was waiting for him when he entered the parlour. This was a cosy room normally for spending winter evenings with friends by a blazing coal fire. It was also where the best furniture was displayed and the only room with a carpet.

'Boggle Hole Jack, that's where you need to go in,' said Tommy.

Jack rubbed the sleep from his eyes and pulled himself together.

'Who or what the hell is Boggle Hole?' he said to Tommy.

'It's the old drift son, they were mining the same seam over a hundred years ago where it poked out of the ground. Now they've gone down sixteen hundred feet, but that's up there on the top of the hill.'

'So why didn't they go in here in the first place?'

'A water inrush son, the workings caved in under the weight of hundreds of tons of water, poor buggers never had a chance,' he looked at Ruth, 'beggin your pardon miss.'

'But how do you know that it will lead us to the victims Tommy?' Jacks voice was becoming excited.

'Look son.'

He overlaid the plans with his own drawings, the coal seam of the drift and the mine ran into each other

'Where did you get that from?' Jack was poking the drawings.

'Careful son that map is very old and not as accurate as

today, but the fact is it's the same seam and there's still water down there so you're gonna need boats.'

Jack looked at Tommy as if he was mad.

'Where are we going to get boats around here, there's only streams and one small river, it's not like we live in a fishing village is it?'

'Calm down son, the surveyor whose working with you is chairman of Ebchester boating club and they've just bought half a dozen collapsible canoes. It can be done lad and you will save those poor men and boys, I knew there was a reason why we had crossed paths.'

'Tommy the whole lot might be blocked from the entrance in, it could take months of digging.'

'It won't.

'How do you?' his voice trailed away when he saw the look on Tommy's face.

'You've been down haven't you,' it wasn't a question because he already knew the answer.

'You'll get to the water fairly easily but then you have to cross it, that's where they are Jack believe me.'

Jack thought for a few moments, if he was right they had a chance and he would prove himself as not just a body collector but as leader of a real rescue team, was it vanity? Yes some of it was and why not, anyway he didn't have time for this and what if he failed, there was always that.

'Will you guide us Tommy?'

'I'll show you where the entrance is, but then it's up to you Jack.'

'Right, we better get started then.'

'Jack,' said Ruth, he turned to her, 'take these, you may need them.'

She handed him a water bottle filled with cold tea, a pitman's favourite, a bait tin filled with some thick pork and dripping sandwiches and a small silver flask.

'Thanks Ruth, you obviously know how to look after a man,' and he kissed her on the cheek before she had a chance to move.

She felt her cheeks flushing and half turned so that he wouldn't see but it was too late, this man was having an effect on her and it was obvious to both of them.

'I better get on with things,' she said quickly and dashed off into the scullery out of the way where she stood with her hand on her cheek, remembering the gentle way he had kissed her.

The men made their way to the pit offices where over a hundred miners were standing.

'We're your volunteers Jack, just tell us what to do,' said a big brute of a man his hands like shovels and burn marks on his arms showing him to be the pit blacksmith.

'Thank you, all of you, I need ten minutes and then if you're up for it we're going to get those men and boys out of there.'

There were no cheers, only grim nods of determination.

Upstairs he explained the details to the pit officials and faced their scorn with the same grim determination of the men downstairs. He was going to do it and nobody was going to stop him now.

Tommy had stayed downstairs and was waiting for Jack.

'It's on Tommy.'

'Good lad, I'll be watching out for you.'

Jack turned to ask a question but Tommy had gone, a surge of panic overcame him and then disappeared as he remembered Tommy's last words, he didn't doubt him for a minute.

'Brophy,' he shouted over the noise.

'Aye Jack I'm here.'

'Get the men equipped with food, water and all the tools they can carry. Send a deputy to the Infirmary to get an ambulance organised, filled with blankets and medical supplies. I need twelve men to go with the surveyor to the boat club, I'll explain later, I'll meet you at the pit gates in about thirty minutes.'

Brophy nodded and started giving out orders.

'Brophy,' interrupted Jack, 'thanks marra.'

Brophy's chest seemed to swell and his face glowed with pride as he nodded and went back to his task. Jack had called him marra again.

* * *

Underground, the cavern was filled with the clamour of working men, they had made inroads into the direction of the airflow, Seth cursing and praising and bringing down the wrath or otherwise of God depending on the incident. The sweat ran down the bodies of each team as they worked at the face but there wasn't enough water to replace what they were losing. The men were weakening in body but not spirit, but they couldn't go on forever and Seth prayed over and over to God to save them, especially himself. He didn't deserve to die he had work to do, anyway he was protected by Him and he would be saved, he hoped.

'Down,' screamed a voice and everyone dropped to the ground, it was a command nobody disobeyed no matter who gave it.

It was deadly quiet, they lay on the ground waiting, they could hear the drip of water but what was behind it? Maybe thousands of gallons of the stuff just waiting to drown them all, or maybe gas, the deadly firedamp, highly explosive as they had seen, but even if they survived, what followed would be even worse, the lethal afterdamp or carbon monoxide. The devil, or Auld Nick as he was called, controlled the underground world and these were three of his weapons. The drip increased to a trickle then a stream, then a torrent of freezing water burst through the tiny hole made by the pick of the man who had raised the alarm. Then the water stopped. They stood silently, waiting for the death blow, but it never came. What they did see was an opening into another chamber.

* * *

Jack was at the head of the rescuers as they made their way down to Boggle Hole, he heard a voice at his side.

'Mister Walker.'

Jack looked down to see a familiar face but without the beaming smile, it was Bobby Samms, the lad who carried messages for Bassett.

'What is it son? I haven't got time to idle today.'

Bobby was alarmed by Jack's manner and stopped. Jack immediately relented, remembering the lad wasn't a full shilling.

'I'm sorry son, it's just that I've got a lot on my mind at

the minute, what can I do for you?'

'I want to help, I want to do what I can because we are all one family in this.'

Jack thought what an effort that must have been for the lad, but it was probably Madge that had put the words into his head, but the lad's heart was in the right place.

'Good,' he shouted, 'do you hear that everyone? Bobby Samms wants to help, so what do you say?'

'Aye,' was the response but shouted at the top of their voices.

'I reckon he should be the rescue team runner, what do you say?'

Again a huge' Aye,' was heard. Bobby's face lit up in gratitude, but there was something wrong.

'What's up son?'

'I've got a friend sir, he's a new friend but he's my marra and he's stuck down there and marras look after each other don't they?' he looked at Jack for agreement.

Jack nodded his head solemnly.

'You're right lad and you and me are going to get him out along with the others, so let's get going.'

Jack began to jog along the road, Bobby was at his side glancing up and trying to copy the same serious and determined face of the man beside him.

* * *

Seth poked his head through the hole, his lamp held out in front of him, the flame didn't alter. He was testing for gas. If the flame reduced and a pale blue haze surrounded the lamp then gas was present. The gauze on the inside of the lamp allowed oxygen to pass through, any gas that entered the lamp would be extinguished in the wire gauze preventing an explosion, most of the time, it worked

Seth noticed a pair of wooden rails reaching into the darkness. He pulled his head out of the hole.

'Right you lot, we've got a chance,' the miners teeth were showing bright white in the darkness as they grinned at each other, maybe just maybe they would get to see their families again.

'But don't build your hopes up, we are in the hands of the Lord and if he has decided to take us then no matter what we do He will take us if He wishes, but I will pray to him for mercy.'

He giggled quietly, if he got them out of here he would be a hero, that would teach the bitch a lesson when she found out, walking out of his life when she saw his disfigured face and leaving the bairn with him. He had no choice but to give the baby to a childless family. A voice interrupted his thoughts.

'God will decide without your help you daft bugger,' the man's crackers,' he said to the miners.

'Oh it's you again Telford,' hissed Seth, 'all you've done my lad is complain you bastard and when we get up top you're finished, you mark my words you pile of shite.'

The miners recognised the dangerous edge to Seth's voice and kept quiet.

'Shut up Telford, he's got us this far and we're still alive so leave him alone,' said Henry, the man who had shut him up earlier.

'Right,' said Seth, 'let's widen this hole and get through into the old workings.'

The men were stunned into silence, old workings? Seth had never mentioned that, maybe he did talk to God, in these conditions they would believe anything if it saved them.

'Yes, old workings. If Telford had shut his fat mouth then I would of told you,' he cast his eye over the miners swinging his lamp to and fro like an archbishop tending his flock of worshippers.

'Stick with me lads and you'll be all right.'

* * *

Jack stood looking into the darkness of Boggle Hole. A lot of vegetation had been cut back to allow access to the wooden gates closing off the drift mine. The gates were rotten and easily pulled off their hinges, a pair of wooden rails stretched away into the gloom, wooden trackways hadn't been used for years and it was obvious to Jack that the drift was very old and that meant it could be dangerous. He turned to Brophy.

'Did you see Tommy pointing to the drift entrance? I don't think we would have ever found it, if it hadn't been for him.'

'I never saw anybody Jack,' he gave Jack an inquisitive look.

'You must have been busy with something else eh?'

'Aye, that's it Jack,' said Brophy even though he knew he had been looking in the same direction as Jack. 'You've been working hard Jack, I think we all need a break once this is over.'

Jack cocked his head on one side.

'You think I'm cracking up don't you, I know what I saw,' an edge of anger entering his voice.

Brophy held up his hands in resignation, Jack was about to speak then clamped his mouth shut, they had more important things to do for now.

'Get a party of men with props and wedges and a deputy in charge, any sign of weakness in the gallery can be shored up as we go, and I'm sorry Brophy.'

Brophy nodded and ran off.

'You men,' called Jack to five men sitting on the broken down wall of the drift. 'Get shovels and picks and follow me. There wasn't likely to be gas at this level so Jack lit his carbide lamp, the big reflector gave more light than a Davy lamp, anyway they had a finch in a tiny wicker cage. If the bird fell off its perch unconscious, then firedamp was present. Before long the sounds of shovelling and hammers knocking props into place could be heard. Men were shouting at each other to be heard over the racket, they were making progress at last.

The little bird was chattering away as happy as it could be considering its surroundings, an occasional crumb of bread would be pushed through the bars of the cage. The bird was expendable but that didn't mean it was treated cruelly. Four hours later the rescuers stood on the shore of a huge pond. The floor had fallen away and there was no way around the edges of the water. The surveyor was frowning as he examined the rock wall.

'Got it,' he said. 'The coal seam runs down there under the water which must have been above the miners. The rock must have been so thin over their heads that the weight of water caused the roof to collapse, the poor sods never had a chance. No wonder the place was abandoned, there must be a void of twenty feet or more above us if we could see it. I need to get across in one of the canoes to get a look at the other side. By the way Jack, how did you know this would be here?'

'Call it a feeling maybe or somebody told me, I can't remember exactly but we're here to save some men if you haven't forgotten.'

The surveyor gave Jack a cold stare but it was lost in the darkness, that's the trouble with the lower classes he thought, give them a bit of authority and they think they've moved up in the world. He would take him down a peg or two when this was over, can't have an underground savage strutting about.

'You'll need to send some men to the boathouse Jack,' said the surveyor.

'What's your name anyway?' was the retort.

'It's mister Henderson to you Jack.'

'Shite, if you call me Jack then I want your first name your lordship.'

The man stared at Jack for a moment.

'It's Hector,' he said quietly, as though revealing a secret.

'Great, Hector,' Jack spoke loudly making the surveyor cringe, 'how many men do we send?'

'Nine,' said Hector.'

'Do you mind telling me how the hell are we going to get them here?'

'Let me worry about that Jack, it's only a mile to the river, please just send the men.'

Jack shook his head at the impossible request but nevertheless turned to Brophy who had returned and overheard the conversation. Jack raised his eyebrows, Brophy nodded and was off again. Thirty minutes later the nine men returned with what looked like a carpet bag in each hand. Jack stopped driving a wedge above a pit prop and stared dumfounded.

'What the hell is going on,' he said to Hector.

The surveyor smiled.

'Two bags each, weighing ten pounds, six canoes and not long to set them up. They've been updated slightly and can carry six men at a time. Designed by a German fellow called Alfred Heurich, I bet he never thought they would be used like this.'

Jack watched in amazement as each bag was opened. A folding bamboo frame was opened out to form the shape. Then a canvas preformed cover was pulled over the frame. The whole exercise took no more than five minutes, it even had folding oars.

'Right, I need to get across that water,' said Hector.

The first canoe was launched, a rope was fastened to the prow, if danger arose or the thing capsized then it could be hauled back to dry land hopefully. The surveyor jumped in.

'I'm the best one to handle the boat Jack, give me three men and we'll get to the other side while you build the other vessels.'

Jack raised an eyebrow.

'Mind you don't get your feet wet,' he knuckled his forehead in a sarcastic manner.'

'Argue later Jack, we've got some men to save, or had you forgotten?'

Jack turned away.

'You three, you heard the man, get in the damned boat.'

'By the way Jack, the boat's called Dolphin one.'

He was about to carry on when Jack cut him short.

'Yes, I know,' he said curtly.

The canoe slowly disappeared into the darkness, the carbide lamp growing fainter with distance until it became a tiny pinprick.

'Secure that cable men, if we have to pull them back it will need to be fast,' shouted Jack.

Brophy stepped forward.

'Wedge a prop up as tight as you can and run the rope around it, the more leverage we can get the better.'

The canvass canoe reached the other side of the water, the surveyor swung his lamp in the air, there was nowhere to moor the craft. It was one of the men who spotted it.

'There,' he gestured with an outstretched finger, 'just there, right in front of your bloody nose man.'

The surveyor ignored the caustic remark as he spotted what the man was gesturing at. A piece of wooden railway was sticking up out of the water. It was obvious to Hector that the ground had heaved at the time of the water inrush. The floor rearing up, the roof falling down, followed by thousands of gallons of water. It must have been a terrifying sight for the men and boys working at the time, they didn't have a chance, he thought. He tied the heavy rope around the timber to secure the craft.

'Give me your handpick,' he said to one of the men.

He grabbed the short handled tool and started pounding on the wall, he soon realised that it was part of the coal seam.

'We can do this,' he said to the others, 'get us back across as quick as you can.'

A tug on the rope was all Brophy needed to start pulling the canoe back across the water.

'Gimme a hand men,' he shouted, he wrapped the rope once around the pit prop and began to heave, more men joined him. The thin edge of the wedge at the top, facing opposite the pull on the rope.

They soon had the canoe back across the water. Hector jumped out of the vessel.

'Jack we can do this, the seam carries on directly opposite where we are, the coal is at the surface and I believe that the roof of the old workings is just above that. When I sounded it with a pick it feels and sounds quite a thin wall and I think that the workings carry on at the other side of the face. If we can get three canoes across with men and equipment then God willing we can get through.'

Jack had been nodding in agreement all the time.

'Right lads you heard the man, the surveyor takes over at this point, do what he says and let's get bloody moving.

The atmosphere had suddenly changed, there was hope, or at least a very faint chance of rescue but it was worth it and a new energy seemed to drive the men on.

CHAPTER THIRTY FOUR

The desperate situation had become too much for one of the miners who jumped to his feet and began to shout at the others.

'What's the point of this lot? All we've done is ended up in old workings that don't go anywhere,' there was panic in his voice.

'Shut up for Christ's sake you stupid bastard.'

There was silence.

'Didn't you hear that? You're so far up your own arsehole that you're not listening to what's around you.'

Seth slowly turned towards the voice, a malevolent glitter in his eye.

'And who might you be? You little bag of shite,' he had spotted his victim, another boy, not even in his teens, but the lad stubbornly held his ground.

'The names Johnson for what it matters.'

'You've got spunk boy.'

'There, listen,' said the boy, his voice dropping to a whisper.

A faint tapping could be heard.

Heads turned in the direction of the sound, ears cocked to pick up the noise.

'It's regular,' whispered a voice, and then the sound stopped. The men were galvanised into action. Maybe they wouldn't starve to death without ever seeing the sun, maybe just maybe they would see their wives and mothers and families again. A boy started to cry.

'Shut it,' shouted Seth, 'all of you listen to me. This is our chance and I am going to lead you out of the valley of death into the Lord's hand. But first let us pray.'

The miners knelt while Seth spouted short verses from a bible that only existed in his head. They knew he was bonkers and let him get on with it. Eventually he finished and stood up.

'Right you useless buggers let's get moving. Boy?' He pointed at Johnson, 'you're with me and keep those big ears of yours cocked.'

They headed into the darkness, jogging along in the curious gait of miners in confined spaces, their legs bent at the knees. They soon reached the end of the workings where the old wooden tracks were standing almost vertically against the wall. They stopped, the only sound the wheezing and gasping of dust filled lungs.

Tap, tap, tap. The trapped men began to shout at the top of their voices, whoever it was must be human.

Seth shouted above the noise.

'Shut your bloody gobs you stupid bastards you'll bring the friggin roof down.' Eventually they became quiet.

Seth swept his yard stick from under his arm, the noise incredibly enough was coming from above. He stretched up and began to rap on the roof of the tunnel. Immediately the tapping stopped, he rapped again, three times, there were three taps and he rapped again.

'We're saved men, oh praise be we're saved,' said Seth. Some of the miners were on their knees praying, some were crying, others stared vacantly into the darkness. None of them ever believed that they would be rescued, but now!

* * *

Mary Bassett was also offering up a small prayer, not for the miners but for herself. She wasn't that concerned about what was going on, anyway George never told her anything. What she was more concerned about was her gardener. She was pleased she had brought him with her when they moved house. This was the chance she had been waiting for as she watched him from a downstairs window. Ed knew he was being watched but carried on clearing the weeds from the overgrown garden. It was wet but it didn't bother him, he had a cosy brick potting house with water, a stove and even a small camping bed in the corner. He did have his quarters in the big house but didn't use them often. He threw the big bundle of grass and weeds onto the compost heap and glanced at the windows of the big house. She was there all right but what was she up to? At eighteen he was still naïve and had faith in his fellow man, or woman as the case may be.

He looked up at the sky, the heavy rain clouds were moving in again so he decided to take cover in his shed. Mary Bassett quickly slipped a heavy coat on and left the house making her way down the garden path towards the shed that stood in a clump of fruit trees. She opened the door of the shed and stepped inside just as the rain began to pour down. Ed stood up quickly.

'Yes mistress Bassett, can I help?'

'I think you could help by taking a lady's coat from her, don't you think? she said with a little smile turning up the corners of her mouth.

He helped her shrug the coat off her shoulders and put it

by the stove to dry. She was wearing a simple bodice that was tied at her bosom with a lace, which was straining to contain what was underneath. Ed couldn't stop staring.

'You're a naughty boy Edward, staring like that,' he immediately lowered his head.

'I didn't say that you had to stop staring and anyway, I like naughty boys,' her voice had become husky.

Ed risked his job and lifted his eyes again.

'I'm sorry mistress Bassett.'

'Call me Mary, but only when we are alone.'

She lifted his hand again and rested it on her breast. Ed's eyes widened in astonishment, there was no doubt that she was a good looking woman and those tits.

'Anyway I've come to see what you're doing, I've always loved gardens and I hope you are going to do a good job for me, yes?' she swept his hand away.

Ed wasn't able to hide his disappointment which she duly noted, she was enjoying herself now.

'I'll do anything you want me to, er Mary.'

'I was hoping you would say that Edward. You see, I don't get much pleasure these days.'

'But what about your husband,' Ed had decided to go along with her, she was obviously bonkers and was simply going to torment him and then go away.

'He's not the same as he was,' she said, her voice rising.

'In fact I haven't had a man for months,' she lifted his hand to her breast again and he squeezed, gingerly at first and then with more confidence.

She loosened the lace on her bodice.

'There,' she said, 'that'll make it easier for you.'

All of a sudden her husky voice changed to the sharp tone of mistress to servant.

'Now take off your trousers,' she ordered sharply.

Ed was startled by her tone, it was more like an order. He smiled inwardly, but wasn't that what he was, a servant? He did as he was ordered. She lowered her hands and began to stroke and play with him. Her eyebrows lifted as he instantly grew in her hands.

'Very nice,' she whispered, now lie on the bed.'

Her prayer had been answered and when she looked down at him she saw that her prayer had been answered very generously indeed.

'Thank you,' she whispered quietly, then lifted up her dress and straddled him, sitting on his hard belly.

She felt his hard dick throbbing between the cheeks of her backside then cupped her breasts in her hands, lifting them slightly.

'Suck me Edward, now.'

He grabbed a nipple between his lips and began to suck noisily, she swung the other breast in his face.

'Now this one,' she gasped, the sensation unbearably exquisite. She lifted herself up and sank down onto his dick, a cry of ecstasy escaping from her parted lips.

She began to ride him like a horse, her hair falling over her face hiding her closed eyes.

'Don't hold back,' she gasped, 'shoot whenever you're ready, I'm in my safe week.

He shot his bolt as he groaned with pleasure. She had reached her orgasm at the same time and shivered with delicious ecstasy and then rolled on to her side, a smile on her face. After a few moments she got dressed, watched by Ed who had started to become erect again.

'My, my, you are keen,' smiled Mary, 'but I have to go.'

She turned back to Ed as she was leaving the potting shed.

'Now you must keep quiet about this Edward, do you understand?'

'You don't think I would tell anyone about this Mary, I want you all to myself.'

'Good, you're a good boy, a naughty boy and a big boy. Oh, perfection. I will be back Edward. Oh, by the way, consider your probation over, you have the position.'

She was singing to herself as she strolled up the garden path.

CHAPTER THIRTY FIVE

Hector had heard the rapping below him.

'Quiet,' he said.

He tapped on the coal again and was immediately answered by more rapping.

'Good heavens, I think we have found them.' Quickly, you two men get back across the water and inform Jack.'

With the combination of paddles and the draw rope the men were soon back at the tunnel.

'We've found them Jack,' said one of the men, a huge grin on his face.

Jack's eyes widened in surprise.

'No,' he said, 'is it possible? Brophy,' he called. The man came running.

'We've found them.'

Brophy stared at Jack.

Suddenly Brophy swung round.

'Don't just stand there you lot, get this man across the water,' he was grinning, as were the men he faced. 'Get a relay of canoe's spread in a line over that water and let's get some gear across there.'

He turned back to Jack who nodded his agreement. Jack clapped Brophy on the shoulder and jumped into the first canoe which carried him swiftly to the other side where Hector was waiting for him. Jack explained what was happening, the surveyor nodding his approval.

'Listen Jack,' the surveyor tapped on the coalface the tool causing a hollow sound in the wall.

'It's not very thick as you can hear, maybe only eight inches in the centre, beneath me we've got about two feet. I suggest we break in here,' he said as he reached up and pointed to a spot just above his head.

Jack's frown was noticed in the gloom.

'If we go in anywhere other than up their then we run the risk of the wall down here collapsing under the weight of all this water, but all the same we are going to have to be very careful.'

Jack realised that it wasn't over yet, if they made a mistake the whole lot of them including the rescuers could drown.

'I understand what you say,' said Jack, 'let's get started.

Seth and the trapped miners stood silently as they heard the unmistakeable sound of picks hitting the coalface above them, every head peered upwards waiting for the impossible to happen. Dust began to float down, then lumps of rock and coal, nobody moved out of the way.

'Look,' called a voice that was thick with dust but also emotion, 'there, can you see it?'

'Aye lad, I can see it,' said Seth, 'praise be to the Lord as he comes from above,' nobody noticed Seth's face twitching violently.

'The Lord my arse,' shouted a familiar voice, 'It's thanks to the rescuers.'

'For once Telford will you shut that great arsehole under your nose, the man has pulled us through so give him a break or you'll be the next shaft accident you bastard,' the voice came from one of the older and more respected miners. The rest of the men murmured their agreement and nothing else was said by Telford.

Suddenly a lamp was thrust through a hole high up in the wall.

'Hello,' called a voice.

Immediately a barrage of voices exploded in the cavern, the surveyor turned to Jack as he withdrew the lamp, a huge grin on his face.

'I think we can definitely say that we've found them, all yours now.'

Jack nodded his thanks, the difference in class was too strong to allow his barrier to drop. He stretched up and peered through the hole. A sea of white eyes and white teeth stared back at him.

'My name's Jack Walker, who's in charge down there lads?'

'Seth Ridley is in charge Walker, nice to see you son.'

Jack was taken aback by Seth's response he'd never said anything pleasant to him ever.

'Seth, this is the situation, I'm standing on the edge of an underground pond, the water is probably thirty feet deep, the coalface and rock separating you from the water is only about two feet thick. We are coming in from here and intend to set up two ropes, one to hold onto, the other to tie around yourselves so that we can haul you up. Got that?'

'Aye lad, do we have a chance?'

'Ask God Seth.'

Seth nodded as the head withdrew, the hole was soon widened and two stout ropes dropped to the floor.

'It's about ten feet to the top,' said Seth to the men, 'I want the injured and those weakened by our ordeal at the front.'

No one moved.

Seth glared at them, a bit of the old style Seth was needed he thought to himself.

'Right you bunch of shites, pull your bloody selves together, I don't want any heroes, I want miners who are going to be fit for work and that means the weakest first,' his voice was cracked and hoarse but he still managed to get some clout into it.

'Now move, you useless buggers.'

A shuffling of feet and one or two moved forward soon followed by others.

'There's nowt the matter with you Telford, unless your mouth's worn you out,' Seth pulled him from the line of men.

'You're with me my lad, right to the bitter end,' he tapped the man's helmet with his yardstick and winked with his right eye which immediately started his face twitching, causing Telford to step back in alarm.

'Right, we're ready down here son.'

That's the second time he's said that thought Jack, maybe he's gone totally bonkers.

The operation began to move ahead smoothly, the miners were taken swiftly across the pond and given cream crackers and sweet warm tea heated by the miner's lamps. It was going well, there were only about thirty miners left. Then everything went wrong. It was one of the trapped men who spotted it first, just a weep of water coming from the wall above. He pointed it out to Seth.

'Jesus save us,' groaned Seth, his eye darted to and fro, a gleam of panic in it, his greatest fear, water. Would it always torment him he wondered. He tried to control his voice.

'Jack, are you there?' he shouted, the edge of panic in his voice was picked up by the others.

'What's up?' said one of the men.

'Shut up,' roared Seth. The men became silent, but the news had spread and the hope once again turned to fear.

'I hear you,' said Jack, then a low groan shook the earth, a long crack began to open in front of his eyes. It slowed as it reached the surface of the water but the pressure would soon cause the wall to cave in sending a torrent of water onto the remaining men in the tunnel below him.

'Seth, get moving you haven't got long, let's get those men out of there and fast.'

The rescuers doubled their efforts and soon had four canoe's filled to capacity, there were only a dozen men left.

Seth was watching the seep as it turned into a stream then a waterfall as the water cascaded down the rock face. The sixth man was through the gap, only six left.

'Please God don't let me die this way,' called Seth out

loud. Four men were fighting for the rope.

'Get back you useless bastards,' shouted Telford. 'One at a time or we're all finished.'

He took command when he saw the look of terror on Seth's face, they were through, only two left.

Jack and Brophy threw a rope each into the hole.

'Tie them around your waists,' Jack shouted above the noise of the water. Jack and Brophy were in one canoe, ropes tied around them that were held by miners at the other side of the water. The canoe was securely held by ropes as well. One other rescuer was in the vessel with them holding the canoe steady. It was the quiet man , Ralph Henderson, always willing to help.

Suddenly the wall above Seth began to crumble away, the water blasted through the wider gap pouring down onto the men threatening to carry them away. Brophy and Jack heaved on the ropes fighting against the ever strengthening current. Panic gave Telford the extra strength he needed and he was through the gaping hole in seconds, only Seth was left. They were running out of time. Jack and Brophy were praying that the rope would hold against the rapidly increasing speed of the water as it turned into a raging torrent.

'Is it holding, Brophy?' yelled Jack as the roar of water increased. Brophy merely nodded.

The canoe was in danger now of being swept away. The gap in the wall was widening. The quiet man reached over and took the rope from Jack, he gave a mighty heave and Seth appeared through the gap, the water forcing him backwards. The man pulled out a sheath knife and began to saw through the rope.

'You killed my daughter you bastard, you drowned her and now you're going to drown as punishment.'

'No,' roared Jack as he tried to grab Ralph's wrist. But Brophy beat him to it.

'You're wrong,' shouted Brophy. He tore the man's arm away and chopped down with his other hand, the knife instantly disappeared into the torrent of water. The man reached forward for Seth's throat but Brophy stopped him again by grabbing his belt. Ralph beat at Brophy's hands until he let go. A smile crossed his face as he reached out for his victim. With a huge crack, the wall gave way altogether. The smile disappeared as Ralph was swept past Seth. He bounced off the rock wall with a terrible crunch of breaking bones, his screams echoed in the chamber as he was swept away to his death.

The miners across the pond were already pulling the canoe back. They had seen the danger and took action. Seth was in the water by the canoe as Jack and Brophy hauled him over the gunwale sodden but alive. Jack sat him up and Seth began to cough up water.

'Thanks son, blood is thicker than water after all eh,'

Jack looked astonished for a second then put it out of his mind, they needed to get back across before the water level dropped too far.

An almighty groan split the air. The earth was moving. The release of thousands of tons of water had caused a slight upsurge in the floor of the cavern. The centre rose up and the sides dropped. It was only a fraction of an inch. But it was enough. High above in the roof of the cavern a huge boulder was released from the grip of surrounding rock and began to fall. The canoe in front of Jack was carrying six men, three boys and two rescuers. The rock landed in the middle of those miners. The two halves of the canoe snapped shut as the boulder smashed through the middle. Most were killed instantly. The rest were swept away through the hole in the wall. The men on the ropes pulled as hard as they could. The water level was dropping fast. There was a tremendous crack that echoed around the chamber, the wall had collapsed altogether and the water was rushing through the opening at a terrifying rate. The level was dropping. Brophy had to look upwards now as the level rapidly dropped. He looked at Jack, the glance not missed by Seth.

'Save us for God's sake,' Seth pleaded and then began to

sway as he chanted some made up hymn from his personal bible. The canoe had reached the other side now but was six feet below the floor level.

'Keep hauling,' shouted Jack, 'It's our only chance.'

The canoe lurched upwards and a man and his son were thrown into the water. There was nothing anyone could do. The boy would never realise his dream of asking the girl he loved to walk out with him. Mary would have to choose another.

'Dad, dad, I'm frightened,' screamed the boy. His father cuddled his son as they were hurled at the rocks around the opening where their bodies were broken. But the man held onto his son as they disappeared over the edge and into the mine workings to die with their comrades.

* * *

The huge pond was gone. Jack and Brophy stood on the edge of the parapet staring down at the macabre scene below them. A pair of broken and twisted wooden rails wormed their way across the floor, wrecked when the earth had slipped and the water poured in from above. Corves lay scattered about, the old type of coal tub made from woven willow branches. But they could just make out with their lamps a more grisly scene. Piled up against the far wall were a jumble of bones, the skeletons of those that had perished, some lay with boots on, others still wearing their flat caps.

'How many were lost?' asked Brophy.

'Not sure, about fifty to sixty or thereabouts,' said Jack. 'Poor buggers never stood a chance. Come on, let's get these men out of here, those poor sods are beyond our help now.'

He turned and cupped his hand to his mouth. 'Where's that runner of mine,' he roared. A few seconds passed then the clatter of boots was heard tearing along the tunnel. A huge smile appeared in front of Jack, the boy's eyes gleaming in the murkiness

'Yes mister Jack, I mean Walker, sorry.'

'Bobby, get yourself up top lad and down to the village and tell them their men and boys are coming home.'

Bobby turned to run off.

'Wait lad, just a minute,' Jack knelt beside the boy. 'That lad who you had made friends with, he decided to stay with his dad, there was nothing we could do to save him.'

Bobby stared across the chasm, the smile gone, but then he turned back to Jack.

'Thank you mister Walker, I'm sure that you did everything you could.'

'Is that it son?'

'No sir I don't suppose it is, but I've got my family now

to help me.'

Jack was astonished at the boy's maturity and shook his head in disbelief.

'Aye Bobby, I suppose you're right there, it's better than some have,' he ruffled the boy's hair and asked him to wait for a moment.

Seth was sitting with his back to the wall when Jack approached him.

'Seth, how many didn't make it back there?'

'Eleven, that's including the two rescuers, nine different families.'

'Would you write their names down for me?'

Seth nodded, then unscrewed the top of his yardstick, the ferrule came away and he pulled a small piece of paper from inside. It was folded around a stub of pencil and still dry. Jack smiled to himself, you've got to hand it to the man he thought. Seth scribbled down the names and handed the paper to Jack.

'Jack,' he said, 'thanks for saving me, you're a good lad.'

Jack was about to say something then changed his mind, instead he turned to Bobby.

'Right son, this piece of paper is very important, give it to Madge, yeah?'

Bobby nodded vigorously to show he understood.

'Thanks mister Walker for trying to save my friend,' he

wasn't smiling.

'It's Seth you need to thank, he was the one who brought most of them through this. Go on hop it, you're supposed to be my runner.'

Bobby turned and sped away.

He reached the drift entrance and burst out of the undergrowth and stopped suddenly. In front of him, in a crescent, stood the village community. They were quiet, the gentle patter of rain could be heard on the ground and on the clothes of the villagers. They were waiting, and would wait forever or until they had news. Madge stepped forward and Bobby ran to her handing over the note.

She opened it and glanced at the names knowing exactly what the note meant.

'Wait there awhile,' she said to Bobby, she turned to address the people. 'I have eleven names here of men who will not be coming back,' a long groan was returned like an animal in pain.

'I will read those names out first.'

Families tensed as they waited, cries and wails of sorrow followed as she read out the names one by one, in those pit cottages there would be no celebration. Others gathered round the stricken families offering help but there was nothing else they could do for now. Those who had lost their loved ones shambled away from the scene and back to the village. One woman was noticed by a girl called Mary. The woman had fallen to her knees and was sobbing. The tears began to fall from Mary's eyes, they gathered on the point of her delicate chin and dripped onto the ground that had destroyed so many lives. Her mother noticed and glanced at the other woman. The she understood and pulled her daughter to her.

'Come here my bonny bairn,' she said and embraced her child. A momentary feeling of guilt ran through her when she saw the first of the miners coming out of Boggle Hole. It was her husband and that was all that mattered.

Madge breathed in deeply.

'They are coming home,' she said to the waiting crowd. This time a babble of excited voices began to talk in excited tones, but soon went quiet again as others reminded them of the families on their way back to the village and to show a little respect.

The first of the miners appeared, there was a silence as the man peered through the drizzle trying to adjust his eyes to the blinding light. His face and clothes were filthy and he was unrecognizable to the villagers, except for one that is. A woman ran from the crowd, her voice a mixture of sobs, laughs and near hysteria. She flung her arms around her husband ending up covered in coal dust. He pulled her arms away.

'Let's have a look at you lass, I thought I'd lost you forever, is Mary with you?' a tear ran down his cheek but he hastily wiped it away before anyone noticed.

'Yes pet, but she's a bit upset.'

He frowned.

'It's all right love I'll explain some other time,' she grabbed his hand and led him away. The scene was repeated many times until only Madge and Ruth were left.

'Bobby? Get yourself back along that tunnel and ask our men if they are ever coming out of that hole.'

Ruth looked at Madge, 'Our?' she said.

'Aye lass,' smiled Madge, 'I've been around long enough to know what smitten looks like.'

Ruth turned away to hide her reddening face.

'Don't worry pet, your secret's safe with me, you've just got to let that man of yours see it.'

Bobby came scampering back.

'You two have got to go home because we still have important work to do.'

'Well at least he knows he's your man now eh, but I'm not going anywhere, are you?

Ruth shook her head.

'Not a chance,' she said.

'Thanks Bobby,' said Madge, 'tell them we are staying

put.'

Bobby scratched his head trying to understand then gave up, smiled and ran off with the message.

Down in Boggle Hole Jack was confused enough after what Seth had said and now the message from up on the surface, her man! He wondered what that was about.

'Jack.'

He turned to see one of the older miners.

'I need to have a word, in private son if you don't mind, it won't take long.'

Jack had stood up into a crouched position out of respect, Daniel Laidler was the most respected and oldest miner in the village.

They stepped back into a recess in the wall and hunkered down.

'I've spoken to Seth and he says it's time Jack, so let me say my piece and then the rest is up to you. Seth was married once, had a bouncing bairn that was nearly one when the accident happened. His wife, a bonnier lass you'd ever see, rushed to the hospital when they pulled him out, took one look at him and ran away. She's never been seen again, broke his heart, though he'd never admit it. He passed the bairn on because he had to work to live. There was a childless couple in the village who were happy to take him, seemed a good couple then. It wasn't till later that he found out that they weren't treating him properly. He asked a deputy to keep an eye on his boy underground, didn't want to interfere with the lad, he reckoned things would sort themselves out. They did in the end.'

'That deputy saw the man fall into the shaft when his boy stood and watched. He deserved it Jack, he was a bad'n and I think by now you'll be putting two and two together lad. You were that boy who watched and you might remember now that I was that deputy.'

Jack leaned closer to the man to make out his features, there was something oddly familiar about the grizzled face that stared back.

'You mean that Seth is?' Jack shook his head in disbelief.

'Like it or not son, what you're thinking is true, he is your father. Go easy on him Jack, he's had a hell of a tough life, but he's kept an eye on you as well son, blood is thicker than water. There, I've said my piece, it's up to you now.'

'Why couldn't he tell me himself?' retorted Jack angrily.

'Because you wouldn't have listened, you're a stubborn bugger Jack Walker, just like your dad.'

Daniel raised a hand.

'So long kid and good luck.'

CHAPTER THIRTY SIX

Jack was staring across the fields from the back upstairs bedroom of fourteen North View, or official Row to give it its more common name. The events of the previous day were hard to get into perspective for him. He had acted instinctively and somehow he and his team had rescued men and boys from deep underground who thought that they were finished and were waiting to die. But Seth, his father, how could that be? He was the son of a man who was most likely mad and almost certainly evil. Yes he resented the man. Yes he understood a little, but he also felt ashamed that he was Seth's son. Yet underground Seth was the last to leave, he had made sure that everyone went ahead of him and it couldn't be denied that he had held those men and boys together down there. He was going to have to come to terms with a lot of things.

Yesterday, after Brophy had left he had stood alone looking at the scene of the rescue. This is what I want to do, he had thought. Now he knew where his future lay and he was content. He was alone now as he left Boggle Hole. Ruth was waiting for him. He was about to protest but decided against it. Instead he rested his hand on her shoulder and gently kissed her on the cheek. She smiled, took his hand in hers and they walked home through the rain.

Once in the house, he had lain on the settee and fell fast asleep. Ruth wakened him when evening was setting in and they sat together in front of the fire. Jack stared into the flames.

'You're very quiet Jack,' she said quietly.

It was a few moments before Jack looked at Ruth and answered her, his voice gentle.

'For the first time in my life I feel the urge to tell someone about my past Ruth. Can you understand that?'

'Funny that Jack.'

He frowned at her words.

'You're not the only one with a past Jack and believe me when I tell you, I was just thinking the same.

She stood up and crossed the room to the wooden sideboard, opening the left door she reached inside and brought out a bottle of whisky.

'It's nowt flash, but it'll do tonight,' she said, smiling. She put the bottle on the hearth and went into the pantry, returning with two small glasses.

'He used to drink this,' she said, lifting up the bottle,

'when he couldn't handle his problems.'

'Problems?' said Jack.

'My husband didn't care much for me Jack, I don't mean as a person, but physically. I'm sure he loved me,' she hesitated, 'but he preferred other types of relationships, if you know what I mean.'

Jack was nodding his head slightly, she was talking about something disgusting to him and admittedly he was shocked at first, but he wouldn't show her that. He would try to understand instead.

They sipped whisky and talked. They talked more about their lives, leaving out nothing. Ruth pretended to drink more than she had but Jack had sought sanctity in the bottle of whisky, just as her husband had. He began to slur his words then lay his head on the arm of the settee. She took the glass from his hand and placed it on the hearth beside the almost empty bottle and lay her head on his arm.

'Goodnight Jack, I love you,' she whispered.

* * *

It was the morning sun that woke Jack.

'Ruth?' he called.

She peeped from behind the scullery door, a happy smile

on her face.

'Morning Jack, breakfast?'

'Yes please,' he responded.

As they sat at the table eating their breakfast of eggs and toast, Jack was watching Ruth intently.

'You're chirpy this morning pet.'

'Why shouldn't I be? I've told you everything and you haven't thrown me out yet.'

'Don't be daft lass, why would I do that?'

'Well then, you must want me to stay then,' she said.

'Well that works both ways doesn't it?' retorted Jack, enjoying the game of cat and mouse.

'Yes, but it's you're house,' she replied again.

'Rubbish, you've as much right to be here as me and you're not leaving,' he said.

'Why?' was the response.

'Well, because I would prefer you to stay, here, with me, I mean, well dammit woman you know what I mean.'

'I love you Jack.'

He was speechless.

'Well?' she said quietly.

'I think I know how I feel Ruth but let me be sure love, no sorry I didn't mean it like that flower. I need to go out for a while.'

There was a knock at the door followed by. 'It's only me.'

'I will be back Ruth. Coming Brophy,' he called out.

'I can wait,' she said, not sure of her confidence now.

He smiled and left the room.

* * *

Brophy was waiting outside the back gate with the new horse and trap that had been supplied, so that emergencies at other local pits could be attended quickly.

'Do you know how to ride that thing,' Jack asked.

'Drive Jack, the word is drive and the answer is yes I can. We had one on the farm when I was a liitl'n.'

'All right, I only asked.'

He pulled himself up into the trap and Brophy drove off. The sun was slowly disappearing behind an ominous looking cloud bank but at four miles an hour it didn't take long to get to Allansford. When they arrived they noticed that the pathway was overgrown.

'There's been a lot of rain Jack,' Brophy had noticed the look of puzzlement on Jack's face.

'Hmm,' said Jack. 'Brophy, do you think those candy men were buried deep enough in the sand pit?'

'I hope so, for all our sakes,' he replied then added, 'do you think of it as murder?'

'Sometimes, but then I remember what they were about to do to my,' he broke off.

'Say it Jack, it's as plain as the nose on your face what you think about her, she's your bloody woman,' said Brophy.

Jack looked at Brophy, a big smile spreading across his face.

'Thanks marra,' he said. He knew he had the answer now. He jumped down from the trap and headed for the path, pushing the undergrowth out of the way as he barged through to where Tommy lived. Brophy was close on his heels laughing out loud at Jack's sudden change.

'What the hell are you laughing at, you great oaf?' shouted Jack.

'You're happy.'

'Bugger off you Cumberland clod.'

Brophy was about to retaliate when they suddenly burst into the clearing. They stopped in their tracks, all thought of banter gone. A derelict building stood before them, blackberry bushes were growing through the door and weeds were sprouting up around the walls. They walked towards the wreckage and then a voice called out.

'State your business lads and if it's good I won't pull the

triggers.'

They looked to the left and their eyes were drawn to the double barrels of a Harrington and Richardson double barrelled hammerless shotgun, held in the capable hands of a burly red faced man.

'We're looking for Tommy,' said Brophy.

'You two know who I am? If you don't then I'll oblige you, I'm the gamekeeper on these lands and I controls it and I don't take kindly to folk telling lies to me.'

'We aren't telling lies mister and I suggest you take back that insult afore I take that gun off you and shove it up your arse,' Jack was getting angry.

The gamekeeper ignored him, he was staring intently at the two of them, a look of recognition spread across his face.

'Dammit,' he said.

Jack and Brophy looked at each other, Brophy shrugged. The gamekeeper was hurrying towards them now, his shotgun now at the rest in the crook of his arm, he had broken the gun open making it safe for now.

'I would sincerely ask you two gentlemen to accept my humble apologies. You're Jack Walker and William Brophy aren't you?' It would be a pleasure and an honour if you would allow me to shake your hand sirs. It was magnificent what you did down at Boggle Hole, we all thought they were gonners,' he grabbed the right hand of each man in turn and vigorously shook their hand.

'Tommy?' asked Jack.

'Well that's an odd thing mister Walker,' his manner had completely changed, 'the hermit was never called that until he died you see. There's one or two who claim to have seen him and even been helped by him. They reckon if you're worthy, he could just appear so that he can help you. I'm not saying I believe that but the woods are a strange place and even stranger things have happened.'

Brophy shivered and looked around, the gamekeeper carried on.

'Like I said the odd thing is, Tommy died in Boggle Hole, so how could he be here?' I figure it must be just old wives tales.'

Tommy helped us,' said Jack. The gamekeeper looked as though he wished the ground would open up and swallow him.

'I'm not implying that you are wrong sir, it's just that, well, you know what I mean,' his voice was trailing off as he ran out of reasons for what he had said.

'C'mon Jack,' said Brophy, as he pulled Jack away from the scene.

'Aye, mebbe's your right mister, we must have got it wrong,' said Jack.

'So long mister,' they said in unison as the gamekeeper turned and disappeared into the undergrowth.

'We didn't imagine it Brophy, it makes you wonder if that man was real as well doesn't it?'

Brophy began to run.

It was raining when Brophy dropped Jack at official Row and then headed home to Madge.

Jack was soaked but it was his grim face that Ruth noticed first.

'What's wrong?' she asked, afraid of the answer.

He stood in front of her, a pool of water at his feet spreading wider all the time. She didn't care.

'I think I would like to see a lot more of you, if you would allow it.'

'Oh Jack, you don't know how long I've been waiting to hear you say that.'

He swept her into his arms and kissed her.

The next morning Jack was standing by the back door in his newly washed, starched and ironed clothes.

'By lass, you've done a grand job with my clothes, I never thought they would look like this again.'

'You look a picture pet,' she handed him his cap. Go on, off you go then, your father's expecting you.'

'Aye, who would have thought, Seth Ridley, my dad. It's

a funny old world isn't it?'

'And what next Jack?' said Ruth.

'Who knows? It depends on where the next accident happens, but we'll be ready next time. There's one thing for certain though lass.'

'What's that then?' she said.

'Wherever I go I'll always have you to come home to,' he winked and left the house.

ABOUT THE AUTHOR

I am a coalminer's son and born at a time of poverty and hardship. I would never have thought that those tough years would ever be of use to me, but an era has passed and I was lucky, I see now, to be involved in those times. Through my personal experiences and much research I have tried to capture a little of the day to day lives of those folk. But first and foremost I am a storyteller. I love to write and at the end of the day I hope you enjoy my work. I have had many non-fiction articles published in national magazines, but it is historical fiction that I enjoy most of all. It allows me to escape as it will you, I hope.

My Jack Walker series of novels are intended to give the reader a flavour of the mining communities of Durham in Northern England. Those miners and their families were indeed;

A BREED APART

16903604R00198

Printed in Great Britain
by Amazon